THE REMEMBRANCE

ALSO BY T. C. PARKER

Saltblood
Hummingbird
A Press of Feathers
Salvation Spring
Maiden (with Ward Nerdlo)
The Long Con: An El Gardener Omnibus

THE EL GARDENER TRILOGY
The Debt (Book 1)
The Push (Book 2)
The Remembrance (Book 3)

THE REMEMBRANCE

TC PARKER

PUBLISHED BY NEFARIOUS BAT PRESS

2022

THE REMEMBRANCE
Second Paperback Edition

Published by Nefarious Bat Press

Copyright © 2022 by TC Parker
Cover design by Kealan Patrick Burke | Elderlemon Design
Interior design by Todd Keisling | Dullington Design Co.

All rights reserved.
No part of this book may be reproduced in any form or by any electronic or mechanical
means, including information storage and retrieval systems, without written permission
from the author, except for the use of brief quotations in a book review.

For everyone who's stuck with El, Ruby, Sita and the others to the end -

thank you

BETHNAL GREEN, LONDON

January 1941

She'd been under a table when the bomb hit, scrabbling around for a coin she'd spotted on the floor. It was a shiny, well-polished thing, bright as a sliver of moonlight; a casualty, most likely, of some half-cut drinker's carelessness as he stood up from his seat and dug into his pocket for another fivepence to swap for a pint at the bar.

That coin, Dolly had thought later, had probably saved her life - or kept her, at least, from injuries more serious than the high-pitched ringing in her ears and the sporadic headaches she was left with, after.

Her parents weren't so lucky.

Her Dad had been at the bar too, queuing up to get her a glass of water and himself another bitter; she'd seen his work boots shuffling impatiently on the carpet just before she felt the blast, before the shockwaves sent the glassware flying and blew the joists and beams to smithereens, pulling the ceiling down on top of them and carving out a man-sized hole in one of the walls.

Her Mum had been sitting down, perched on a stool on one side of the thick wooden table that had unwittingly sheltered Dolly as she'd hunted for her treasure. The exposed side; the *wrong* side.

Dolly was on her hands and knees, eyes stinging from the smoke and trickles of fluid spilling from her perforated eardrums, when one of her Mum's severed arms rolled - soundlessly, or so it seemed to her then, through the cotton wool veil of silence that had fallen over her - off the stool and under the table, stopping just shy of Dolly's downturned palm.

It was the left arm, Dolly saw: her Mum's diamond wedding band still fixed to the scorched ring finger of its blackened hand. And it was whole: cleaved from its trunk at the shoulder joint, if not exactly what Dolly would have called cleanly.

She wasn't, she found, at all distressed to see it; nor to realise, in seeing it, what seeing it *meant*. Only surprised, and very mildly repulsed - the way she might have been had she stumbled on an uncooked side of beef from the butcher's shop on the pavement, raw and bloody and unwrapped.

That her Mum was dead was a foregone conclusion; no body could have survived a blast strong enough to do *that* to it. It was a miracle Dolly herself had come out of it alive.

She couldn't see her Dad at first, through the smoke and her streaming eyes and the heat haze pouring off the smouldering rubble - even after she'd crawled away from the wrenched-off arm and used what was left of the table to lever herself upright and stagger four or five paces across what had been, until recently, the pub. So dense and toxic was the air around her that it took her a minute or two to become aware that she was standing almost on top of him - that the smoking pile of wood and half-melted metal just in front of her were the ruins of the bar, and that the remains of *him* were buried underneath it.

He wasn't dead, though. Not quite.

He'd been crushed: pinned into place by the heavy, splintered plank across his chest and stomach. Bone rose up through the charred, torn meat of both his shins; a second, smaller piece of wood pressed down onto his throat. A broken piece of someone's pint glass, she saw, had wedged itself - grotesquely - into the jelly of one of his eyeballs, forcing the eyelid upwards.

She edged closer to him, unsteadily, and he seemed to register her presence - his other pupil darting in her direction even as his stoved-in head stayed fixed to the spot. His lips moved, and she got the sense - though she wouldn't have been able to hear what he was saying, even if he'd been capable of speech - that he was trying to tell her something. *Ask* her something.

Help me. Please.

Get me out.

And just as she'd found herself unmoved by the evidence of her mother's death - sudden and brutal as it must have been - so it struck her, as she took in the smashed remnants of the man who'd given her piggybacks and tucked her and her sister into bed at night since both of them were little, that she had no interest at all in getting him help.

The fire brigade would be there soon enough, she reasoned; might well be on their way already, sirens blaring. They'd be able to dig him out; to help him, if there was anything left of him to help.

She didn't think there *would* be, though. He was too far gone.

And what she really wanted, she realised, was to watch him die. To see the look on his face, as the life drained out of him.

Something moved to the side of her - in what she'd come to know later as her peripheral vision. Close to where her Mum had been sitting, before the bomb went off; close to the hole in the wall.

She ducked down, on instinct; hid as much of herself as could be hidden behind the pile of wood, a hand over her mouth to stop the smoke from choking her.

If it was the firemen, then they could come and find her. If it was the soldiers or the police, then they'd find her too, eventually, just as soon as they started digging.

And if it was the Germans chasing after their bomb with a land invasion, unlikely though she thought *that* was... then hiding from them made a lot of sense, didn't it?

It wasn't the Germans, though. Or the police, or the army, or the fire brigade.

It was a man - a buck-toothed, thin-faced man in a flat cap and overalls, leather boots like her Dad's on his feet, brown kid gloves covering his large hands and his back bent nearly double under the weight of something that looked to her like an enormous sack of potatoes.

He didn't *seem* like an air warden - he didn't have a helmet or a uniform, for starters. And he was on his own, not with a rescue party, which was out of the ordinary - didn't they normally come in teams, the rescuers?

There was something else about him too, she thought. Something slippery in the way he slithered through the hole in the brickwork; something shifty in the way he scanned the wreckage before he took another step inside. As if he was hunting - not for survivors, but for an opportunity.

She ducked lower behind the wood; held her breath.

The floor was hot to the touch, singed though not quite burning, but the thin-faced man navigated it lightly, nimbly, even with the heavy sack slung over his body; as if, Dolly thought, he was doing nothing more demanding than strolling down the pavement on a warm summer's evening.

In the centre of the newly formed bomb site, where the largest portion of the ceiling had come away and heaped itself into a bonfire of oak and lath and plaster, the man stopped in his tracks. He seemed to study the ground below and around him for a moment with great intensity and then, apparently satisfied with what he found, laid down the sack, untied the knotted length of rope that held it closed and reached his arm inside, all the way up to the elbow - reminding her, just for a second, of a stage magician preparing to pull a recalcitrant rabbit from an oversized hat.

There was a body in the sack: an old man, grey-haired and fancily dressed, jowls like Churchill's drooping from his yellow jaw and a square of green handkerchief pressed neatly into the top pocket of his dark suit jacket. He looked to Dolly like a banker or a businessman: someone rich and important.

He had to be dead, though - as dead as her Mum, as dead as her Dad soon would be. There was a dent in his forehead, a bloody crater dripping red gunk down his cheeks and into his snow-white sideburns. His lips were blue.

The thin-faced man dragged him from the sack by the armpits, hoisting his body upright until they were chest to shoulder, looking to Dolly as if they'd stopped to catch their breath in the middle of dancing a tango. Then, with not so much as a glance behind him to check the path was clear and still cradling the dead man in his arms, the thin-faced man took two steps backwards over the rubble, paused again, and laid the body down like a human sacrifice on top of the wood pile.

With one gloved hand, he pulled a brick from a smaller pile of debris to his left - and, with a turn of speed that took Dolly so completely by surprise she had to press her fingers tighter to her mouth to hold in her gasp, dropped to a crouch and dashed the brick, hard, against the dead man's head, on almost exactly the spot where the crater had been made.

He's hiding the body, Dolly told herself, in awe of the thin-faced man's ingenuity. *He killed him, and he needs to get rid of the evidence, so he's leaving it here for the firemen to find so's everyone'll think the old sod died in the air raid.*

And it'll work, too.

Because who's going to know in all this mess whether it was a flying brick or a blackjack that got him?

It's a stroke of genius.

The thin-faced man rose up from his crouch; walked with the same fleet-footedness as before to his rope-tied sack where it lay on the ground; picked it up, folded it neatly into a rectangle no bigger than a tablecloth and tucked it away in the capacious expanse of his overalls.

Then, fast as a rattlesnake, he took to his heels and disappeared from the crumbling shell of the pub the exact same way he'd come, through the hole in the wall.

NORTHAMPTON

March 1998

El Gardener wasn't a dog person.

She wasn't *opposed* to dogs, per se - even found some of the bigger eyed, better groomed ones quite appealing, from a comfortable distance. But the particular circumstances of her childhood had precluded much meaningful interaction with animals of any sort, much less the kind that might lead inexorably to a spaniel or a Labrador curled up in her lap on the sofa. And if, she reasoned, the urge to rear Yorkshire terriers or take long, slow walks in the countryside with a pack of Border Collies at her side had failed to strike her in the thirty-four years of life she'd already accumulated, then the odds were good it never would.

She was more than a little uncomfortable, therefore, to find herself not so much surrounded by dogs as *drowning* in them.

They were miniature Dachshunds, all of them: small, smooth little bullets of fur and enthusiasm, clambering over the furniture - over *her* - with their stubby legs, tails wagging and ears flapping in excitement at the presence of visitors. She'd counted eight of them when she'd been shown into the living room, drawing up a mental tally of wet noses and wetter tongues as she lowered herself onto the hair-covered sofa. But there were more in the house, she was sure of it, more Dachshunds and other breeds, besides; she could hear them, scratching at doors and yapping at the strangers they could sense but couldn't see, desperate to be released.

It'll be worth it, she told herself, as one of the dogs - a chocolate brown puppy with the doleful, faintly accusatory eyes of a disappointed toddler - leapt down from a sofa cushion to position itself on her shoulder like a ship's parrot. *You've suffered worse for less before.*

"We don't like to keep them locked up," said the man on the larger sofa opposite her, in lieu of apology for the Dachshunds' misbehaviour. "It's just cruel, isn't it, Lauren?"

"Cruel, that's what I say," his wife agreed, nodding vigorously. "*We* wouldn't like it, would we? Cooped up all day long in a little space like that?"

El took in the narrow confines of her current environs, the four walls of a lounge overflowing with cushions and knick-knacks and teeming with excess canine life, and suppressed a sigh.

"I couldn't agree more," she said.

There was a depressing banality to the Robinsons, she considered; a petty, priggish, proudly Middle Englander quality to their conversation - to the structure of their lives - that seemed to sap the air from the room and the energy from El's body. He was white, red-faced and beefy, in his mid-fifties but ostentatiously toupee-d, his lips perennially puckered in a moue of low-level distaste. She was very slightly younger; permed, petite and sinewy, her makeup an orgy of blue eyeshadow and her fingernails painted a nonthreatening coral. Their patterned knitwear didn't quite match, but had almost certainly been ordered from the same department store catalogue.

They were nothing at all like her usual marks. And they certainly weren't the marks she would have chosen, had the choice been hers to make.

But they had something she needed. And while the scope of their ambitions was small and unlovely, it gave her just enough room to manoeuvre her way into their home, if not their hearts.

"Let's get down to brass tacks," she said, transferring the wandering puppy from her shoulder to the armrest and settling into the blunt, no-nonsense, Yorkshire-tinged bark she suspected would appeal to the couple's sensibilities. "What is it you want doing? 'Cause I might as well tell you now, I won't put 'em down. I'll dock a tail, if I absolutely have to, but I don't believe in killing 'em."

The Robinsons startled as one unit.

"What?" the wife yelped, the timbre of her voice not vastly dissimilar, to El's mind, to the high-pitched wailing of the Dachshunds. "Kill them? Who said anything about *killing* him? Good God, no! We don't want him *hurt*, do we, Colin?"

"We most certainly do *not*," the husband replied firmly - the moue, El noticed, growing so pronounced at even the possibility that his lips seemed in danger of disappearing entirely into the corrugated trench of his mouth. "I don't know how you normally do things, Miss Cutler..."

"Call me Annie," El told him. "Everyone does."

"Right. Well, I don't know how you normally do things, *Annie*, but we don't hold with harming poor defenceless creatures in this house. Me and Lauren, we're animal lovers. *Dog* lovers. And if you think we'd ever, *ever* want something like *that* to happen..."

"What *do* you want, then?" El said, stopping him mid-flow. "Because *you* told *me* you wanted this Erasmus out of the picture in time for the show, and there are only so many ways I can do that for you."

"We didn't mean *that*!" Lauren Robinson spluttered. "We thought you could, you know... shave his fur off, or something. Make him *look* bad, so he couldn't compete."

El believed her; had anticipated exactly the reaction she received, when she'd made the suggestion. The Robinsons, she suspected - disagreeable though she found them - would conceive of animal cruelty as a hanging offence, on a par with premeditated murder and the desecration of war memorials in their personal hierarchy of punishable ill deeds. The question for her had been how close to actual *physical* harm they'd be willing to go in pursuit of their goal.

Their quarry, Erasmus, was a mustard Dandie Dinmont, the prize pet of a pair of retired dentists from Kettering and Best In Show three years running at Marfett's, Northamptonshire's somewhat lower-key answer to Crufts. He was also the chief rival, for Marfett's much-coveted winner's rosette, of the Robinsons' Horatio, an energetic beagle who'd been runner-up for the last *two* years at that same event - and who was, or so the word on the Northamptonshire pure-breed grapevine had it, set to sail into second place behind Erasmus for a third year, too.

The Robinsons, though, had other plans.

"*Shave* him?" El said, as if the idea hadn't previously occurred to her. "Yeah, alright. I suppose we could do that, if that's what you're after. What do you reckon, Lola?"

She turned to the red-haired girl sitting beside her on the sofa, shifting uncomfortably in her seat to accommodate the wheezing - and, it seemed to El, very elderly - Dachshund that had taken up residence between her knees.

"Don't see why not," the girl answered - her own approximation of a northern accent only half succeeding in masking her usual, cut-glass pronunciation.

She was younger than she looked, aged a handful of years older than the fourteen she actually was by strategically applied foundation, adjustments to her posture and a tailored white shirt that El herself had hand selected. Her name wasn't Lola but Sophie, and she was, in a roundabout sort of way, something approaching El's stepdaughter.

"Mind if we take a look at Horatio, while we're here?" El asked, pivoting back to the Robinsons. "It'll help us get a sense of how far we need to go, with

Erasmus," she added, pre-empting the inevitable *what would you want to do that for?* she knew was apt to follow. "How *much* fur we need to take off him."

The Robinsons looked anxiously at one another, and then, apparently simpatico, shrugged in unison.

"If you must, I suppose," Colin Robinson said, only slightly begrudgingly. "He's downstairs, in his bedroom."

Horatio's bedroom, El had learned in her early reconnaissance, was the Robinsons' basement, now converted into an air-conditioned sleep-and-play area that kept Horatio himself not only calm and entertained, but away from the other, more boisterous dogs that might startle him or nip at his perfectly maintained coat.

It was also, she happened to know, where they kept the painting.

They hadn't *bought* it. Though partial to pastoral portraits of smiling Whippets and blue ceramic renderings of thoughtful-looking Westies, neither Robinson was much of an art aficionado. In fact, the painting, one of the very few oil-on-canvas pieces produced by the American comic-book artist Melinda Hogan, had belonged to Lauren's Auntie Vanna, an unmarried radio producer and amateur fine art collector of whom both Robinsons had faintly disapproved, and whom Colin had long suspected of harbouring lesbian tendencies - but whose estate in its entirety, in the absence of a valid will, had fallen to her niece and only surviving relative at the time of her death.

The current location of the painting had come to El by way of Ruby Redfearn, her long-time friend, mentor, frequent collaborator and godmother in all but name. Ruby, herself an enthusiastic and knowledgeable connoisseur of anything with a sufficiently hefty price-tag, had known Vanna in life; she and Sita, El's *other* almost-godmother, had been at one time frequent visitors to Vanna's Paddington flat, and in Sita's case (because Colin Robinson wasn't *entirely* wrong about his wife's aunt and the trajectory of her desires) to her bed. The Hogan canvas, a gothic reworking of Lichtenstein's *Crying Girl* titled *Weeping Skeleton*, had captured Ruby's attention from the moment she'd seen it resting, one evening in the late nineteen-eighties, against the crushed velvet walls of Vanna's sitting room. So, when Vanna finally succumbed to the renal failure that had plagued her for going on a decade, and the Robinsons had helped themselves to her worldly goods, or at least those worldly goods they felt might prove valuable, Ruby felt, or so she claimed, almost obligated to retrieve it from them: to restore it to a place - specifically, the first floor of the West Hampstead duplex she shared with her twin sons - in which it might be better cared for and appreciated.

It was testament to the strength of the older woman's affection for El that, when El mentioned that she might *also* have a suitable home for *Weeping Skeleton* in mind, Ruby didn't just pull her hat out of the ring and step aside: she made an active contribution to the plan that would, all being well, help El to obtain the painting.

"It's not for me," El had told her, but Ruby had known already, or had at least suspected as much. Extensive though El's working understanding of contemporary art was, after years of running cons on gallery owners and exhibitors and private collectors, she had no real passion for acquiring any of her own.

Rose, however, was a different story.

Rose - Lady Winchester to Tatler and the tabloids, Sophie's mother and, as of the previous Autumn, El's significant other - loved Pop Art: lived, breathed and purchased it so vigorously that she was known, among those with any interest in the subject, as one of the foremost collectors of Hockneys, Rothkos, Blakes and Warhols on either side of the Atlantic. Much of the substantial fortune she'd inherited from her late husband Sebastian - and augmented thereafter through myriad astute stock-trades - she'd invested in artwork, bidding thousands, hundreds of thousands and occasionally millions of pounds at a time on the pieces she coveted.

There were no Melinda Hogans in her collection, though. A situation that, with Rose's 42nd birthday on the horizon, El - ably supported by Sophie, on her first live job - was on the road to rectifying.

El wasn't, she knew, the most adept at romantic entanglement. Even plucking up the courage to ask Rose to dinner in the first instance had taken a year and a half of the two of them working very intensely together, one eventful trip to California, a pointed pep-talk from Ruby and no small amount of literal bloodshed. Now, six months later and on the verge of packing up her cottage in the Midlands and moving permanently to London to join Rose and Sophie in their Bayswater apartment, she was happy and something very close to secure in the relationship - and in the not-quite-parental rapport she'd established with Sophie. But she was also aware, sometimes subtly and sometimes more painfully, that both her happiness and her new-found security could evaporate in an instant, should she take her eye off the ball.

Long-term relationships, she knew - from observation, if not necessarily from practical experience - took effort to maintain; required hard work and sacrifice from their participants, if they were to go the distance. And since she wanted - really quite a lot, she was discovering - for her relationship with Rose to succeed, she was determined to put in the necessary effort. To *try*.

Hence, the painting, and the elaborate con she and Sophie - with Ruby's input - had devised to extract it from the plywood crate that currently housed it, down in the Robinsons' basement.

"He'll be asleep," Lauren Robinson warned them, gesturing to the hair-lined carpet and, presumably below it, Horatio in his bedroom. "He always has a nap after he has his lunch."

El smiled, warm and trustworthy.

"Don't worry," she said, rising from her seat. "We won't disturb him if he's resting. A quick look, that's all we're after."

She'd borrowed one of Ruby's cars for the trip: an olive Land Rover Defender, tall as a Jeep, its tyres and bodywork artfully splattered with the mud and agricultural detritus she thought a couple like the Robinsons would expect of the cash-strapped farmer and show-dog-incapacitator-for-hire they imagined her to be. The afternoon traffic was light, and they made it out of the suburbs and onto the motorway quickly and painlessly, Sophie grinning and humming along to Celine Dion on the radio all the way.

"I can't believe they fell for it!" she cackled, for the third time since they'd left the house, her voice beginning to settle back into an excitable Oxford English. "I can't believe you *got* them to fall for it!"

"It's my job," said El neutrally. "And can you turn that down a bit? Those high notes are a bit much, when you're trying to concentrate."

"It's amazing, though! I mean, I know it's what you do, you and Ruby and Sita - and Mum, even, sometimes - but *seeing* you do it, *helping* you do it... It's just *amazing*, isn't it? Just fucking *amazing*."

"Don't swear," El chided her, glossing over the more problematic parts of the preceding statement. "Your mum doesn't like it."

It was a source of some anxiety for El, and not a little for Rose, that Sophie had become intent on learning the con, since their busman's holiday to San Francisco the previous year - and that both Ruby and Sita had been amenable to teaching her. They'd started small, introducing her to the pigeon drops and fiddle games that had so completely fascinated El at fourteen – but they had plans, Sophie had hinted, to bring her into some of the larger, higher-stakes jobs they had on the boil, once the kid had garnered a little more experience.

"It's not ideal," Rose had said, when El had asked her how she felt about this development. "But what can I do? As she's pointed out so many times, both you and I were up to very similar things at her age. *Worse*, in fact. And she's done nothing so far that could actually land her in any trouble, even if she were caught - or so Sita assures me, anyway."

The first argument, at least, had been difficult to counter, since Sophie had been entirely right. Both El and Rose *had* been up to worse, in their teens: El pulling short cons and getting to grips with the long game under Ruby's tutelage, and Rose helping her adoptive father steal paintings and jewellery and whatever other rare and expensive objects took his fancy from museums and climate-controlled cellars and private collections across the North West.

About the veracity of the second argument, however, El had her doubts, though she'd elected not to share them with Rose.

It had been Sita's idea to take Sophie with her to the Robinsons as an assistant, ostensibly - although Sophie had been a more than willing accomplice.

"Don't you see, darling?" Sita had told El, when she'd made the initial suggestion. "It makes such *sense* for her to tag along. She won't rest until she's able to get her feet wet, or at the very least dip a toe in the water. And how much better for her to do that with *you*, one of the very few people we can be sure will look after her and keep her safe, than for her to go running off on her own, trying her luck doing who *knows* what with a perfect stranger?"

It was a logical assertion - but also, like so many of Sita's arguments, so blatantly Machiavellian that it had left El with the sensation of having been manipulated by unseen hands, even after she'd agreed to the idea.

Sophie, of course, had been overjoyed - albeit not quite so overjoyed as she was *now*, having seen the con in action.

"What's next?" the kid asked, making no move to turn down the volume on the radio. "How are we going to get the painting? No, wait - don't tell me, I bet I can guess. You got a replica made of *Weeping Skeleton*, didn't you? A forgery. And when we go back there, one of us is going to swap it in for the original when those people turn their backs on us."

"No," said El, who'd yet to commission the forged painting but had planned to do more or less exactly what Sophie had outlined on her next visit to the Robinson house.

"What, then?"

"I'll tell you once I've sorted it. And can you at least change stations? That song's giving me a headache."

Just outside of Luton, El pulled the Land Rover into a service area, parking close to the entrance of a fast-food restaurant that smelled, even with the windows rolled up, like cooking oil and mystery meat.

"Why are we stopping?" Sophie asked.

"You need to eat something. I told your mum we were going out for burgers, so I can't very well take you back unfed, can I? She'll get suspicious."

"She's already suspicious. You're a terrible liar, she can read you like a book."

"You just told me how convincing I was, back at the Robinsons'."

"Sure, when you're *working*. But when you're just... *you*, you're rubbish at it. *So* bad - like, it's painful to watch."

"I'll bear that in mind, next time Ruby and Sita take you out for the day and you want me to tell your mum you're going ice-skating with the girls from gymnastics."

She climbed down from the driving seat, closed the door behind her and waited for Sophie to follow.

"I don't even *like* burgers," Sophie grumbled, when she eventually extricated herself from her seatbelt and joined El on the pavement.

"Then I'll get you fish and chips. Doesn't matter to me what you eat, as long as you've got the scent of *something* deep-fried clinging to you when you walk into that flat. But I need to get a tenner out of the cashpoint first so I can actually pay for it, if that's alright with you?"

"You're going to *buy* it?" Sophie said, disappointed. "With your own money?"

"What were you expecting? I don't know what Ruby and Sita have been telling you, but you can't *con* a cash machine. Karen could probably do something elaborate to it with a piece of cardboard and a screwdriver and trick it into coughing up someone's life savings, but that's not really my area."

Karen Baxter - technically Karen *Armstrong*, El supposed, now she'd got married - was another frequent collaborator: a thief, sometime-grifter and perennial tech-head whose skill with a lock-pick, an algorithm and a motherboard - not to say a complex security network - never failed to make El's head spin. If a system could be hacked, Karen could hack it - and if it couldn't be, then the odds were good that she'd be willing to give it a go anyway.

"You can con a *person*, though," Sophie insisted. "The counter assistants - you could persuade one of them to give us a free meal, if you wanted to."

"And get their wages docked for giving away food, when *I* know I can afford five quid for a fizzy drink and a portion of fries and whatever *you* decide you want to eat?"

"I didn't mean..."

"I know you didn't. And I'm not trying to make you feel bad. But if you really are set on doing this, on picking up the con... don't punch down, eh? There's no joy in it."

They walked to the ATM in silence, Sophie's stare fixed to the floor and El's stomach - the barometer by which she tended to judge any shift in her mood - tensing with guilt at having chastised her.

She's a kid, she told herself. *She doesn't know any better. What were you thinking, shaming her like that?*

And what would Rose *have thought, if she'd heard you?*

She pulled her wallet from her jeans, grabbed the first bank card she could reach - the most easily retrievable of a dozen or more cards she kept for everyday use, not one of them registered in the name El Gardener - and slid it into the machine; typed the corresponding pin into the keypad, and waited.

The machine beeped at her, ominously.

"Insufficient funds?" Sophie said, craning her neck to read the message that appeared in green neon text, immediately after the beep, on the machine's dark screen.

El jabbed at another of the machine's buttons, and it spat out the card. She plucked it from the slot, held it up to the light, and studied the account number embossed in the corner of the plastic.

"It's a glitch," she said, confident that it *was*. "There's nearly…" She stopped herself, before she could let slip the intimate details of her personal finances. "There's money in that account. The machine's playing up, that's all."

She dug back into the wallet, snatched another card between forefinger and thumb - this one corresponding to an account that held, she was certain, somewhere in excess of £500,000 - and pushed *that* one into the ATM, punching in the pin with slightly more force than the action necessitated.

Again, the machine beeped.

"I don't get it," Sophie said, as a second message notified El that there were *insufficient funds to proceed with the transaction.*

"Neither do I," El said.

She was reaching into the wallet for a third card when her mobile rang.

"Darling," said Sita, the instant El flipped open the phone cover. She sounded breathless, El thought; breathless, and worried. "Have you spoken to your broker today?"

Another voice shouted something inaudible in the background; Ruby's voice, by the sound of it.

"No," El told her, the acid in her stomach beginning to rise and roil. "Why? *Should* I have done?"

Another muffled shout, a scuffle of footsteps, and then it was Ruby on the line, not Sita.

"Ring 'im," she said, in the familiar, authoritative tone El knew would have no patience for counter-argument. "Ring him now. We need to know if it's just us, or if it's happened to you an' all."

"If *what's* happened?"

More scuffling, another muffled exchange, and then the sound - what El *thought* was the sound - of the phone being passed around again.

"It's not good news, I'm afraid, darling," Sita said, clearing her throat. "I spoke to my financial advisor earlier, and Auntie Ruby to hers, and it *seems* as if..."

"As if..?" El asked, duodenum burning.

"As if we've been cleaned out," Ruby answered, over Sita's protests. "So I should check your money, if I were you. 'Cause me and Sita here... we ain't got none left. I don't know how, but it's gone. Every penny of it."

MORNINGTON CRESCENT, LONDON

February 1941

It was a stroke of luck, seeing him again.

She'd been back in Camden Town, waiting for a bus by the Black Cat Factory, her Dad's old haversack on her back and loaded up with the few odds and ends she had left to transport. They were all but moved now from their house off Hampstead Road - what *had been* their house off Hampstead Road - to her Uncle Jim's in Bethnal Green: the place it had been decided that she and her little sister would be living, with their parents gone, though neither one of them had been consulted about it, even after the decision had been made.

She'd half-wondered, before she'd found out what was what, whether they'd be evacuated: sent off to the seaside or the countryside to stay with some Lord of the Manor or an old maid with no family of her own. Had been in two minds about whether she might actually prefer a change of scenery to knocking around London, until Uncle Jim had come to see them with his news; whether the soft bellies and softer hearts of a load of country bumpkins might be made to work to the advantage of a city girl with a good head on her shoulders.

It was *another* stroke of luck that the man - as thin-faced as he'd seemed to her that day at the bomb site but more spiffily dressed, a toff now rather than a workman, with his brogues and bow tie and silver-tipped cane - had stopped to admire the big cat statues by the factory entrance; that he hadn't walked straight past her as she'd stood at the bus stop.

He hadn't spotted her - or if he had, had paid her no heed. And why should he have? She'd noticed *him*, sifting through the rubble with a dead body in a sack over his shoulder, but he hadn't noticed *her*.

She'd never forget that face, though. It was burned into her, the impression of him; the lines and ridges of him seared onto the film at the back of her eyes as deeply and as permanently as a cattle-brand. Something had changed in her, when she'd seen him - had changed irrevocably. She imagined it as a sound, the change: a soft whirr and a clank, the hiss and click of a combination lock sliding into place the second before the door released and the safe popped open and the diamonds inside spilled out into your hands.

What he'd done... concealing the old man's body, most likely doing away with him before that: she wanted to do it, too. And not just do it - do it *well*. Do it as cleverly as he had; as flawlessly.

Do it, and get away with it, so she could do it again.

When he'd had his fill of the cat statues, he took off on his heels, heading north towards Camden Market. She'd followed him - followed him all the way to Haverstock Hill, where he'd let himself into a grand old terrace next to a boarded-up cafe and failed to come out again. She'd hung around outside, watching; waiting for him so long that the balls of her feet had grown sore.

She'd gone back to the terrace, though: gone back the next day, and the day after that, lurking in the shade of walls and trees and parked-up motor cars in the hope that he'd show himself. Show her more *of* himself.

After nearly a week of watching and waiting, her good luck struck a third time.

It was the middle of the afternoon, and she was beginning to get hungry:

wishing she'd had the foresight to slip one of the oranges Uncle Jim never seemed short of into her coat before she'd left the house, or even a bit of bread and jam. She was debating whether to nip across to the market and help herself to something from a greengrocer's stall when he limbered out of the front door - as lithe and sure-footed as he'd been the night she'd seen him trip-trapping through the wreckage of the pub.

He looked different than he had both of the other times she'd seen him, though that didn't catch her off-guard; she'd been expecting as much, after his last transformation. *This* time he had on a peaked cap, button-down shirt and striped apron that made him look exactly like a butcher's shop assistant. The impression was only reinforced when, after disappearing for a minute or so down the side-alley of the terrace, he reappeared by the front gate, wheeling a bicycle and delivery cart behind him; the cart - a wooden box far bigger than she was - advertising *Arden's Meats: Fine Cuts Straight To Your Door.*

He opened the gate, mounted the bike and began to pedal, slowly, along the pavement, cart trundling heavily along behind him - weaving in and out of the passers-by that met him at the speed of a snail. And a good thing he *did*, she thought: there'd have been no chance of her keeping up with him, if he'd been taking the road at any sort of lick.

Still, she was out of breath when, finally, he put the brakes on: drawing the bike to a halt by the front of an even grander, white-painted mansion in a little street off Belsize Gardens, its entrance separated from the road by a waist-high brick wall and a hedge of rhododendrons so high she could barely see over them, but which, she had to admit, did a bloody good job of keeping her out of sight.

She'd expected him to take the cart around to the back of the house, to what were probably the servants' quarters - any man who owned a place like that, she reckoned, *must* have servants, the full complement of cooks and maids and butlers whose job it was to take in food deliveries and deal with any tradesmen who came knocking, so the gentleman of the house wouldn't have to.

But he didn't. Instead, he hauled both the bike and the cart a foot off the ground - his thin face seeming to strain under the weight of it, cheeks puffing out like a circus strongman's - and pulled both, with no small amount of effort, up the steps to the front door.

He knocked, and before she could count to ten, the door opened, revealing a middle-aged man - not much older than her Dad had been, before the ceiling beams flattened him. The man had a pencil moustache, a boxer's build and a crop of curly black hair slicked down with coconut oil; his thick body was wrapped tightly in a pair of Oriental silk pyjamas. He looked around, furtively; opened the door as wide as it would go to let the thin-faced man inside, cart and all, and then, casting a final - and, she thought, slightly nervous - glance around the empty street, slammed it shut again.

She considered having a nose around outside, to see if she could find a pane of glass to peer through or an open window to listen at. But it was clear even from a distance that it would be pointless, trying to snoop. The house was a fortress: blackout curtains already drawn shut and every point of ingress and egress sealed off from the world outside, probably by design. All she could do was stay where she was, in the shelter of the bushes, until the thin-faced man came out again; wait, and keep waiting, for as long as it took.

It was nearly dark when he finally emerged from the house - gone five o'clock. She was ravenous; the stomach that had been growling when she'd started following him now roaring like a wounded animal, screaming to be fed. Seeing him totter down the steps, though, sucked the appetite from her. Her mouth dried to sandpaper, and the light-headedness that had been leaving her dizzy turned, in a heartbeat, to the electrified pounding of her own pulse in her ears, a fibrillated fluttering she'd associate, much later - when she'd learned about these things, and what they meant - with the spike of adrenaline that was nothing more or less than her own body telling her to *sit up* and *pay attention*.

The cart was even weightier coming out than it had been going in - that much she could tell, even in what little remained of the early evening light. If getting it *up* the steps had been a struggle, then getting it *down* was a feat so Herculean that he groaned aloud as he lugged it and the bike towards the more even ground of the pavement. There was something in there that hadn't been before; something heavy.

There was blood on his apron: red-black streaks of it, and the smudged remains of what might have been a bloody handprint.

Nothing out of the ordinary, for the uniform of a butcher's boy whose job called for him to handle slabs of dripping meat day in, day out.

But it hadn't been there *before*, had it? When he'd gone *into* the house, the apron had been clean.

Once he'd wrestled the bike and cart upright and perched himself on the saddle, his movements were more fluid, his handling of the contraption more controlled. He was still slow, thankfully, wobbling his way along the darkening stretches of road from Belsize Park back to Haverstock Hill, and she just about managed to match his pace - losing herself in the shadows so she'd be hidden from him, should he have cause to throw a look backwards over his shoulder.

He didn't stop at Haverstock Hill, though.

Instead, he pushed on - past the Underground and around the corner towards Euston Station. Just before he reached the turning onto the Euston Road itself, he dropped what little speed he'd picked up - veering the bike into a tiny slice of passageway between a tobacconist and a sandstone Methodist chapel that had just about room, it seemed to her, for twenty parishioners and a priest, if they squeezed in tight.

She edged as close to the mouth of the passage as she could without giving herself away, banking on the darkness covering her, and peered around the wall.

There was a cigarette lighter in his hand. Yet more good luck, because the way he was holding it - close to his face, the palm of one hand cupped around the flame - meant she had a decent view of him, as he leaned the bike to rest against the wall. A decent view, that was, of what he was *doing*, as he tugged the crate from its moorings and prised the lid of it open with his fingertips.

They were bloody too, she saw; red raw.

She couldn't have said she was surprised, when the flame flickered across the open crate and she saw, just before the light passed over it, the bare white foot of a dead man - of someone she *thought* was a dead man - protruding out from the rim. Truth be told, she'd been expecting to see something like it.

What *did* surprise her was the other thing he'd been wheeling around in the crate.

The official name for it, though she didn't know it then, was a *bundle charge*: a cluster of hand grenades with the handles and fuses removed, strapped to a larger, more fully assembled grenade by a length of wire and capable of discharging the explosive power of all seven of its component pieces, when properly deployed.

He pulled it from the crate and held it upright, close to the flame; *dangerously* close to the flame, if you'd asked for her opinion on the subject. Though she knew it was an explosive - the look of the casings on the defused grenade parts told her so, even in the dark - there was something faintly comical about its appearance; a strange circularity. In another time and place - not in the thin-faced man's hands, and not six inches from another dead body he'd very likely made dead *with* those hands - she might have thought she was looking at a toilet plunger, or a funny-shaped rolling pin swiped from someone's kitchen.

With the same turn of speed she'd seen him call on in the pub that night, he replaced the lid on the crate, spun around and, leaving the crate and the bike and the unfortunate cargo in the passageway, strode towards her, the bundle of explosives in his fist.

No, she corrected herself; not towards *her*. He wouldn't have been able to see *her*; not when it was as damn-near pitch-black as it was becoming.

He was heading *past* her, for the street.

She side-stepped, quietly as she could manage, into the doorway of the tobacconist, hoping its canopied arch would be deep enough to protect her, to give her the camouflage she needed.

But, as it had been before, his attention was fixed on another point entirely - in this case, on the chapel.

He made quick work of the lock on the door to the church; had it unfastened, and had slipped himself and his improvised bomb inside almost before she could blink.

Then, before she'd had time to steady her breath, he was out again - away from the church and back down the passageway, a torn-off piece of what looked to her like cotton wool shoved in each of his ears.

And she knew, in a flash, what it was that he'd done the last time; what he'd done, and why he'd done it.

Knew what was coming - and had sense enough to understand what to do with the knowing.

Sense enough to run, as quick as her legs would carry her, towards the Euston Road and away from the chapel, before the grenades went off and the roof caved in.

WEST HAMPSTEAD, LONDON

March 1998

W e're skint," Ruby told her, draining her coffee and sinking back into her overstuffed recliner with the weary resignation of a Romanov empress recounting the news of a peasants' revolt. "Brassic. Not got tuppence to rub together, neither one of us."

She seemed, El thought, less alarmed by this development now than she had on the phone earlier that day: philosophical, stoic even, rather than panicked.

"You don't sound too upset, for someone who's had God knows how many million quid vanish into thin air," El replied, trying to keep her own panic out of her voice.

Ruby shrugged.

"I've had nothing before," she said. "And I daresay I'll have nothing again someday, once we've get all this lot back. Wouldn't be much cop at this game if I didn't know how to make something out of nothing, would I? You keep hold of your wits and you'll do alright, no matter how much you got left in the bank. Ain't that right, Sita?"

Sita, who as far as El was aware was more than five decades removed from anything like poverty, nodded grudgingly - but looked, to El, decidedly little green about the gills.

They'd assembled at Ruby's for an emergency summit meeting: El, Sophie, Sita and Rose, with Ruby presiding over them from her armchair. Neither Dexter nor Michael, Ruby's twin sons - and current cohabitants - had yet made an appearance, but it seemed likely to El that they'd be arriving home at any moment. For both of them, their mother's distress was a kind of Bat-Signal: calling out to them, wherever they happened to be, and summoning them back to the familial roost.

"Do we have any sense at all of *when* it happened?" Rose asked - sounding surprisingly untroubled herself, for a woman whose entire fortune, like Ruby's, had dematerialised from the vault like so much leprechaun gold in more or less the blink of an eye.

She'd been the first person El had called, after her initial conversation with Ruby and Sita and the shock of her experience at the cashpoint. Before her accountants, before her Filofax of bank managers, before the ethically dubious but refreshingly competent broker who oversaw the ebb and flow of her income and savings from his one-man office in the Caymans - and who, unlike the others, knew her by her real name, and not a pseudonym.

El had expected to do most of the talking; to be speaking rather than listening when Rose finally picked up her mobile, after it had rung unanswered for so long that El had begun to believe that she'd gone out and left it plugged into its charger in the kitchen.

Instead, she'd found her heartbeat accelerating and the acid cauldron of her stomach dropping as Rose had told her, with far less composure than she was now exhibiting, that there was something wrong with *her* accounts, too. That her business manager and her financial advisor, both in some distress, had been in touch to break the news; to tell her, the financial advisor very nearly on the verge of tears as he choked out the words, that her assets - personal as well as professional - had been inexplicably frozen; rendered inaccessible, and thus effectively useless.

"I've spoken to the police," Rose had said - a phrase that had caused El, for whom the police generally represented a bump in the road around which to swerve and not a go-to solution for pecuniary difficulties, to jump that bit further out of her skin. "They're on their way over now. The boy I spoke to said it sounded like... what did he call it? A cyberattack. You know - *hackers*."

"The police are coming to the flat?" El had answered, as perturbed at the prospect of the police paying a visit to her home - to the place that was about to *become* her home - as by the both of them apparently having been made suddenly and inexplicably penniless.

"God, no! Do you think I'm insane? They're going to Highgate - I said I'd meet them there."

Highgate, El had known, meant the gated four storey house in the north London suburbs in which Rose kept the most expensive of her collections: one of a handful of properties she owned in London and Paris. It had served as the venue for their first, strange meeting two years earlier - and still served, to the best of El's knowledge, as a stand-in for Rose and Sophie's *real* home whenever they were in need of a little anonymity.

"Do you want us to head out that way, too?" El had asked.

"Not unless you really want to. There *is* one favour you could do for me, though. Would you mind calling Karen? I feel like she might be better placed than either of us to find out what the hell is going on."

It was a sensible next step; El had planned to give Karen a bell herself about Ruby and Sita's pecuniary conundrum, and her own, just as soon as she'd talked to Rose and the finance guys. If anyone could follow the digital breadcrumbs left by a small nation's worth of evaporated money, it was Karen.

"Wait, though," she'd said, before Rose could hang up. "There's something I need to tell you. The reason I rang."

"Is it Sophie? Did something happen?"

"No. *No.* She's fine."

"And you're alright? You're safe?"

"Yes. Sort of. More or less."

"Then... can it wait, whatever it is? I really need to get to Highgate."

El had taken a deep breath; placed a splayed, self-soothing palm across her churning belly.

"No," she'd said, "I don't think it can."

They were connected - the thefts, and the freezing of the assets. Ruby and Sita were sure of it, as both had made abundantly clear when El and Sophie, and then Rose, had eventually landed in West Hampstead. Rose had been quick to agree.

"But what I don't understand," Rose had said, after she'd despatched Sophie to the kitchen to put the kettle on, "is why whoever did this didn't take *my* money, too. Why they'd leave it just... *sitting* there like that."

"Could be they *couldn't* take it," Ruby had suggested. "A lot of your cash is tied up with your business, ain't it? So maybe it's locked up too tight for whoever doing this to do much more than just stop you getting to it. Maybe the security on the accounts is that bit too hard for them to hack. Especially if there's, I don't know... firewalls and that set up to stop any thievin' bastards getting their mucky hands on what's inside."

"Could be," El had murmured - wondering, absently, where Ruby had picked up enough IT lingo to drop references to *hacks* and *firewalls* into the mix.

"*When* it happened?" Ruby said, parroting Rose's question back at her. "Sometime today, I should think. Everything were fine at my end when I spoke to Bernie yesterday."

Bernie was Ruby's money man: a crooked, decidedly old-school IFA who'd handled her finances since at least the seventies, and whom - despite all evidence suggesting she should do nothing of the sort - she trusted implicitly not to cheat her.

("He's bent," as she'd told El more than once, when the subject was raised. "But he *knows* he's bent, you know what I mean? He ain't trying to pretend he's anything else. You know where you are, with a bloke like that").

"And at mine," Sita added morosely. She reached for the flat gold case and box of matches laid out on the coffee table in front of her, unlatched the case, took a slim white cigarette from inside and lit it, inhaling so deeply that her exhalation, when it came, wreathed her head and shoulders in a fog of near-Dickensian density.

"Do you have to do that in here?" Ruby coughed, batting the smoke from her bright blue, now slightly watering eyes. "If the boys ain't allowed to stay indoors when they smoke them little cigarillo things they like when they've had a drink, then I don't see why *you* should be able to light up left, right and centre."

"I think you'll find these are somewhat exceptional circumstances," Sita replied, taking a second, equally long pull on the cigarette and tapping the ash into her teacup. "A *small* suspension of your usual rules is hardly a gargantuan ask."

El found herself, instinctively, reaching for her own pocket, her own cigarette packet, and came up empty. Annie Cutler the dog-shearing farmer, she remembered, didn't smoke, for reasons she could no longer recall but which had felt compelling when she'd started to build out the persona; neither therefore, for the duration of the con, did El.

She stared at Sita's cigarette, fixing the burning tip with a look of what must have seemed, to Sita, great yearning. The older woman took pity on her: opened the case and thrust its contents El-ward.

"No, you don't," Ruby snapped at Sita, before El so much as extended an arm. "Bad enough I've got you puffing away and stinking up the place - I ain't having you corrupt *her* an' all."

"The girl smokes twenty a day," Sita said, gesturing languidly at El. "I'm hardly the serpent in the Garden, leading her into temptation with my nicotine apples."

"Not in here she don't. And you want to be thankful I ain't making *you* go and stand out on the balcony."

"So you believe it happened today, whatever it was?" Rose said - trying, El could tell, to draw Ruby and Sita away from their habitual bickering and back to the problem at hand.

Ruby glowered at Sita and allowed herself to sink down further into the cushions of her chair.

"I do," she said. "But if you ask me, the question we'd all do better to ask ourselves is: *who* done it? Who is it that's been at my money, and yours, and Sita's, and young El here's? Or perhaps I should say: who do we know who hates us, hates *all four* of us so much that they'd be wanting to hit us in the wallet where it hurts?"

"You think it was her?" Rose asked her, when at least a minute of silence had elapsed.

"You're damn right I do," she answered. "You mean to say you *don't?*"

Hannah, El thought. Hannah fucking D'Amboise. The one that got away, but refused to *stay* away.

Hannah D'Amboise was, at least genetically, Rose's half-sister, and every bit as sociopathic in disposition and in practice as their late biological father - something Rose and El and Ruby and Karen and Sita had discovered that bit too late for the information to be useful, sometime *after* Hannah had nearly killed their then-colleague Kat Morgan with a blow to the head that took out half her skull.

She'd also, they suspected but couldn't prove, been behind a blackmail attempt on them the year before - orchestrated via *another* sociopath with a grudge, the now-imprisoned Charlie Soames - that had almost ended with Ruby stabbed to death on her own kitchen floor.

It was fair to say, therefore, that Hannah had it in for them, individually and as a group. And Ruby, though it pained El to admit it, was probably on to something with her supposition: if someone *was* targeting them through their bank balances, targeting all of them at once - and not just Ruby or Sita, who'd amassed more than a few enemies in their fifty-plus years on the job - then Hannah was a very likely candidate.

"I suppose it's a reasonable conclusion," Rose agreed, looking so forlorn as she spoke that El thought she might cry.

"She's upped her game, that Hannah - I'll say that for her," Ruby said. "I'd never have thought she'd have it in her to do that much damage, just with a computer."

"I think we can safely assume she isn't working alone," Sita observed, stubbing out the remainder of her cigarette in the small puddle of liquid left in the bottom of her teacup, where it hissed and then, with a final wisp of smoke, expired.

"No?" said Ruby.

"With that amount of money to move, and all at once?"

From somewhere close to Sita, a phone rang. She shifted position in her seat, drew a very small mobile from her purse - gold, to match the cigarette case - and, with only the most cursory glance at the screen, brought it delicately to her ear.

"*Yes,* darling?" she demanded of the caller. El heard a pause; the faint, distorted sound of someone speaking, very quickly.

Sita's perfectly cultivated brow creased in response.

"Now isn't the *best* time you could have chosen," she told whomever the caller was. "My hands are rather full, at present."

More talking: as tinny as before but the delivery rapid, urgent.

Sita's eyes widened.

"Good lord," she said. "Are you certain?"

"Who is it?" Ruby hissed at her, in her variation on a *sotto voce*.

"Gerry Adler," Sita whispered back, momentarily covering the receiver on the handset.

"*Adler*?" said Ruby, more loudly. "What does *he* want, when he's at home? Has something happened?"

Gerry Adler, El had learned during their run-in with Charlie Soames, was an old friend and on-off lover of Sita's: a senior officer with the Met, now close to retirement, who'd taken it upon himself since the events of the previous year to watch over Sita - and by extension Ruby, and the rest of them - from a discreet distance, and to alert them to any difficulties that might be coming their way in the not-too-distant future.

"Gerald," Sita said, dropping her own voice lower, "I really must go and deal with this. *Yes*, now. I shall call you back just as soon as I'm able. Yes, darling - *today*. You have my word on it."

She closed the phone, ending the call, and slid the handset back into her purse, her mouth tightening and face paling to wheat. She turned ninety degrees in her seat, until she and El were face to face.

"El, darling," she began, with unexpected gentleness, "It appears I have some rather bad news. Gerry tells me... well, he tells me your house is on fire."

Ruby snorted.

"I'd bloody say so," she said. "Hers and all the rest of ours, an' all. Some bleedin' use *he* is. He couldn't've told us that *before* that harpy sucked my pension dry?"

"I'm not speaking figuratively," Sita snapped, eyes swivelling back to Ruby's. "The girl's house is quite literally *on fire*. The police are there now, with the Fire and Rescue Service. And I'm sorry to say, darling," she added to El, more sympathetically, "that there may not be very much of it left standing."

HAVERSTOCK HILL, LONDON

February 1941

Dolly was worried, walking up to his doorstep, that her nerves would get the better of her: that the thin-faced man would look right through her and tell her to bugger off, or that her tongue would freeze up altogether and she'd end up able to do not much more than stand there staring at him, mouth flapping open like a goldfish's.

Or worse.

There was no sense in entertaining the worry, though - not if she wanted to get from him what she'd come to get. And he didn't strike her as someone who'd have much time for timidity.

It was early in the day, just gone ten o'clock; a normal bloke, she thought, would be out at work. But he *wasn't* normal, was he? And everything she'd seen of him so far had led her to believe that he was the kind of man who did his best work at night, with the darkness of the blackout wrapped around him like a pair of dragon wings.

Besides: not everyone kept to a regular calendar. Her Uncle Jim didn't, for starters. He was up and about at every hour of the day and night, letting himself out through the kitchen after supper and sneaking back in before the break of dawn - though she couldn't truthfully say, even after going on a month under his roof, what it was he actually *did* for a living.

She'd tried asking her sister what *she* thought, in bed one night with her mind galloping a mile a minute with the puzzle of it. But the kid had been practically mute since their Mum and Dad had passed; getting her to answer even the most straightforward question was like shouting at a brick wall, and eventually Dolly had grown tired of trying, turned herself around and gone to sleep.

Ah, well. She'd find out for herself, eventually. He wasn't stupid, Uncle Jim - but he wasn't as clever as he must have thought he was, either. And if it came right down to it, Dolly had an idea she might be cleverer still.

There was no answer, at her first knock; no noise at all behind the door. But she wasn't willing to give up. Not yet.

She tried again. This time there *were* noises, drifting out through the sealed wood from the hallway inside: footsteps on tile, light but audible.

The door opened. And, instead of freezing up or choking on her words or any of the other dozen scenarios she'd managed to persuade herself might play out, as she'd made her way across to Camden from the East End, she smiled; had to bite down hard on her bottom lip to stop herself from laughing.

He was dressed for bed - how was *that* for a turn-up? White Long Johns on his legs and a light blue nightshirt down to his knees; a pair of little round spectacles balanced on his nose and soft grey slippers on his feet. Even a nightcap on his head, like Wee Willie Winkie. The very ordinariness of him seemed, to her, ridiculous - even if (or perhaps, she thought later, *because*) she knew what he was capable of. That he'd have no qualms at all about killing her stone dead where she stood.

"May I help you?" he asked, peering down at her and rubbing at his tired-looking eyes behind the lenses of his specs. He sounded posh, she thought; plummy and well-educated, not at all the sort of gent who'd need to go around doing people in and setting off bombs in churches to cover his tracks.

She cleared her throat. She'd rehearsed this; she knew what she wanted to say, what she *needed* to say.

"Can I come in?" she said, the words flowing out of her as smoothly as if she were reciting the lines of a poem from a page or a Bible verse at Sunday school.

He took two steps backwards, the soles of his slipper-shod feet delivering a silky, whistling shuffle as they pulled him along the floor, and rubbed again at his eyes - blinking back at her in surprise. The gesture lent a bird-like cast to his features; gave him the look of a professor or a librarian, not a habitual killer.

"What do you want?" he answered, warily. "I'm rather tired, and I haven't been up for long, so I'd prefer not to stand around here chatting, if it's all the same to you."

"Bit of a night-owl, are you? I thought you might be."

"Are you selling something? Because the sign says very clearly that I'm not interested in that sort of thing."

He pointed to a square bit of ivory card someone had stuck above the doorbell, a bit of card on which that same someone - perhaps the thin-faced man himself - had stencilled, in bold letters: NO PEDDLERS, HAWKERS OR SOLICITORS.

"I want to know why you do it," she said, still unexpectedly calm.

"Why I do *what*, for heaven's sake?"

"Kill them. I want to know why you kill them."

Something shifted, very subtly, in his bearing. The dazed bookworm veneer was still there, still in place behind the spectacles and the night shirt, but there was something else there now, too: a hard, appraising quality to his eyes, a sharpness to the lines of his jaw as he sucked in a lungful of freezing smog through his oversized teeth. The strange contrast between the two expressions - the flash of wolf showing just beneath the sheep - reminded her of a fish she'd once heard about on the wireless, a deep-sea fish that disguised itself as another sort of fish altogether to lure in its prey. Or the Devil, in the skin of a man.

"I can't imagine what you're talking about," he said, curling his lips in a smile that was more than half a grimace, "and I'm sure you find it terribly amusing to make these ... *accusations*, but I'm going to have to ask you to leave, if you don't mind."

I could go, she told herself. *Leg it now, back home, and hope he doesn't come after me or find a way to hunt me down.*

Or I could stand my ground and see how all this unfolds.

The decision came so easily, it hardly felt as if she'd made a choice at all.

"I'll just be off, then, shall I?" she said lightly. "Nip off down the police station and tell 'em what I saw you do the other day to that big bloke over in Belsize Gardens?"

It was a gamble, baiting him that way. Technically, she hadn't *seen* him do anything to the big man in the silk pyjamas; couldn't have done, with the curtains drawn and that bloody rhododendron bush in the way.

But *he* didn't know that, did he? He couldn't be sure she hadn't seen him.

He didn't answer - just kept staring at her with those hard eyes like she was a funny-looking spider he'd trapped under a glass. One he wasn't sure wanted to bite him or scuttle away through a crack in the wall.

She stared right back at him. Then, when it had been so long since either of them had said anything that she was starting to question whether she'd got it all wrong, whether maybe she'd dreamt the whole thing up and he really *was* just some posh bloke trying to sleep off a hangover, he sighed through his teeth - a sound like air being let out of an inner tube - and took a handful of steps towards her, edging her backwards.

"If I really *had* done what you say I have," he said, so casually he could have been asking her for the time, but with an edge of something else to the utterance that might have scared another person, someone softer than Dolly, "which of course I *haven't*, because even the allegation is absurd... then wouldn't it be somewhat incautious of you to challenge me on it - and on my own turf, so to speak? Rather like diving into a mangrove swamp to pull at the tail of a crocodile."

He's trying to scare you, she told herself. *Trying to scare you, so he can get the measure of you.*

Don't let him.

"Only if I'd been too stupid to cover my arse," she replied, pulling her spine straight and her shoulders back and making a point of looking him in those granite eyes of his, even with him towering over her.

"What *can* you mean by that, I wonder?"

"I *mean*, I ain't daft enough to try to go after someone I know is a murderer without making damn sure I've got at least one person who'd know where to come looking, if I should happen to, let's say, turn up dead. Or, I don't know... disappear in mysterious circumstances. I *mean* I've got enough brains in my head to have wrote down what I saw you doing the other week, put it in an envelope and left it for someone to open and read, if I ever need 'em to."

His eyebrows rose in what might have been consternation - as if what he'd thought was a garden spider had turned out, after all, to be a tarantula with a mouthful of venom. Still littler than him, and still confined to a glass, but capable of doing him some damage, if he didn't handle it just right.

"How *old* are you?" he asked - looking her up and down and sideways, taking her in. "No more than thirteen or fourteen, surely?"

"Twelve," she told him. "Thirteen in September."

"And do you have a name?"

She hadn't expected him to be asking *her* questions. But the fact he *was* asking didn't throw her, either - though she reminded herself that she needed to be cautious, to tread carefully, just in case. He might've thought she had a bit of poison to her, but she couldn't let herself forget what *he* was, either.

"Dolly," she said. "And that's all the detail you're getting, so don't think you can go asking me no more. Like I said: I ain't daft."

This response seemed to amuse him. Then his smile faded, and he sighed.

"Alright, Dolly-with-no-last-name," he said, opening the door wide and stepping back again to let her inside. "In you come. Perhaps we *do* have things to talk about, after all."

KINGSTON, LONDON

April 1998

From the outside, Karen's bungalow looked much the same as it had, the first time El had laid eyes on it. Dark beige, net curtained and gardened to within an inch of its life, it seemed every inch the residence of a house-proud pensioner: one with a penchant for outdoor ornaments of the bearded gnome and ceramic hedgehog variety.

Inside, however, it was radically different than El remembered: the kitchen, living room, bedrooms and store cupboard (which, El knew from experience, had held its own peculiar secrets), and the flock wallpaper and antiquated fittings that had littered them now replaced by a black and white, entirely open-plan arrangement so starkly minimalist it could have been designed by Walter Gropius. There was no bathroom in sight, a feat of architectural courage El admired but elected not to enquire about.

"We've been renovating," Karen explained, entirely unnecessarily - plonking herself down on a Wassily chair opposite El in a section of the now-enormous room that had previously been the hallway. "Fergus kept telling me how sick he was of living like a little old lady. Didn't you, babe?"

Fergus - the tall, redheaded boy who was now Karen's husband - placed a cup of hot chocolate in her hand, passed another to El and sat down, crossed-legged, on the flagstone floor beside his wife.

"Just fancied a bit of a change," he said, his soft Highlands accent a marked contrast to Karen's London vowels.

Like the house, Fergus himself was somewhat different than he'd been - even two months earlier, at their wedding. Though still thin as a rake and pale as the undead, he now sported yellow-tinted contact lenses that gave his eyes an unsettlingly panther-like appearance - and, more disconcertingly still, a pair of stubby, stainless-steel horns jutting out from the stretched white skin of his forehead.

("I keep asking him to tell me what he's fucking playing at, getting *them* put in," Karen had said, in response to El's apparently obvious surprise at seeing the horns when Fergus had greeted her at the door. "The lenses I get - they're meant to block out UV light, so they stop him getting headaches when he's sat in front of a screen all day. But those nubs in his head ... what do they even *do*, except make him look like he's auditioning for the role of back-up faun in The Lion, The Witch And The Wardrobe?"

"I like them," Fergus had replied, running a protective hand over his left-side horn.

"You can *like* them all you want," she'd told him, showing El inside, "just as long as you put a hat on when we're out together. Last thing I want is some smart-arse coming up to me in Tesco to ask me if I'm Mrs Tumnus").

"It looks great," El said, making a show of scanning the room: the exposed brick of the walls and industrial-chic pipework of the ceiling and, she noticed now, the double futon and tatami mat folded out in a far corner by the plank bookshelves. "Sort of... spartan. But in a good way."

"Severe, you mean?" Karen laughed. "Yeah - can't argue with that. Good news is, we've kept downstairs more or less the way it was. Only thing that's changed is how we get to it."

She gestured to a thin but incongruously wide grey and ochre rug covering a portion of the floor to her right.

El stared at the rug - then, mentally restoring the bungalow to its previous configuration, understood its significance.

"There's a door underneath?" she asked.

Karen smiled.

"Leads down to the basement. It's still got the fingerprint lock on it," she added, as if to pre-empt any security concerns El might have. "So nobody's getting in or out of it but me and Hellboy here." She reached down and ran a hand, affectionately, over one of Fergus' horns. "But we thought, you know... if we're gonna have an underground lair, we might as well have a trapdoor as well. Go, you know... full-on supervillain."

Lair, it occurred to El, wasn't an entirely off-base description of the couple's joint office-cum-workshop. It was a huge, cavernous space, one that housed not only their computers and the various pieces of electrical equipment that Karen, at least, seemed to need to work whatever tech-magic it was she worked on the job, but a mind-boggling array of files, lockpicks, blades and pliers - all of which she'd assured El that she used, and on a semi-regular basis.

Whether it also served as a vault and safe-haven for even a portion of Karen's (she assumed pretty significant) fortune, El didn't know - though it struck her that, given the circumstances, she might very soon find out.

"Should have got one of those done myself, shouldn't I?" she said, ruefully. "Might've helped."

Karen looked down at her feet.

"Sita told me what happened to your place," she said, with unusual awkwardness. "I'm sorry. It's just shit, innit?"

El considered her own feet; the trainers she'd borrowed from Sophie - who was, against all odds, *her size* - in the absence of clothes of her own. And the absence, moreover, of any available money with which to buy new ones.

"Yeah," she said. "*Shit* about covers it."

She'd had more to say, at the time; a lot more, much of it in anger. In the two hours it had taken her, in the panicked wake of Gerry Adler's off-the-record call to Sita two weeks before, to drive herself and Rose from the flat in West Hampstead to her cottage in Leicestershire in Ruby's mud-splattered Land Rover, with Sophie sitting in awkward silence in the back seat, she'd cycled through four of the five stages of grief: from denial of the veracity of Adler's claim, all the way to depression at the thought of her worldly goods, or the vast majority thereof, disappearing in what had to be a cloud of arson-smoke.

Acceptance, she suspected, would be a long time coming.

The cottage, when they'd finally got there, had been every bit as damaged as Gerry Adler had said: a black, roofless exoskeleton of smoke-ravaged timber and melted appliances; nothing left of its organs but hot, choking piles of ash and soot. She'd been so shell-shocked she'd barely made it out of the car, and the fire crew still there would doubtless have made it their business to keep her away from the scene if she'd tried to get close, but even from a distance she could tell that almost everything she'd had in there was gone: every book, every album, every bra and toothbrush. Every scarf and wig and makeup kit and stack of research notes she'd ever used to transform herself from usefully nondescript El Gardener to geologist Tara Ashworth, or sushi restauranteur Dipti Agrawal, or crime boss Angela Di Salvo.

All of it, gone, in no more time than it had taken for whichever bastard did it to light the fuse and leave it to burn.

With no access to Rose's money and no money at all in El's account, they'd considered driving back to London and coming back to Leicester to assess the damage up close the following day - but had been spared that, at least, by the intervention of June Martin next door.

An elderly widow and owner of a hideously ugly hairless cat named Jenkins, whom El had occasionally had cause to feed and water, Mrs Martin been watching the blaze and the ministrations of the firefighters from her front window for quite some time before El and Rose and Sophie had arrived. She'd taken pity on them; had ambled out from her own cottage in her nightgown and curlers, Jenkins at her heels, and urged El to spend the night on the fold-out bed in their front room, if she needed to.

"And your friends, too, duck, if they like," she'd added. "Does you good to have people stopping with you, times like this."

So dazed she might as well have forgotten how to speak, El had nodded her agreement - and, with Rose's arm around her doing much of the work of keeping her vertical, had followed the old lady and her pink, wrinkled familiar where they'd led.

She'd woken early the following morning, unfolding herself one stiffening limb at a time from the makeshift sleeping space she'd constructed for herself out of cushions and a blanket on the floor - the popping of her joints waking Rose and Sophie, who'd come around almost immediately thereafter, the ancient springs of the camp-bed she'd insisted they sleep on creaking under the weight of them with every shift and stir of their bodies. All of them had snuck out before either Mrs Martin or Jenkins could intercept them in the hallway - though El had left an effusive thank-you note on the kitchen table, and resolved to send the old lady a very large bouquet and a bottle of something expensive, once the current storm had passed.

The cottage had looked, if anything, even worse in daylight than it had the night before. El had imagined, lying there on June Martin's threadbare carpet with her hips aching and her shoulders seizing, that she'd want to pore over the remains of it: to pick through the charred lumps of microwave and mattress and refrigerator to see if there was anything - anything at all - for her to salvage. But standing on the edges of it, the barbecued-plastic stench of cooling white goods flooding her sinuses, she'd wanted nothing but to get away: to jump back behind the steering wheel of the Land Rover, press a foot to the accelerator and not stop until she and Rose and Sophie were back at the apartment in Bayswater, and she could lick her wounds and mourn her losses somewhere she wouldn't be confronted quite so viscerally by the still-smouldering evidence of them.

There was no question of the fire having started accidentally. The police and the fire brigade had said as much, when she'd eventually spoken to them, although neither service had any leads they'd felt able to share with her, nor any sense of *why* her cottage had been targeted - and the several hours of discussion she'd had with the overzealous young officers in charge of the investigation had veered, at times, towards full-on interrogation of her life and history.

No, she'd told them when they asked - she didn't know of anyone who might want to harm her.

No, she didn't have any enemies, that she knew of - personal *or* professional. She was a self-employed management consultant, as her tax records would demonstrate if they'd care to look; she worked mainly away from home, in London and elsewhere, and almost always alone. She had no colleagues to speak of; certainly no-one they'd find it worth their while to talk to.

Yes, she lived alone: no partner, no children.

Yes, the cottage was her only asset. They were welcome to check for themselves, if they'd like.

No, she hadn't been at home when the fire had been started. And thank God for that.

"But did she *know* you wouldn't be there?" Rose had asked her in bed that night, after El had relayed the highlights of her conversation with the police.

The *she*, of course, had been Hannah. Rose had long been paranoid about the threat her sister might pose - to all three of them, but especially to Sophie. The fear of Hannah's return had been the driving force behind her decision to move them from the house she'd loved in Notting Hill to the rented apartment overlooking Hyde Park: a block of flats so heavily guarded and comprehensively alarmed that it was effectively a fortress.

"She must have known the odds were good I wouldn't be," El had answered, counting the small indentations in the ceiling above them and avoiding Rose's eyes. "I mean, when am I *ever* there? Even before I was *here* every night, I was usually in town somewhere if I was on the job."

"I can't say I'm convinced."

El had torn her gaze from the ceiling and rolled onto her side, pulling Rose closer.

"I'm know what you're thinking," she'd said. "And you don't have to convince me she's a fucking lunatic. I was there in the hospital that night, just like you were - I remember what she did to Kat. But you're safe here. *Sophie's* safe here. You'd have more luck trying to break into Buckingham Palace than you would this building."

Rose hadn't been convinced, however - and a week later, grey in the face and biting anxiously at her bottom lip, she'd taken El aside and told her, in no uncertain terms, that she wanted them to move again.

"Not forever. Just for a few months, until we've worked out what Hannah's up to and what we can do about it."

"Where?" El had asked - knowing Rose well enough to be fairly sure that there was nothing to be gained in trying to dissuade her, if she'd already made up her mind.

"To Harriet's. Hannah... she wouldn't think we'd go there, would she? I doubt she even knows that Harriet and I have a relationship. And Harriet loves Sophie. She'd do anything for her. Protect her with her life, if it came to it."

El couldn't fault her logic. Harriet Marchant, another recently discovered half-sister with whom Rose shared a biological father, had proven herself to be - in the year or so that Rose had known her - an especially attentive aunt, as well as a reliable friend and confidante to Rose.

On El herself, Harriet had seemed less keen; had seemed suspicious, even. But if Rose was happy, then El could learn to live with the odd arched eyebrow or harshly worded comment over soup and sandwiches.

"Sure," El had replied, suppressing her disappointment. "Go for it, if you think it'll stop you worrying. I doubt Ruby'll mind having me stay with her and the boys for a bit."

At that solution, though, it was *Rose* who'd seemed dismayed.

"I mean, of course," she'd said, her face flushing in a way El knew it tended to, when she'd been thrown a curveball and was trying to keep her surprise from showing. "Absolutely, if you *want* to. Though I was rather hoping you might want to come with us. You know... to Harriet's."

And what else could El have done but acquiesce?

Karen swirled an index finger in her hot chocolate and licked at it, thoughtfully.

"You want to know why she's not come at *me*, don't you?" she said. "Why *I've* not lost anything, the way you lot have."

It seemed a waste of energy to deny it. It wasn't *why* El had come all the way out to Kingston to see her; wasn't the *main* reason, anyway. But she'd been dying to know - ever since Ruby had told her that Karen had so far dodged the bullet that had torn through the rest of them. That Karen's house and money and everything else she owned were, or seemed to be, entirely intact.

"I'm curious, yeah," she admitted. "Do *you* know?"

Karen dipped the finger back into the hot chocolate; stirred it around the gloopy not-quite-liquid like a teaspoon.

"The trouble with money," she said - unnecessarily elliptically, El thought, "is, it's not real. It's symbolic, know what I mean? A medium of exchange.

It's only useful 'cause everyone's willing to *believe* it's useful, that it's worth something. If everyone stopped believing in it, it'd be nothing but tin and paper. Even more, when the money's electronic - all the ones and zeros on your monthly statement, all the lines of digits that come up on the screen when you go to make a transfer. People stop believing in *that*, and you'd be just as well off trying to buy a new pair of Levi's or whatever with a load of hieroglyphs scribbled on papyrus as you would with a roll of banknotes, for all the good they'll do you."

"You can't wear money," Fergus murmured from his cross-legged position on the floor. "Can't eat it, either."

"Exactly," Karen said, rewarding him for his agreement with a pat on the horns.

"So, what?" El asked. "You don't believe in currency?"

"Didn't say that, did I? 'Course I *believe* in it. I mean, it exists, yeah? Objectively exists. Or everyone *thinks* it does, which is basically the same thing. But let's just say I'm not one hundred percent convinced we're all gonna *keep* thinking it does, the way we do now. So when, from time to time, I come into a bit of money... I like to make sure it's not gonna *stay* as money very long, if you get what I'm saying. I like to turn it into something else, so it's not just sat there in a bank vault or getting pegged to *more* imaginary money on the global stock exchange."

El considered what she knew about Karen: about her likes and dislikes, the Byzantine workings of her complicated brain.

"Gold?" she said, taking her best guess. "You buy gold?"

Karen, to her surprise, seemed to find the suggestion hysterical. Even Fergus cracked a smile.

"Gold?" she laughed. "What am I gonna do with *gold*? Civilisation collapses and I end up bartering with some shopkeeper for a couple of chickens and a bag of flour, you think he's gonna want a bit of metal that'll do nothing for him but make him a medallion he can show off 'round his neck?

Fuck that. You buy gold, you might just as well be keeping a pirate treasure-chest under your floorboards."

"What, then?"

Karen leaned in towards her.

"I'm only telling you this 'cause you're a mate, you get me? 'Cause we've been through the wringer together, and I trust you."

"I'm glad. So tell me."

She hesitated, then leaned in a little further.

"Silver," she told El, so quietly it was nearly a whisper. "Silver bullion."

El frowned.

"Silver?" she said. "The metal? I don't... Isn't that like gold, but cheaper?"

Now Fergus laughed too, the both of them chuckling heartily together at her expense.

"Sorry," Karen eventually answered, dabbing at her eyes. "Sorry. Think it just... took us by surprise, that's all. You not knowing. But to answer your question: no, silver's not like gold. It's fucking *nothing* like gold, actually. Gold's got no *intrinsic* value, you know what I mean? It doesn't *do* anything, just sits there and looks pretty. But silver... silver's in *everything*."

"Everything," Fergus added, sagely.

"*Everything*," Karen repeated. "Heavy industry, tech and electricals, photography... it gets fucking *everywhere*. It's the best electrical conductor out there, silver. Plus it's got medicinal value. Turn it into silver sulfadiazine, and you've got yourself a proper old-school antibiotic. So, yeah - it might not *cost* as much as gold, right now... but you better believe it's what people are gonna be scrambling 'round for, come the apocalypse."

El was genuinely speechless, albeit only temporarily.

"Where do you keep it?" she asked, when she could move her lips again. "These bullions bars - where have you got them stashed?"

"Not *here*, I'll tell you that," Karen said, more cagily. "And not somewhere that psycho bitch Hannah'd ever know to look. Take my word for it, I got 'em locked up tight. Don't I, goat-boy?"

"She does," Fergus nodded. "Safe and sound."

There was a knock at the door: a quick, impatient rapping, the progenitor of which El would have recognised even if she *hadn't* been expecting her.

"Will you bleedin' shut up about it?" was the first thing she heard, once Fergus had got up to let Ruby inside, and Sita with her, and the two old women had insinuated themselves into the bungalow. "It was one bloody train ride. *One.* And you didn't even have no-one sat next to you for most of it."

"Has our stint in that godforsaken Tube carriage slipped your mind?" Sita said tetchily. "That man in the windbreaker was practically on *top* of me. And did you see him *eating*? There'd be a place in the stocks for people like that, if there were any justice. Fish and *chips*! With vinegar! *Vinegar*!"

"You wouldn't be saying that if he'd offered you any. I saw you eyeing up them chips."

"*Glowering* at them, not *eyeing them up*! This cardigan is vicuña. And now it smells like a haddock."

"Turns out, she ain't so good on public transport," Ruby explained to the rest of them, elbowing El in the ribs to make room for herself on the tubular steel construction Karen and Fergus had fashioned into a sofa. "Spent so long getting her arse warmed on hand-stitched leather in the back of a Rolls, she's forgotten how the other half travels."

"Uncomfortably, on recent evidence," Sita groused, lowering her own body - tarnished knitwear and all - down at the opposite end of the sofa and compressing the oxygen from the other half of El's ribcage.

"Christ, woman - you'd think you'd never set foot on the Underground before, the way you go on."

"Well, you're here in one piece, anyway," El said, more breathlessly than she'd have liked - rising from her seat and feeling her lungs re-inflate to their regular capacity.

"Barely," Sita muttered.

Unlike Ruby, Sita had made no secret of her struggle to adapt to their currently reduced circumstances. Where Ruby had remained in West Hampstead with her sons, and El had trailed after Rose and Sophie to Harriet's place on the Holloway Road, Sita had had no choice but to throw herself on the mercy of her own family. In practice, this had meant her son Rohan who, though based in Copenhagen, had been wise enough to channel a percentage of the profits from his civil engineering firm into the acquisition of an apartment on Ludgate Hill with space enough to accommodate periodically-rotating families of tourists - and, at present, a disgruntled sixty-something woman with a very extensive wardrobe who'd returned home to her flat in Kensington a fortnight earlier to find, dangling from the letterbox, an eviction notice from her landlord giving her, in a move she found particularly perfidious, only the barest minimum of notice.

She'd refused point-blank to sell or even pawn some of her more liquid assets: the jewellery, art and furniture collections she'd spent a lifetime assiduously assembling, and which, El was sure, would have raised her more than a few million, either at a reputable auction house or via one of the fences she and Ruby had worked with over the years.

("I'd rather sell a *kidney*, darling," she'd answered, when El had enquired).

And so, with the rest of her assets frozen and unable to stretch to the chauffeured Corniche in which she typically travelled - and with the fleet of classic vehicles Ruby kept at her lockup in Colindale impounded - she'd been forced to endure what she considered the ultimately indignity: traversing the city by bus, or on the Underground.

"Let's have it, then," Karen said, taking a final slurp of the hot chocolate and laying the mug on the floor beside Fergus. "What have you got?"

"Not a bleedin' lot," Ruby told her, with a shake of her head. "Either a lot of people have suddenly got very, very tight-lipped, or that Hannah's better at keeping to the shadows than I'd have gave her credit for. 'Cause we must've got a round in for half of North London this last week, and not one of 'em there said a dicky-bird."

While El had been in mourning for her cottage, and she and Rose and Sophie had been adjusting to life under Harriet's roof - and while Karen, apparently, had been stocking up on precious metals in anticipation of societal breakdown - Ruby and Sita had been probing their network for intel: on the hacking and the arson, but also on Hannah herself.

The plan had been for the two of them to come to Kingston and share what they'd discovered, and for Karen to pick up the thread: to follow the clues they'd assembled down the inevitable electronic rabbit-hole and, eventually, back to whoever had done them over so comprehensively.

All of which was predicated on there *being* clues to follow; on the myriad thieves and grifters and kiters and cracksmen Ruby and Sita knew between Waterloo and High Barnet having something worth telling them in the first place.

"Fuck," said Karen. "Nothing?"

"Not a peep," said Sita. "And it didn't seem to me that any of them were holding back some morsel of value. I'm afraid the whole undertaking may have been rather a waste of time."

"Which means," Ruby added, "we ain't no closer than we were to getting back what got took."

"What now, then?" El asked - an unappetising short-term future of spare mattresses and borrowed clothes and queuing for the bathroom flashing before her eyes.

"We keep going," Ruby said. "Keep asking and keep looking 'til something turns up. Which it will, 'cause it always does."

I'll do a job, El told herself. *It can't be a long con, because I've got nothing to offer upfront as a convincer and I haven't had to find a mark in so long I might as well have forgotten how to do it. But I used to* like *the short con; used to be good* at it.

I can get good at it again, if I have to.

Then, when I've got a bit more cash to play with...

"I can just about *see* you schemin'," Ruby told her - her uncanny ability to read and interpret El's thoughts never less than unnerving. "You're thinking about doing a job, ain't you? Something to bring a bit of money in?"

How does she *know*? El wondered. How does she know, *every bloody time*?

"Maybe," she conceded.

"Stands to reason. It's no fun, having your pockets emptied. 'Specially when you're used to working with a bit more capital than we got between us here and now. Lucky for you, I've been doin' a bit of thinkin' about that myself."

"Thinking about what?" Karen asked.

"About a *job*, darling," Sita said. "A little something to keep us afloat while we're trying to restore ourselves to dignity."

"You've found a mark?" said El, suspiciously.

Ruby looked to Sita, and Sita to Ruby - the same quick, furtive trade of symbolically loaded glances that had been driving El to distraction since she was a teenager.

"In a manner of speaking," Ruby said. Then: "Though *found* ain't exactly the word I'd use. It's not a *new* mark we're talking about. More like... one I've been savin'. For a rainy day."

"And I think we can all agree," Sita added, "that since the clouds have rather drenched us these last few weeks... that day may be upon us."

KENSINGTON, LONDON

February 1941

They walked in lockstep, her smaller strides working to match his longer, quicker ones as they passed the Albert Hall and rounded the corner onto Kensington Gore.

They might have been father and daughter, Dolly thought: she in the nicest, cleanest party dress she had, the green one with the polka dots that went in at the waist; he in his dinner jacket and bow tie and a pipe like Clark Gable's clenched between his teeth, and the both of them in long black coats and soft, warm leather gloves. Father and daughter or uncle and niece, strolling home together after a night at the theatre or a double-bill at the Majestic.

"This is madness," he said quietly, taking the pipe from his mouth but still walking, not losing his pace. "You are aware of that, aren't you? Sheer and utter madness."

"You said you'd do it," she replied, just as quietly, not letting her own step falter. "Said you'd show me how."

"Because, for now, you have me over a barrel. But what sort of child *are* you, to want this? It's monstrous."

"*You* do it."

"And I have no qualms about confessing to my own monstrosity. But it's hardly something to *aspire* to, now is it? A girl your age ought to be stuck on... oh, *I* don't know, dolls, or Hopscotch, or something. Climbing trees or playing marbles with your friends. Not *this*."

"I don't see why you think it's so peculiar. Someone must've showed *you* how to do it."

"Not as a *child. Good God.*"

"Well, I know my own mind, whatever you think I am. And you *said* you'd do it."

It sounded petulant, even in her own head; made her sound, she thought, every inch the child he'd accused her of being.

But he *had* said; *had* promised to take her along with him, if only because she'd told him she'd get the law on him if he didn't, and because he'd believed her when she'd told him there'd be consequences for him, if he did anything to shut her up.

"I want to know why you do it," she'd told him, that first day in his house in Haverstock Hill - when she'd jumped through enough hoops to convince him that she wasn't going away, no matter *what* he said, and that he couldn't make her. "Why you kill them. And what it's like."

He'd given her the same uncertain stare he had on the doorstep, before he'd invited her in - like she was a tiger he'd picked up by the tail, thinking she was a ginger tom.

"What it's *like*?" he'd said, his mouth hanging open. "You want to know what it's *like* to kill someone?"

"Yeah. When you, you know... wrap your hands 'round their throats, or stick a knife in them, or however you do it. Wait, though - it the same every time? Or have you got a few different tricks you like to use, to keep you from getting bored?"

She'd been so excited, the words had just spilled out of her - a long, exhilarated cascade of them.

He'd looked back at her as if she'd slapped him in the face.

"What *are* you?" he'd said - caught, she'd thought, between revulsion and morbid curiosity.

"What am I? *You're* the one who's been going 'round murdering people, not *me*. Anyway, you've not answered the first thing I asked you."

"Which was? You seem to have come armed with rather a lot of questions."

"*Why. Why* you're doing it. Are you a Jerry, is that it? One of them secret assassins? Did Hitler send you over here?"

He seemed almost offended by the accusation.

"A *Nazi*? Certainly not. I'd swallow cyanide before I bowed to *that* madman."

"What, then?"

He'd narrowed his eyes at her, behind the pop-bottle spectacles.

"You're not going to go away, are you?" he'd asked her, with a sort of resignation.

She'd shook her head.

He'd regarded her a minute longer, as if he'd wanted to be absolutely sure of something, before he told her anything else. Then he'd taken off the spectacles, rubbed at the bridge of his nose - exactly like the librarian he wasn't, but could have been mistaken for at a distance - and walked across the sitting room to the drinks cabinet, where he'd poured two fingers of what she'd come to recognise later as a *very* good Scotch into a brandy glass and downed it in one.

"Little girl," he'd said, when the glass was empty, "do you happen to know of the phrase *contract killer*?"

He came to a stop in front of one of the fancy-looking blocks of flats that lined the road, so suddenly she almost ran into the back of him as she skidded to her own, jerking halt.

"Is this it?" she said, the thrill of it - of what they were about to do, the pair of them - rising up in her like champagne bubbles. "Are we here?"

He spun around and forward, until there was barely an inch of air between them, and pressed a hand to her mouth. Not gently, either.

"You do not speak," he told her, practically whispering into her ear. "Your being here at all is an idiocy. A *dangerous* idiocy, and for both of us. But if you *are* to be here, then you *do not speak*, is that understood? Not a word, not a breath, not a sound."

She nodded, entirely silently.

He released the hand that covered her mouth, grudgingly slowly, and reached with it into the inner lining of his dinner jacket.

When he withdrew it, there was a key tucked between the gloved knuckles of the fingers: small and silver and gleaming so bright it might've been cut only the day before.

Silent as a cat-burglar, he pressed it into the lock on the door leading into the building; twisted it right, with surgical precision.

The door sprung open, and he crept inside, leaving her just enough time to follow before he let it fall shut behind them.

There was a lift in the vestibule, a chunky-looking copper coffin inside a black steel cage, but he ignored it, leading them instead up three flights of stairs and along a narrow hallway with a moss-green carpet, thick and dark enough under her feet to make her feel like she was trekking through a forest.

The door he seemed to be searching for was at the very end of the corridor:

a solid mahogany affair with the number 308 above the frame and a discreet bronze plaque identifying the occupant or occupants as Caster.

On reaching it, he stopped again, though this time she was ready for it and was able to still herself before she went flying forward. As before, he reached into the lining of his jacket - the left side, this time - and retrieved a key; slid it into the lock, opened the door and let the both of them in.

It was dark inside; not quite pitch black, the way it had been outside with the lampposts off, but dark just the same, and it took every bit of concentration she could muster to keep up with him as he moved, fox-like, down the hallway and towards a set of double-doors at the bottom.

They passed a desk along the way - a sort of writing bureau with the roller down that she nearly but not quite bumped into in the murk. Something big and heavy had been placed on top of it. A statue, she saw as her eyes adjusted: a great charcoal-coloured, foreign-looking thing with a long-nosed head and shoulders but no body, rough enough around the edges that she wouldn't have been surprised to discover it had been carved out of a lump of mountain rock.

He picked it up in one fist; held it up in front of him like an oil lamp, and kept right on walking.

It was a bedroom, behind the double-doors - she could make that out even in the gloom. A bedroom with a man in it: a young man, good-looking and clean shaved. Almost a boy, really - curled up fast asleep in the four-poster bed in the middle of the room with the blankets pulled up to his neck and a plump pile of pillows supporting him from behind. He was snoring, gently; out for the count.

With great care, the thin-faced man set the statue he'd picked up down on the bedroom floor; unbuttoned his coat, took it off and passed it to Dolly. She took it wordlessly, slinging it over her forearm; he ducked his head at her, in acknowledgement if not thanks, and took hold of the statue again, his grip tightening around it.

He was across the room in a heartbeat, statue raised above his head. The man in the bed didn't stir; didn't so much as roll over in his sleep.

The statue didn't crack, when the thin-faced man brought it down onto the skull of the sleeping man in the bed. But the man's skull did - the breaking-eggshell sound of it cutting through the dark silence in the bedroom like the crack of a whip.

Something like an electric current raced through Dolly's veins, under her skin. It was something else, the sight of it, even in the gloom. She'd never known anything like it; never felt anything near as alive as looking at the cracked skull made her feel.

She wanted more.

She inched closer to the bed; to the thin-faced man, the bloody statue in his hand.

The second blow brought gouts of dark red blood and something grey-green that she thought might have been liquifying bits of battered brain-matter spilling from the skull onto the pillows. For the third blow, the thin-faced man changed course - aiming the statue not at the skull but at the no-longer-snoring, very likely dead man's face.

His nose and cheekbones shattered like glass; more blood and fragments of bone flew from him onto the pillows, the blankets, the thin-faced man's dark shirt and dickie-bow.

That seemed to be enough.

The thin-faced man stepped away from the bed, opened his palm and let the statue roll out of his hand and onto the carpet.

"*Now*," he said, taking a handkerchief from his trouser pocket and wiping the blood from his face with it, "you may speak, if you absolutely must."

The excitement had left her flushed and breathless, sent her heart bouncing like a jackhammer in her chest; it took her a second or two to pull herself together enough that she could speak without tripping over her words.

"Who was he?" she asked.

She'd asked before; first, when the thin-faced man had told her where they were going, and then again on their walk from the Underground to the Albert Hall. Both times he'd ignored her.

This time, at least, he answered.

"Just a boy," he told her. He finished with the handkerchief, replaced it in his pocket, snatched the coat from her hands and, slipping both arms inside, began to button it all the way to the throat. "A boy with an inheritance, who married unwisely. You might be surprised how often those two sets of circumstances converge."

She considered what he'd said.

"His *wife* paid you to do it?" she said.

"With some minor monetary assistance from her lover, I believe. How else would I have got hold of the keys to the marital home? How else would I have known for sure our boy would be... let's say... too *tired* to put up a fight?"

"She knocked him out? Slipped him chloral hydrate, or something?"

"A sleeping pill or two, that's all. But it seemed to do the trick, didn't it?"

He looked back across the room at the pummelled corpse with something like professional pride.

A job well done, she thought. *Bloody well done.*

"What now?" she asked him.

"That really depends," he said. "Since you've insisted on inserting yourself into the proceedings - how useful do you think you might make yourself?"

It wasn't quite so exciting as the bludgeoning had been - didn't give her *quite* the thrill of seeing the brains of the young man in the bed tumble out of his head onto the mattress. But it was something. And after what she'd just seen the thin-faced man do, she'd take any crumb he'd throw her way.

"I can help," she said, trying to come across more nonchalant than she felt.

He fixed her with yet another one of his stares. It was like being x-rayed, she thought; like having your mind dissected under a microscope.

"Yes," he said, still looking at her through the darkness. "I think you probably can, at that. Pull out some of those drawers, then, will you? If this young man's wife is going to be calling the police about a robbery when she eventually comes home, we're going to need to leave her more of a mess than *this*."

"Are you satisfied?" he asked, on their way back to the Underground. "Have you taken whatever it was you felt you needed from this experience?"

He was making fun of her, she knew. *Sneering* at her.

Perhaps he thought she'd seen enough to frighten her away - to scare the curiosity out of her, enough that she'd not see fit to darken his door again.

If he did, though, he was wrong; dead wrong.

Because how was she supposed to go back to normal, knowing what she knew now? After feeling what she'd felt in the blackness of that bedroom, with that symphony of hot blood and mashed-up bone echoing through her body like a high note through a tuning fork?

Whatever it was she'd been keeping locked up inside her, whatever darkness of her own she'd known she had in her but had never thought to lay claim to... it was out of her now. She'd seen it, and it *hadn't* frightened her; *hadn't* scared her away.

It was as she'd suspected. Now she'd done what she'd done in that bedroom - or, at least, what she'd been party to, which was almost the same thing... she didn't want to stop.

Except she didn't want to *watch*, next time. She wanted to be the one to hold the statue in her hand; the one to bring it down on the skull.

And she didn't want to wait to do it, either.

KING'S CROSS, LONDON

April 1998

In the soft, low light of the wine library, Kat Morgan looked healthier - if not happier - than she had even three months earlier: her face fuller and less consumptive, her smile wider, her blue eyes clearer and less bloodshot.

"I thought it was just me, when it first started happening," she said, tapping a long red nail irritably against her thigh. "That I'd typed in the wrong pin, or something. I still get a bit of, you know... brain fog. Trouble remembering the odd word. The odd number. It's not as bad as it was, nowhere near, but it happens, still. From time to time."

"Sorry," El said, grimacing. Mild though they were, the cognitive impairments - like the weakness in her legs and the intermittent balance problems that demanded she still, periodically, needed a walking stick to get about - were among the more enduring reminders of Kat's run in with Hannah D'Amboise two years before.

"Not your fault, is it? Wasn't you that did me in the head with that bastard wheel lock. Anyway. Like I said: I thought it was just me, having one of my moments. Then when I tried the other cards, and none of *them* got the job done either..."

"You knew something was up?"

"I had an inkling, yeah. And then those two old baggages rang me out of the blue and told me what'd happened to all you lot, and I thought to myself: well... probably not a coincidence, is it?"

The way El had heard it, Kat had lost millions, like the rest of them - but had managed, through the now apparently quite extensive property portfolio she'd been developing, to retain several of her more valuable assets, albeit in less liquid form than she might have liked.

She'd agreed immediately to the job, when Ruby had suggested it - not so much, El suspected, because she needed the money, but because helping the rest of them stay afloat while Karen used every backdoor trick in the technical manual to ferret out Hannah would give Kat her best shot yet at getting even with the woman who'd maimed her.

That she *wanted* to get even was a given, as far as El was concerned. She liked Kat, and she respected her - respected her skills on the job, especially. But she was a tough woman, hard-edged and unforgiving, and El couldn't conceive of a situation in which, after the attack she'd suffered and the damage she'd been left with, she'd pass up the opportunity to nail Hannah to the wall.

"But you're coping?" Rose asked, sipping delicately at one of the complementary glasses they'd been given - a gritty Cabernet that tasted, to El, like it had been stored under a heat lamp.

"Keeping it together," Kat said. "Just about. And you two doing alright, are you?"

"Not so bad," El answered, flashing Rose a quick smile and pressing all recent memories of Harriet Marchant's sagging spare mattress and decidedly cat-stained guest duvet to the very back of her mind.

The glass door connecting the wine library to the wider drinking club beyond slid open, and the bearded sommelier who'd seated them stepped discreetly through, immediately ahead of a very tall, very angular middle-aged white woman, her thick platinum hair piled up on the crown of her head like a braided loaf and an ivory fur coat slung, Cruella De Vil-style, across her thin shoulders.

The two walked towards their table, and El took her cue.

"I don't know *what* I'm supposed to do now," she wailed, in a voice an octave and at least two social classes higher than her usual register - one she'd modelled, in fact, on Rose's, though she'd die before she'd let *that* slip. "He just *left*! Took the bloody Jag, and everything. Thank *God* he didn't take Valeria, is all I can say. I don't know *how* I'd have coped without her to come home to. Animals are such a comfort, aren't they? *Such* a comfort."

She downed the remainder of the stewed Cabernet with a melodramatic flourish reminiscent of one of Sita's, and placed her forearm over her eyes, as if to cover the tears that threatened to well there.

"You mustn't worry," Rose drawled, loud enough to be overheard by anyone with an interest. "It's *your* money, isn't it? Every penny. Not his. He's got no claim to it. And you've still got that pre-nup in place, so even with *Anthony Julius* on his side he'd fall flat on his face. Let him try, I say. Let him *try*!"

"But what's the use of money when you *have* no-one?" El replied mournfully. "I don't even have a *job* to throw myself into anymore. There's nothing to do all day but lie around the house feeling *sorry* for myself."

"You need a *purpose*, darling," Kat chipped in, her Welsh lilt lost to an artificial upper RP. "Something to get you up in the morning."

Through the obstructive canopy of her own arm, El saw the angular woman's head tilt towards them - as if, somewhere on the wind, she'd caught the scent of a fox she hadn't expected to be hunting.

"Her real name's Patricia Swift," Ruby had told them, when she'd first mooted the job back at Karen's place. "But she goes by Doctor Upgrade. Ain't a real doctor, mind - she's one of them, what do you call 'em? Life coaches. Pay 'em a couple of grand a week and they'll tell you whether to have pork or salmon for your dinner, sort of thing."

"She's at the higher end of the affordability scale," Sita had said. "*Terribly* expensive, for what she offers. And, if I may say, a rather nasty piece of work."

"Specialises in the sort of rich, posh bird you get out west." This had been from Ruby again. "Bored, neurotic types with no self-confidence and enough time on their hands to want to dick about *finding themselves* and what have you."

Sita had wrinkled her nose in disapproval - of Swift, of her clients, or of both, El hadn't known for sure.

"It's really rather sad, the way they flock to her. Brainless lambs to the slaughter, every one."

"And Christ knows, she fleeces 'em," Ruby had agreed. "We're talking fifty, sixty grand a pop, just to make 'em a to-do list reminding 'em to drink enough water and get an early night and have a clear-out of the attic. Talk about money for old rope."

"And you like her for a mark?" El had asked.

The two old women had nodded in unison.

"*Very* much," Sita had replied. "She's quite appalling."

"Greedy, an' all. Prides herself on gettin' what she wants, and not lettin' nothin' stand between her and whatever that might be." Ruby had grinned, the action splitting the lower half of her face into a thousand small crevasses. "Just our type, in other words."

Did they have an in? El had wanted to know. And Sita had affirmed, with some pleasure, that they did - if, that was, El would be willing to working the inside.

"Wine," she'd said. "Our Doctor Upgrade is quite the oenophile. Especially now she's accumulated sufficient funds to indulge her more costly enthusiasms."

"Bloody loves the stuff," Ruby had concurred. "Gets her arse to Rioja and Barbaresco for the weekend once a fortnight. Owns a stake in at least one vineyard in Stellenbosch too, that we know of. Ain't afraid to pay top dollar for the right bottle, neither - she splashed out ten thousand on a crate of Montrachet, and that was just *last* month."

A bottle scam, El had thought. It'd have to be. A bent bottle, or a falsified label. Both, if they could find a way to spring for them.

"Seems like the more straightforward way of getting her on the hook, don't it?" Ruby had confirmed, when El had pressed her on it. "Not too original, I'll grant you, but ain't the old ones meant to be the best?"

"And we were wondering," Sita had added slyly, as if the idea was such an afterthought that she'd considered it barely worth mentioning, except in passing, "whether you might ask Rose to put in a membership enquiry to one of the wine clubs Auntie Ruby happened to stumble upon, in her research? There's a little place just off the Pentonville Road of which Ms. Swift is *particularly* fond, and I daresay they'd kill to have a Lady on the books..."

"I must go," El said, smoothing down her poker-straightened hair and slipping the Thierry Mugler sunglasses Ruby had lent her for the occasion from her forehead until they shielded her eyes. "Valeria will need her supper."

She climbed down from the high metal stool on which she'd been perched, came to rest on the four and a half inch heels of the shoes she'd borrowed from Rose - and the toes of which she'd liberally stuffed with tissue paper, to compensate for the difference in their foot sizes - and draped the Louis Vuitton handbag Sita had donated to the makeshift wardrobe department of the con over the padded shoulder of her blazer.

"Call me, won't you?" she asked the other women at the table, dropping air kisses on first Rose's cheeks, then Kat's.

And, throwing a nervous smile at Patricia Swift and the sommelier as she brushed past them, she left the building.

"It went exactly as smoothly as we'd hoped," Rose told her later, as they lay together on the dropping cushions of Harriet's tartan sofa while Sophie and Harriet cooked pasta and chopped fresh basil in the kitchen; Harriet's cat, an obese tortoiseshell improbably named RD Laing, resting across El's calves.

"Yeah?" El asked, trying to dislodge RD Laing from her legs, and succeeding only in pushing him onto her ankles.

"Oh, yes. She was *very* interested."

Swift had sidled over to their table almost as soon as El - and soon after, the sommelier - had exited the wine library, claiming the stool El had vacated without so much as asking if Kat and Rose would mind if she joined them.

"I couldn't help but notice," she'd begun, so warm and personable the three of them might have been old friends settling in for a night of drink and gossip, "that your friend seemed a little... upset?"

Kat had jumped in and taken charge of the conversation before Rose could even open her mouth.

"Oh, she's just a little down," she'd said, her delivery treading a fine line between legitimate sympathy and catty schadenfreude. "Husband left her, you know. Gather it came as a bit of a shock."

Rose had scowled at Kat, as they'd planned; castigating her for spilling the intimate details of their friend's misfortunes to the intruder at their table, whomever *she* might turn out to be.

"Ah," Swift had said, helping herself to one of the tasting glasses and wincing as the sour Cabernet hit her palate. "One of *those*."

"I said to her," Kat had continued, with a slight slurring of her speech designed to signal moderate drunkenness, "what *is* it you're so upset about, exactly? She *must* have seen it coming, all those hours he told her he was working - all those Saturdays he was spending *at the office*. Honestly. I've known Archie Moncrieff since we were children, and that man has never spent a *minute* extra at his desk past five thirty."

"Jessica!" Rose had whispered, feigning outrage at the looseness of Kat's lips. "For heaven's sake!"

"Oh, *please*," Kat had said, shushing her friend into silence. "We both know I'm right. And as for all that business about *needing a purpose* and *trying to find herself*... well, *really*. She's still young enough to find a replacement for old Archie if she desperately wants one, she's thinner than she's ever been since she stopped eating, and she's positively *swimming* in money. Really, what else *is* there?"

Swift's eyes had widened, for a split-second - just long enough to show them the avarice there, to let them see that the rope had worked, and they had her on the hook. And then, lowering her gaze, she'd turned her attention back to the commandeered wine.

"Find herself?" she'd asked, casually.

"She gave us her card," Rose told El, grasping RD Laing by his love handles and lowering him to the floor. "Kat said we'd pass it along. She's expecting your call."

"She thinks she can help me find myself?" El replied, with a grin.

"She *guarantees* it, if you believe half of what she told us at the club. So really, I think the bigger question is: are you ready to be Upgraded?"

LOS ANGELES

May 1957

A lady driver?" the man mumbled from the back of the limousine. "Jesus. Now I've seen everything."

He was beautiful, when he was still; as beautiful as he'd seemed, the handful of times she'd seen him on screen, all rosebud lips and tousled brown hair and twinkling green eyes under thick, dark eyebrows. When he spoke, though, he was ugly: his perpetual sneer reconfiguring the perfect symmetry of his face into something wicked, malign.

The drink probably wasn't helping his cause, Dolly thought, as she watched him swig again from the leather-bound hip flask he'd been clinging to like a baby's bottle since he'd stumbled into the car. Some men, she'd seen - some women, too - got calmer, the more they put away; closed their eyes and drifted off, dead to the world. Others, it was like they were possessed: shouting and swearing and hurling punches at anyone who got in their way, or - worse still, to her mind - stabbing jibes and insults with scalpel precision into the soft bellies of whoever they'd decided most deserved it, in the moment.

Castle, she reckoned - even after only half an hour in his company - sat squarely in that last group. She didn't know how much he drank, or how often; he was too young and too pretty for it to have shown up on his face yet, to have ruined his looks. But it was obvious to her, at least, that he was an absolute bastard, with a drop of liquor inside him. A bastard, and a liability. The sort of loose cannon that'd run his mouth off, before he started in with his fists.

"A job's a job, Mr Castle," she told him, in the Mid-Atlantic Katherine Hepburn voice she'd adopted since coming to America. It didn't quite cover the residual sediment of the accent she'd been born to, the one she was still working on shedding, but it was good enough to convince most Americans that *she* was an American, too - albeit one with ideas above her station.

Besides, this was Hollywood: nobody was *from* here. Everyone around her was a shapeshifter, a rootless chameleon trying to be someone other than the person they'd been, sloughing off names and errant vowels and religious identities like so much dead skin.

They just had... different ambitions than hers, that was all.

And it might be, she thought, that she'd benefit herself from a bit more of a change. The name she'd been given by her long-dead parents wasn't the name she'd been using, and it certainly wasn't the one she'd been giving to her clients, when they'd asked, although many of them didn't - preferring to know as little as possible about the hand behind the trigger they were paying her to pull, and who could blame them? But it was the name that remained on what official documents she had, and perhaps it was time to do something about that, too.

"How does a *woman* get to be a limo driver, anyway?" Castle said, whatever was in the hip flask beginning to macerate his words, to take the edge off their cruelty. "Your fella up and leave you or something? Or are you one of those girls who thinks she can be just like a man, if she puts a pair of pants on when she gets out of bed in the morning?"

"It's just a job, sir," she said again, flatly.

She turned left, following the road as it curved around another of the mountainous hills that ringed the city, the high beams of the limo's headlights cutting through the darkness up ahead as it climbed. From the top of *this* hill, she'd discovered in the long hours she'd spent poring over maps of the city, the drop from the edge of the road to the ground below was near-on two hundred feet; almost certainly not survivable. *Definitely* not survivable, if you factored in the sharp, eroded spikes of sand-coloured rock that poked up out of the earth floor like stalagmites at the bottom.

"You gotta make it look like an accident," Rudolph had insisted, the single solitary time they'd met face-to-face after he'd blackmailed Rube Orloff, another producer at the studio, into giving up her name and number. Rudolph had chosen a roadside diner, of all places, for the meeting; one that had looked to her more like an oversized caravan than a bricks-and-mortar restaurant, hidden away at the end of a dusty stretch of track somewhere just north of the San Fernando Valley.

He was a large man, tall and stout and with an appetite so big he'd polished off a plate of bacon, scrambled eggs and waffles before she'd finished her coffee. Large and mean, if his reputation and the snippets of studio tittle-tattle she'd been privy to meant anything - and she could well believe, having met him, that they did. He hadn't told her *why* he wanted the job done, or what Castle had done to earn his ire, but Dolly wasn't stupid, and Castle had quite a reputation himself.

He swung both ways, or so the grips and runners she'd talked to had implied: some with a derogatory grin and a hand gesture, others with an aggressive revulsion evidently intended to let her know, in no uncertain terms, that they, themselves, were *not* like Castle, were *not* that way. Unlike Castle, Rudolph was married, had kids and grandkids - but his own predilection for the better-looking boys that his casting directors brought onto the lot for auditions hadn't gone unnoticed, either. And it didn't take a genius, Dolly thought, to work out how things might have unfolded between the two of them: Rudolph the producer, with a weakness for beautiful young men, and

Castle the careerist, prepared to do more or less anything to make it in front of the camera and, once there, all the way up to top billing.

It would have been Castle's drinking that finally brought the axe down on him, Dolly reasoned. Even if he hadn't threatened Rudolph directly, or tried to blackmail him for a part - and she could easily see him doing both of those things - then his inability to keep his gob shut once he'd poured a couple of Old Fashioneds down his neck would have sealed his fate. Gossip was one thing; it was par for the course, probably, in their business. But having a big-time actor - a star like Castle - actually naming names, maybe even producing evidence... no. Someone like Rudolph wouldn't want to risk it. Not when there were other options on the table.

She stopped the limo at the top of the hill. The view was breath-taking, the way it always was at night. It was one of the things she loved about Los Angeles, about California: the lavishness of the landscape, of a geography as excessive and melodramatic as the culture it enveloped. So much less *gentle* than England; so much less restrained.

She pulled the gun from the holster at her ankle, where she'd strapped it. It was a new model she'd picked up on her way through Chicago, a Smith & Wesson; she didn't like it particularly, compared with the Webley she'd used back home and in France, when circumstances demanded it, but it struck her as a particularly American choice, and that went some way towards compensating for what she considered the unpleasantly rough hand-feel of the weapon.

"Why are we stopping?" Castle said, more confused than irritated.

She turned around in her seat, pulled down the glass panel separating the front of the car from the back and pointed the gun at his throat.

"Get out of the car, Mr Castle," she told him, letting the accent drop.

He didn't fight her, to his credit - was far more compliant than she'd have expected of him.

He stumbled from the back seat, and she followed him outside, making sure he saw that the gun was trained on him at every point from A to B. She gestured to the edge of the hill - which was really more of a cliff, now she thought about it - and cocked the hammer, more for effect than because she imagined she'd have to use it. He struck her as a coward, a loudmouth with no substance; he wouldn't risk her shooting him, even if the alternative was the drop below.

He took a step backwards, closer to the edge.

"What do you want?" he asked her, through his tears. She could smell the booze on his breath. "Why are you doing this?"

"For the money," she told him, pressing the muzzle of the gun against his chest. "Why else?"

He took another step backwards, lost his footing and fell.

She heard but didn't see him land.

It was a long drive back to Malibu, or it felt like it; all the journeys she'd taken in the country seemed to take an age, to a girl who'd grown up with the Tube. Rudolph and his wife lived by the beach, their flat-roofed Modernist mansion looking to Dolly like a tower block that had got itself tangled up in a car compactor. They had no immediate neighbours, which was just how Rudolph liked it.

She parked the limo a five-minute walk from the mansion, out of sight - although the number of limos she'd seen parked up in Hollywood made her doubt that anyone would bat an eyelid at hers - and jogged along the path to the gated entrance, electing to climb the gate rather than press the buzzer and ask Rudolph to let her inside.

"What the hell are you doing here?" he demanded, when she'd knocked at the door and he'd answered, barrel chest barely covered by a fluffy white bath robe. "You're not supposed to come to the house, for Christ's sake! What if someone sees you?"

"Best let me in, then, hadn't you?" she told him.

He did it, with obvious reluctance, but didn't show her into any of the sitting rooms or smoking lounges he used for his guests - stopping her at the bottom of the great marble staircase that led upstairs from the white-tiled atrium and demanding to know, once again, what the *fuck* she was doing there.

She didn't answer him; just bent down as if to tie her shoelace, pulled the Smith & Wesson from its ankle-holster and shot him, twice, in the centre of the forehead.

She'd screwed a silencer to the pistol, before she'd left the hills for Malibu. Neither bullet made a sound.

The shots were perfect - her shots were *always* perfect - and he died immediately, blood pooling around his head and shoulders on the tiles.

When she'd checked his pulse, to be absolutely certain, and had satisfied herself with what she'd felt there, she took off her shoes and walked the stairs to the upper level of the mansion. There were no servants, no assistants to be dealt with; the Rudolphs lived alone, which was also how they liked it.

She found *Mrs* Rudolph asleep in bed in the master suite - the covers beside her unwrinkled, undisturbed.

Separate rooms, then, Dolly thought. Can't have been a happy marriage.

Softly, gently, she tiptoed to the bed, where the woman was dozing, her mouth wide open. Barbiturates was Dolly's guess; if she was anything like the other studio wives Dolly had met since she'd been in LA, then Mrs Rudolph was probably doped up to the eyeballs.

She took the woman's hand from where it rested on the top of the covers - with equal gentleness, so as not to disturb her - and wrapped its fingers around the grip of the gun, pressing the index finger to the trigger.

Then, still gently, Dolly opened the woman's mouth with her own thumb and forefinger, slid the silenced muzzle of the gun inside as far as it would go, placed her own hand on top of Mrs Rudolph's trigger-finger and squeezed.

It was another long drive from Malibu to Bel Air, this one snarling her in so much late-night traffic on the freeway she worried she wouldn't make it there on time.

When she *did* arrive, finally, Orloff was waiting for her by the front steps to his house – though he was nothing less than magnanimous in his greetings. He was a good client; one of the best she'd had. Never argued, never micromanaged; never tried to screw her on payment.

"And everything went smoothly?" he asked, passing her an envelope that felt satisfyingly thick as she slid it into the pocket of her chauffeur's jacket.

"Smooth as silk. They're out of the picture, both of 'em. Rudolph's missus, too."

"Good, good. Let's hope it's the last of the scandals you and I and the studio must deal with, eh?"

"Let's hope," she agreed, smiling - certain, knowing Orloff, that it wouldn't be.

HOLLOWAY ROAD, LONDON

April 1998

Getting dressed for a job in Harriet Marchant's flat was surprisingly challenging, El was discovering.

The problem wasn't just the smallness of the place, although that was a factor: the living room, bedroom, kitchen and tiny bathroom that had been ample for Harriet and RD Laing was threatening to burst at the seams with the addition of Rose and Sophie on the pull-out sofa bed, and El on the single mattress pushed into a sloping crevice between the television and one of Harriet's many Scandinavian shelving units.

It was all the *stuff*: the charity-shop paperbacks and hardback limited editions; the social psychology monographs and journals Harriet kept on hand for her own academic research; the figurines and collectible characters from films El had never watched and comic books she'd never read. And the memorabilia; *so much* memorabilia.

Harriet was a rock fan; El had known this from early on in their acquaintance. She practically *lived* in band t-shirts - the inexhaustible supply of long-sleeved, voluminous, mostly black but occasionally tie-dyed cotton jerseys that seemed to comprise the entirety of her wardrobe, all of them emblazoned with the names of albums by Metallica and Slayer, Kiss and Iron Maiden and the Sisters of Mercy. What El hadn't known, before she'd imposed herself on the flat and on Harriet's goodwill, was the extent of her would-be sister-in-law's enthusiasm for the genre.

It was *everywhere*: on every wall, every surface, every slice of carpet not occupied by book piles or bedding or one of RD Laing's water bowls. There were posters, signed record covers protected by sturdy-looking frames; even a couple of electric guitars strategically mounted between bookshelves. But there were also some more esoteric items: a battered Trilby in a glass display case; a tiny, wheeled replica of a tour bus; an enormous plastic tongue that doubled as a floor lamp.

Navigating it all made the performance of even the most prosaic tasks a Krypton Factor-level feat of mental and physical agility.

Currently El was balanced on one foot in front of the living room mirror, doing her best to apply the makeup and hair products that would restore her to the woman she'd been when Patricia Swift had seen her in the wine library - her other foot resting, of necessity, on a pile of Napalm Death concert programmes so substantial that it forced the accompanying leg outwards at a ninety-degree angle, giving her the look of an incompetent acrobat carrying out an unusually complicated warmup stretch.

It was in this position that Harriet found her upon returning to the flat - the afternoon lectures she'd been scheduled to give unexpectedly interrupted by a fire in the student union.

"Do you normally stand like that when you get ready?" she asked, taking in the scene from the hallway.

"I didn't want to, you know... disturb anything," El answered, half-apologetically.

She drew a final stroke of Spanish red across her bottom lip, ran her steel comb through her hair to augment the severity of the centre parting, disentangled her foot from the programmes and stepped back from the mirror.

"Don't feel you have to stop on my account," Harriet said, picking her way through the doorway to the sofa.

It sounded disdainful, faintly spiteful even, though El was inclined to think that Harriet hadn't intended it that way. She wasn't an especially warm character, except perhaps where Rose and Sophie were concerned, but she wasn't an unkind one, either. Rather, or so El was beginning to suspect, it was as if she'd never learned how to demonstrate friendliness; how to articulate the minor but essential phatic expressions - and attendant non-verbal gestures - that told other people she had any interest at all in what they had to say.

And with a father like James Marchant, El had reminded herself more than once, *is that any surprise, really?*

El's sense that Harriet was wary of *her* specifically, however, hadn't abated since circumstances - and Rose's anxieties - had thrust them together.

Was it, she wondered, that Harriet thought she wasn't good enough for Rose? That El would lead Rose even further down the rabbit-hole of criminality than she had already, if left unchecked?

Or was it only that Harriet was, as Rose herself had pointed out, desperately protective of both her older sister and her niece, and felt obligated - though they'd been in her life barely more than a year - to look out for them, to guard them against anything with the potential to bring them heartbreak, up to and including El herself?

As closed a book as Harriet was, El found it impossible to know for sure, despite the many efforts at cold reading she'd thrown at the problem. And she'd been unable, thus far, to muster the courage to ask her, head-on.

"Unless you were on your way out anyway?" Harriet added.

It *wasn't* in all likelihood a dismissal, El thought. Very likely *wasn't* a demand to make herself scarce, so that Harriet could go back to enjoying the full benefit of her own merchandise-laden living room uninterrupted.

But it *felt* like one.

"I've got a two o'clock with the life coach woman," she replied, laying the groundwork for an imminent retreat from the awkwardness between them.

"Ah. I see. Well, that explains the get-up, I suppose, doesn't it?"

El bit her tongue.

Then scuttled away, like the coward she thought she probably was.

Patricia Swift was waiting for her at the basement bar in Chelsea they'd agreed would serve as the best and most neutral venue for their preliminary session.

El - Allegra Moncrieff, as Swift knew her - had expressed a slight hesitation in them meeting at all, taking greater pause still at the suggestion that they work together.

"You *did* call *me*, though, didn't you?" Swift had purred back at her down the phone, not an ounce of her self-assurance slipping. "You didn't have to - you could have ignored your friends and thrown away my card. But you didn't. And I'd wager that's because a part of you knew that I could help you, if you'd only let me. You should listen to that part, Allegra. Because I *can* help you."

"I don't know," El had said. "I just don't *know*, Patricia."

"And that's understandable. When you've no experience with a process like this - like mine - it's perfectly reasonable to have concerns. But wouldn't it be better for us to thrash them out together? I mean," she'd added, with a throaty laugh, "what's the worst that could happen? If nothing else, you'll get a good lunch and a glass or two of something delectable. I *guarantee* I can do better than that *swill* they served you at the club."

She rose to her feet as El entered the bar, beckoning her over to their table and greeting her with a spattering of air kisses uncannily similar to those Allegra Moncrieff had offered her friends at the wine library.

"Allegra, *darling*," she said, so intimately El was sure even fragile Allegra Moncrieff's suspicions would have been raised, "I'm *so* glad you decided to come."

"I'm not committing to anything," El replied, lowering herself onto the unoccupied chair with a stiffness indicative of Allegra Moncrieff's uncertainty.

"Not a problem. Drink?"

She grabbed the bottle without waiting for El's response, pouring them both a generous splash of an '87 Merlot El knew to be only *marginally* better than the unpleasantly crunchy Cabernet she'd sampled on the Pentonville Road.

They made what Swift - and probably Allegra Moncrieff - must have thought was pleasant conversation for a few minutes, Swift's contributions focusing primarily on the Millennium Dome and what she considered the inadequacies of Tony Blair's leadership, and El giving little in exchange but an intermittent murmur of agreement.

When the first round of Merlot had been demolished and El was midway through doling out the second, Swift went in for the kill.

"What is it you're looking for *really*, Allegra? Your friends told me you've been having a touch of a life crisis recently. That you've been looking for something - a larger purpose. Do you want to tell me about it?"

Allegra Moncrieff was vulnerable, and rich, and cosseted; Swift knew as much already. It made sense to El therefore that she was also more than a little self-centred; that she enjoyed the sound of her own voice to a greater extent than most.

Even the most meagre expression of interest in her personal life, El had decided, would be enough to precipitate an uncorkable outpouring of oversharing.

And thus, with the conversational door opened, she overshared.

It wasn't just Archie leaving her that had turned everything upside down, she said. She'd known *that* had been coming for a while; despite what she'd been telling her friends, and her overbearing mother, she'd been aware for months of his infidelities and the plans he'd hatched to start a new life with the most recent of his conquests.

She *was* lonely, and she *was* depressed, even with Valeria, her Red Sable Pomeranian, to come home to; that much was true. But loneliness wasn't the full extent of what kept her awake at night, nor even the half of it.

The fact was, she felt rudderless - ever since she'd given up the job she'd loved the previous year. Entirely adrift in her own life.

"And what was it you did?" Swift asked.

She'd *been* a merchant, she said - dealing in wine, and spirits, and the occasional very rare case of Champagne. It was one of the reasons she knew the club on Pentonville Road so well. She'd run a little boutique place over in Mayfair - strictly appointment-only, and catering to a very specialist, high-net-worth clientele. The job had taken her all over: Bordeaux, Napa Valley, Marlborough, the Western Cape... anywhere and everywhere she might lay her hands on the singular, high-priced bottles her clients demanded. It was fun, it was lucrative, and she absolutely loved it; couldn't have been happier with her career choice, with the state of her professional life.

Until she'd met the old woman.

"She actually *walked into* the shop off the street," El said, aghast even in the recounting of it. "I usually kept it locked between appointments, but evidently I'd forgotten to put the bolt on that morning, and then suddenly... there she was, just *standing* there, as if she expected me to *serve* her! I didn't know *what* to say."

Old was probably an understatement, she added - the woman was *ancient,* wrinkled as a prune and bent practically double. In her eighties, at the very least, though she could very easily have been ninety.

"I couldn't imagine *what* she might want. But then she brought out this photograph and laid it down on the counter..."

It was a polaroid, El explained. Slightly blurry, as if the photographer's hand had been shaking as they'd captured the image.

"Do you know how much this is worth?" the old woman had said, her voice like dry leaves crackling in the wind.

Morbidly curious, Allegra Moncrieff had leaned in for a closer look - and her eyes, as they'd focused, had very nearly fallen out of her head.

"It was a bottle," El told Swift. "Not wine - whisky. As I say, the shot was fuzzy, very poorly done, but I could just about read the label... and it was a Glenallan. A 1937 Glenallan Duo. Do you know what that is?"

Swift's own eyes widened, cartoonishly, in their sockets.

"The '37 Glenallan?" she whispered. "Of *course* I know it. *Everyone* knows it."

"Then you'll be familiar with the price tag."

"Yes. I mean... yes, *obviously*. Didn't it go for just under a million at Christie's last year?"

"Just *over*, I believe. But *that* bottle wasn't the one she showed me. There were two of them produced - a pair. The one that sold was the first. The one in the photograph, by all accounts, was the second."

Allegra hadn't known that at the time, of course; hadn't known, until she'd been able to do more research, *which* of the '37 Glenallans she was looking at.

"Is this... *yours?*" she'd asked the antediluvian creature before her, scarcely believing such a thing could be the case.

"Damn right it is," the old woman had creaked, the scrape and grind of her vocal cords descending on Allegra's ears like fingernails down a blackboard. "Now, can you tell me what it's worth, or am I going to have to take myself off to one of them other fancy bottle shops 'round 'ere? 'Cause you're not the only one in the phone book, you know."

"Well, I mean... yes, of *course* I can," Allegra had managed, struggling to overcome speechlessness.

"Good. And don't think you can stitch me on the money, neither, 'cause I *know* how old it is, and I *know* it's worth a few bob. My son's had a look at it, and he says it'd go for at least ten grand. At *least.*"

Allegra had executed a brief but thoroughly breath-taking round of mental arithmetic: subtracting ten thousand pounds (*fifteen, let's call it fifteen, just to be safe*) from the hundreds of thousands the Glenallan would fetch, should she take it to an auction house or - better yet - directly to one of her clients, and had alighted on a total that had snatched the remaining air from her lungs.

"Ten... thousand?" she'd asked, her own voice almost as hoarse and scratched as the old woman's.

"Yeah. And I'll not take a penny less, before you go telling me lies about how it's not what I think it is, or what have you. Not a *penny.*"

She'd glared at Allegra through rheumy, pink-rimmed eyes, and snatched the polaroid back from the countertop, letting it drop into the basket of the wicker trolley she'd wheeled in behind her.

"Do you... have the bottle with you?" Allegra had said.

"Ha!" the old fossil had replied, her laughter something closer to a coughing fit than a show of mirth. "Think I'm barmy, do you? Think I'd take a ten-grand bottle of Scotch out for a walk 'round the block, just like that?"

"But... I'll need to see it," Allegra had countered, beginning to gather her senses. "I can't give a valuation without examining it first. I need to see the label, the level, the packaging..."

The woman had scratched her nose and plucked at one of the wiry grey hairs scattered across the leathery folds of her chin, deep in thought.

"See it?" she said.

"Yes. Up close. It's the only way I can confirm that it is what it *appears* to be - and if it is, that it's sufficiently intact. I don't buy anything sight unseen, I'm afraid."

There had followed a long, deep silence.

"I ain't bringing it out the house," the old woman had said eventually.

"Not for all the tea in China. What if I should break it? What if *you* should break it, when you pick it up?"

"I understand. Perhaps I could come to you, then? I'm not entirely averse to making house-calls. Do you live nearby?"

She *couldn't* be from Chelsea, Allegra had thought. Not looking like that; not *sounding* like that.

"I do, as it happens," the woman had replied. "You heard of Drayton Gardens? Not far from there, I am."

The salubriousness of the postcode had surprised Allegra almost as much as the Glenallan itself. Several of her wealthier clients, in fact, kept homes on some of the surrounding streets.

"Have I *heard* of it?" she'd said. "Yes. Yes, absolutely."

"Alright, then. Should save us a bit of time. Got a pen and paper, have you, so's I can write down the address?"

Swift's jaw was now almost on the floor.

"And did you *go* to the house?" she asked El. "Did you *get* the Glenallan?"

El sighed.

"I went," she said ruefully. "The very next day I went - all on my own, just as I'd promised the old bat I would be. Couldn't *believe* where she was living, when I got there. Absolutely *phenomenal* place in Clarington Mews, you couldn't miss it. Bright pink, the colour of candy floss, and the most *enormous* statue of a flamingo by the doorstep. It was like something you'd find in Las Vegas."

"And the bottle was there?"

"Oh, yes. The place was an utter *pigsty*, but she'd stored it in the cellar, thank God. And it was the real thing - I knew it the moment she brought it out from the cheap old lockbox she'd been keeping it in. You can't imagine how wonderful it felt, to look at it. To *hold* it."

El allowed a shadow to fall over Allegra Moncrieff's face at the memory; a strange, bitter sadness quite at odds with the jubilation she'd experienced in the old woman's cellar.

"And that was where the problem began, you see," she continued, more quietly. "I was standing there, the most magnificent specimen I'd ever encountered quite literally in the palm of my hands… and suddenly all I could hear was this tiny voice in my head demanding to know what in God's name I thought I was *doing*, trying to swindle a little old lady. Asking what sort of person I'd become, that I was prepared to do such a thing."

"And then… well, I'm rather embarrassed to say I had something of a panic attack: right there in the cellar, in front of her. It was as if I couldn't breathe; couldn't stand to be in my own skin. All I could do was put down the bottle, make my apologies and *dash* out of there. I've never moved so fast as I did, running back to the shop that day."

"You just left it?" It was Swift's turn, now, to look aghast. "A '37 Glenallan, and you *left* it there?"

El bowed her head.

"I did. The whole thing rather brought home something I hadn't wanted to confront head-on before then - something I'd been shying away from for quite some time. The fact is, Patricia: I didn't like myself very much. Didn't like how I behaved, or who I'd become. You've heard that many times before, I expect?"

"Hmm," Swift agreed, though with less enthusiasm than before.

"I knew, after that, that I couldn't carry on as I had been - that something would have to give. Which is why I… well, I suppose you'd say *retired*. Sold on the business. I hardly needed to keep going with it, anyway - I've been rather comfortable on the financial front ever since my father passed on, and the shop was always more about the joy of it than the profit margins. Even getting the Glenallan… it wouldn't *really* have been about the money, so much as about the *getting* it, you know? The thrill of the chase and the satisfaction of the win."

"Hmm," Swift repeated.

"The challenge, of course, is knowing what I ought to do *now*. As I say:

I've been somewhat adrift since I gave it up. And with Archie gone... I feel so terribly *untethered*. So *purposeless*."

Swift's eyes had begun to glaze over, as Allegra Moncrieff concluded her tale of woe. She was no longer really listening, El thought; had lost her appetite for the pursuit of this particular prey.

"Is that the sort of thing you normally help with?" El asked.

"What?" Swift replied - then, seeming to remember why she'd requested the meeting, added: "Oh. Yes. Absolutely."

But her mind, El thought, was elsewhere - in a cheap plywood lockbox in the basement of a bright pink, flamingo-festooned house in Clarington Mews. A house so bright and so peculiarly decorated, it would be absolutely impossible to miss.

SANTA MONICA

February 1972

She realised, around about the time Charlie Manson and his girls went to trial, that the business was getting too big for her to handle on her own. That if she wanted to carry on at it, she was going to need an extra set of trigger fingers. A hired hand; an apprentice, even.

It would be a risk, taking someone on; a big one, if she didn't tread carefully, didn't start growing eyes in the back of her head. There was nothing like a neophyte for thinking he could get away with playing dead man's boots - hadn't Dolly done it herself with the man who taught *her*, back when the war was still fresh in people's minds and she still called herself by the name she'd been given?

Paris, it had been. She'd been a teenager, still, though old enough that no-one had batted an eyelid at him and her shacking up together in an apartment on the Avenue Montaigne. It had been building in her for a while - the wanting to leave, to strike out for herself without the dead weight of what had seemed to her at the time like an old man holding her back. And he'd been getting handsy, too, especially after he'd had a drink – that hadn't helped his cause. Getting to think that, because she was sharing his flat, she ought to be sharing his *bed* at nights, too.

He hadn't seen it coming, when she'd come at him; hadn't expected the needle in his neck that turned his legs to spaghetti, or the paring knife across his throat that sent the blood rushing out of his body and his buck teeth gnashing at the air in agony.

She was smarter than he'd been, though. Much smarter. And she knew better than to turn her back on anyone - and especially on a lieutenant who might stand to gain a thing or two from having her six feet under.

It was months before she happened on someone she thought might be a likely candidate.

He was young, though not as young as *she'd* been when she started. She'd guessed fourteen or fifteen, from his height and build and the dusting of fuzz on his upper lip, though God knows it was difficult to tell, when none of the kids wore uniforms to school. Physically, he was unremarkable, unmemorable: white but suntanned to a light, all-over brown; straight, white teeth and an aquiline nose; hair down to his collar and curling slightly at the ends, the same as every other boy his age in California. He was neither particularly attractive nor notably ugly; even a sharp-eyed observer could pass him in the street or serve him dinner in a restaurant without his face leaving a lasting impression.

And that was good, she'd thought. If he really *was* cut out for the sort of business she was in, then it would do him well to look ordinary; to fade into the background. To be the sort of person who could be anyone and no-one.

She'd seen him first hanging about by the beach - a can of pop in one hand and a comic book in the other, medium-brown eyes fixed on the blue of the ocean. Except, and she couldn't have said exactly how she knew, they *weren't*; instead, she was sure, he was only *pretending* to stare at the water. Was using it as a pretext, a cover for looking at something else altogether. Something he shouldn't have been looking at.

She'd watched him, covertly enough that he wouldn't have *known* she was watching him, until she got a bead on what he was *really* looking at; what was actually in his line of sight.

Who.

He was an oldish man: grey-haired and long bearded and unkempt, a string of love beads around his neck and a dirty rainbow poncho that she'd known would stink of armpit sweat and marijuana if she ever got close enough to catch a whiff. One of the ageing hippies who lived around the pier, she'd reckoned; destitute, but by design, preferring to pitch a tent on the sand than submit to the constraints of a nine to five. He was crouched on the ground, rubbing a pair of sticks together for a fire; something to cook his dinner on, perhaps, or keep his bones warm when the sun went down.

Another woman might have asked herself, then, what the boy was doing, staring at the old bloke like that. But not her. The more she'd watched the boy, watched the vacant expression he wore crystallise into something like hunger, the more certain she'd been about what he wanted, what he was after. She'd known that expression; had likely worn it herself, back when she was his age.

Curiosity: that was what it was. The sort of dark curiosity that could lead a boy to cut a man's throat or stick a knife in his guts to see the look on his face as the life drained out of him, to feel the ebb and flow of the blood as his pulse ran down like a dying battery.

She'd wondered if he was going to act on it there and then: invent some ruse to lure the old hippie away from the beach and towards a more secluded place where he could do the deed. But he'd been more patient than that - and *that* was a good thing too, she'd thought. A boy who was willing to wait for the kill, to keep a lid on his impulses until he could be a little bit strategic about satisfying them... that was a boy who could learn. A boy she could teach.

She'd followed him home, the way she'd followed the thin-faced man back to his house in Haverstock Hill, all those years ago - back to a plush-looking apartment block on 2nd Street, where the epauletted doorman had let him in through the lobby with a deferential tip of the hat.

A rich boy, then, she'd thought. A rich boy who'd have more to lose than a poor one, if what he was - the abomination he was - was ever made public.

She could work with that.

She'd been following him a week when he made his move; long enough to have worked out his pattern. He'd catch a bus to school in the early morning, Monday to Friday, and *stay* at school for the remainder of the day, like his classmates. But rather than returning to the apartment once his classes were out, he'd make his way back to that same stretch of beach - where, always with a tin of Coke and a comic book by his side, he'd look out at the surf. At the old hippie in the poncho hunkered down on the sand.

The pretext he ultimately settled on to snare the hippie was unoriginal, unimpressive, and she felt a touch of disappointment at his lack of imagination, though she chided herself for the reaction - reminding herself of his age, his inexperience, the likely lack of a guiding hand to steady him on his journey towards self-discovery.

He'd brought an extra Coke with him that day, along with a square package of something greasy - a sandwich, she'd guessed - leaking oil and butter into its brown paper wrapping. This time, instead of standing and looking out to sea, he walked down further onto the beach, across the sand - leaving a trail of footprints behind him, she noted - and squatted down next to the hippie. They talked for a moment, though about what she couldn't hear from the shelter of her hiding place. And then the boy was pressing the brown food package into hippie's open, outstretched palms; placing the can of Coke onto the sand beside the man like an offering to a minor water deity.

The hippie opened the package greedily, a grin blossoming across his weather-beaten face as he took in the contents: a Reuben, she thought, or something like it. He ate quickly, shovelling the bread and meat into his mouth as if he was worried it might be snatched away at any second, and washed down the unexpected meal with the Coke before crushing the can in his fist and belching, loud enough that she caught the echo of it even from fifty feet away.

When he'd finished, the boy squatted down next to him on the beach;

leaned in close, almost whispering in the old man's ear, then - when he looked to have said his piece - stood up again. The hippie cocked his head quizzically, then nodded, and scrambled to his feet.

The boy began to walk away, back in the direction of the city proper: the long, straight, intersecting lengths of road and rows of shops and houses and fancy hotels fading to clusters of yellow light as dusk closed in on the Pacific. And the hippie took off after him, leaving his patchwork tent and dirty sleeping bag behind him on the sand.

There'd have been promises made, she thought, to draw the old geezer away from his home like that. Promises of booze to share, or something harder; of sex, even, though she wasn't inclined to dwell on *that* possibly, given the boy's age.

Stupid.

It was dark out, but it wasn't dark *enough*, not yet. And the beach might have looked empty to the boy, except for the hippie - and except for *her*, though he couldn't have known that - but nowhere was ever *completely* deserted; she'd learned that much. There was always *someone* about: a businessman taking a shortcut home after an afternoon quickie with his mistress; a jogger midway through an evening workout by the ocean; a tourist who'd wandered off the beaten track and stopped to take a photo of the sunset.

People who'd take note of a clean-cut teenager out for a stroll with a shabby-looking derelict three times his age or more; people who'd remember seeing them together, if they were ever prompted.

So bloody stupid.

He didn't go *into* the city, she saw, or stray far from the shore - another bit of idiocy she'd have to chalk up to his inexperience, she told herself. Instead, he led the old hippie down the bit of pavement running parallel to the beach, towards a small, shack-like house along the beach-front, its light blue wooden frontage overrun with moss and mould and beginning to surrender to rot. The house was abandoned, no question: there were boards across the broken windows, rubbish bags and scraps of broken furniture stacked up on the strip of dead grass that passed for a yard. No lights on anywhere inside.

The old hippie looked puzzled, at first, as they walked the path to the peeling front door. But the boy leaned close to him again, whispering what she reckoned were likely more inducements - and whatever he said must have been convincing enough, because the hippie smiled, showing teeth that were nothing but orange stumps even in the darkness, and followed the boy into the house.

If the boy was clever about it, she thought - cleverer than he'd been about everything *else* she'd seen him do so far - then he'd do the job with a knife: something sharp and efficient, even if it was something he'd had to swipe from his dad's toolbox or one of the drawers in his mum's kitchen.

And fortunately, she saw as she peered in through the gap in the mildew-reeking boards across the window-panels, he *had* been clever - about that, at least. The hippie had barely set foot in the empty front room when the boy struck: took his weapon out of his schoolbag - a box-cutter, not a knife, though the blade of it was keen enough for the difference to be negligible in practice - and shoved it, with a thrust that would've done an Olympic fencer proud, into the old man's chest, just about where his lungs ought to have been.

The hippie toppled over onto the dirty floorboards, coughing foamy pink ichor down his chin, the handle of the box-cutter still sticking out of him, and the boy bent down next to him to watch - a satisfied little smile on his face that reminded Dolly of the joy she'd taken in the kill herself, her first few times. It was a bloody good strike, she'd give him that: a sucking chest wound like that, and the old man'd be drowning in his own blood, soon enough.

What then, though? Did the boy have sense enough to know how to take care of the rest?

She suspected he didn't. But there was only one way to find out, wasn't there?

He didn't hear her come in through the door, though perhaps that wasn't a surprise - she'd always been able to tread softly, when she'd needed to. He moved fast when he saw her, though: had the box cutter out from between the dying hippie's ribs and back in his hand and pointed at her with the speed of a sniper.

A turn of speed like that would come in useful, she thought. Very useful.

She had her elbow at his throat, his shoulder in a joint lock and the box cutter in her own free hand before he knew what'd hit him.

"Am I gonna have to break your arm?" she asked him.

"You're hurting me," he winced, his breath coming hard - though he didn't cry or beg, and she had to respect him for that.

"I know. So, am I gonna have to break it, or will you be able to control yourself if I let go of you?"

He ducked his head in what she took to be a nod, and she released her grip, the force of the action spinning his body away from hers and sending him sprawling, not a few inches from the bloody jumble of the hippie's still-wheezing carcass.

"Are you a cop?" he asked, pushing himself onto all fours, then up and into a standing position that left them staring each other out across the room.

His voice hadn't quite broken yet, she realised; was stuck in the discordant seesawing register that seemed to afflict so many adolescent boys.

Her eyes never leaving him, she tiptoed over to the hippie - side-stepping the sticky rivulets of blood seeping into the floorboards from both sides of his upper body - and, lowering herself into a squat position behind his head, ran the blade of the box cutter across his throat in a single, effortless motion.

"No," she said, raising herself back up to her full height, wiping the box cutter clean with her handkerchief, sheathing it and sliding it into her handbag. "No, I ain't a cop. But you'll be seeing one before too long, if you don't get *this* mess sorted."

She gestured to the hippie, now - finally - dead.

"Got a plan, have you?" she continued. "For clearing it up, I mean? Getting rid of the body, so it don't get found?"

He opened his mouth, but nothing came out.

"No. Didn't think so. Lucky for you, I got a bit of experience in these sorts of matters. Question is: do you *want* my help?"

"You killed him," he said, finding his words.

"No. *You* killed him - I just finished him off. And I expect you liked doing it, didn't you? Liked the feeling it gave you, slicing him up?"

The boy fell silent again.

"You're alright," she told him. "I ain't trying to trick you into nothing or back you into a corner. But let's say, for argument's sake, you *did* like doing it... I wouldn't be wrong in thinking you wouldn't mind doing it again, would I? Though perhaps with a bit more thought put into the planning, next time," she added.

He dropped into a crouch, like a wounded animal, and she wondered if he might make a run at her, and how badly she'd have to hurt him if he tried.

"Who are you?" he said quietly. "If you're not a cop, who *are* you?"

"Your fairy bloody godmother, that's who," she replied. "Now, I'm gonna ask you again, and if you don't answer me properly then I'll just take myself off and leave you to clean this up all on your tod. So listen careful. Do. You. Want. Help?"

The boy bit his lip. There was blood on it, she saw; just a smear, probably splash-back from going in too hard with the box cutter, but something he'd have to remedy before he went anywhere with overhead lighting.

"How?" he whispered.

"That a yes, is it?"

He nodded again, this time more decisively.

"Yes. Please."

"Thought you might."

She peered down at the body on the floor; cast an appraising glance around the room.

"It'll take a while to get sorted, this lot. A bit of elbow-grease, too. But that ain't the first order of business. 'Fore we do anything, I'm gonna need you to nip back down the beach and grab the tent and any other bits and pieces this man here left behind when the two of you walked off together. Reckon you can do that?"

His jaw slackened.

"You were watching me?" he said, the possibility seeming to startle him.

"That's right. And good thing I was too, eh? Or something tells me you'd racing 'round like a headless chicken right about now."

He considered this; looked as if he was mulling it over.

Doesn't rush to judgement, then, she told herself. *Can be thoughtful, when he has to be.*

Another tick in the box.

"You want me to go get the guy's stuff?" he said eventually.

Inside, she smiled.

"Yeah," she told him. "And give your hands and face a wash in the water, while you're there. Then I want you to come back here with what you got, quick as you can. *Then* I'm gonna need you to go out again, to that phone booth across the road - you know the one I mean? Next to the liquor store. Ring your mum and dad and tell 'em you'll be stopping at a friend's tonight. 'Cause you and me, even if we work fast... we're gonna be here 'til morning."

CHELSEA, LONDON

April 1998

The house in Claringdon Mews had always been pink. The addition of the flamingo statue, however, had been Sita's idea.

("Just a little something to make it stand out, darling," as she'd put it. "Pink paintwork isn't terribly uncommon in Chelsea, but man-sized effigies of Rose Pompadour wading birds... they're rather rarer").

The house's owner, thankfully, hadn't objected to the temporary ornamentation; though El had wondered whether her neighbours might have had more to say about it, had their opinions been sought.

She was another of Sita's old acquaintances: a romance novelist, well into her ninth decade but still sprightly, and - though herself a law-abiding citizen - sufficiently intrigued by Sita's life of crime to have offered up her spare home in the city as a venue for the con.

("On condition," Sita had said, "that I tell her all about it, in the fullest detail, once the deed is done. So should some ill-disguised surrogate for one of us turn up in the pages of a bodice-ripper eighteen months from now... we'll know why").

El hadn't been there when, immediately after their meeting at the basement bar in Chelsea, Patricia Swift had made a beeline for the house - closing the quarter-mile distance at a clumsy but energetic sprint, according to Karen, who'd been keeping tabs on the woman's movements.

Nor had she been there when Ruby, her already-wrinkled features buried below the weight of half of Sita's makeup case and her spine collapsing under the small false hump secured to the inner lining of her cardigan, had very slowly opened the front door to find Swift waiting just outside - looking particularly rapacious, even by Ruby's own, not un-mercenary standards.

But the description Ruby had passed along to her later had been vivid enough to make up for it.

"Hello there," Swift had said, as if addressing the sticky-fingered child of an old acquaintance or an unfamiliar dog in the park.

"Can I help you?" Ruby had answered cagily, her voice like sandpaper and tobacco.

"I do hope so. Allegra Moncrieff sent me - you know, the lady from the bottle shop on Clifford Street?"

Ruby had frowned - the puckered, latex-loaded face she and Sita had worked to create wrinkling so completely with the effort of remembering that she'd had trouble, she told El, actually seeing out of her left eye.

"She was here before, weren't she?" she'd said eventually, still wary of the stranger on her doorstep. "Few months back. Girl had a fit down the cellar - just about ran away, she did. Ain't seen her since."

"Yes - yes, she said been... taken ill. And she sends her apologies, of course."

"Why's she not here now, then?"

"I'm afraid she's still a little unwell. It's an... ongoing condition. Which why *I'm* here. She asked if I might step in for her, just this once. To finish up the sale."

"The sale? What you on about, *sale*?"

"Of the Glenallan. The whisky she came to value? You *do* remember?"

Ruby had let her expression go blank; had held the blankness long enough for Swift to start to sweat under her own - only marginally less severe - makeup.

"The whisky," she'd said eventually. "Right, yeah. The whisky."

Swift's relief, she told El, had been palpable; had come off the woman's body in waves.

"Now," Swift had said, picking up where she'd left off as she rallied, "Allegra mentioned she'd suggested a price already? But I must say that, while I *obviously* trust her judgement, I'll need to take a very quick peek at the bottle myself, just to be absolutely sure of everything before I write the cheque."

"A hundred grand," Ruby had replied, with a sudden sharpness that had taken Swift quite by surprise. "That's what I said to her. A hundred grand, and not a penny less."

Swift had balked.

"One *hundred* thousand?" she'd said. "Allegra told *me* she'd offered you ten. That ten was what you'd *asked* for."

"Yeah, well. That was *before*, weren't it? Before my boy went and did a bit more homework. Spoke to one of them auctioneers, he did. And a hundred grand, that was what they said to him."

"That's... an awful *lot* more," Swift had spluttered - though, Ruby could tell, she was doing the sums in her head, working out the difference between a hundred thousand pounds and the million the bottle was worth and still, in spite of her shock, liking where the calculation took her.

Still only ten percent of the value, El could imagine her thinking. *Maybe less...*

"You've gone quiet," Ruby had observed. "Can't stretch to a hundred, is that it?"

It had been a well-calculated dig; designed, El knew, to poke at Swift's ego.

"Don't you worry," she'd added, with just a hint of sympathy. "We'll take it up the auction house instead. I should think they'll know what to do with it."

That would have been what did the trick, El thought; what pushed Swift from a *maybe* to a *yes*. The threat of not only losing the Glenallan, but of losing it to *someone else*. And of the world believing that she'd lost because she *couldn't afford to play the game.*

"No," Swift had said abruptly. "No. A hundred should be... more than manageable."

Ruby had scratched at her chin; rubbed a fingertip over one of the little artificial hairs Sita had fixed there with cosmetic glue.

"You makin' an offer, then?" she'd asked.

"Well... we'll have to see about that, won't we?" Swift had told her, shifting gears from alarm and back to confidence with the sort of smoothness that, Ruby said, must have made her bloody good at coaxing the bored rich into trading a piece of their savings for a diet plan and a set of numinous mantras. "I *will* have to come through and have a look at it, before we can talk numbers."

Ruby had grumbled a bit, for the look of it - then relented, and let Swift inside.

("Off like a bleedin' rocket the minute I'd invited her in," Ruby said. "Didn't even need me telling her where the cellar was. I've known *bloodhounds* go slower").

The sight of the '37 Glenallan - a clouded vision of dark amber in the oldest, most authentic bottle Karen had been able to lay hands on, encircled by the finest age-stained label their exceptionally talented document man had been able to forge and stoppered by an original mid-thirties cap - had brought Swift very close to tears.

"A hundred grand," Ruby had repeated.

Swift had picked up the bottle, so gently and so tenderly she might have been scooping up a bird with a broken wing.

"Okay," she'd whispered - looking, Ruby said, as if she'd have agreed to just about anything, if it meant she'd get to walk out of the house with the whisky under her arm.

There'd followed a long and, for Ruby, slightly embarrassing silence.

"What's the best way to do it, then?" she'd asked, when it became clear she'd have to be the one to break it.

"To do what?"

"The money. I'm thinking you ain't got that amount of cash just stuffed into your knickers."

At this, Swift had finally untethered her gaze from the counterfeit Glenallan.

"I'm sorry. *Cash*?"

"Yeah. That's what that other girl said, and I ain't arguing. I don't do cheques, me."

"You want me to give you a hundred thousand pounds *in cash*?"

"Ain't no other way of doing it. I don't believe in banks."

Swift had *had* the cash - El knew it, and so did Ruby and the others. Had it salted away in forty- and fifty-thousand pound increments across three different accounts, but she'd *had* it, and more.

"I'm not giving you *cash* for it," Swift had remonstrated. "That's absurd."

"Then I ain't giving you that whisky."

Ruby had reached out a knotted, arthritic hand and, with startling speed, snatched the Glenallan from between Swift's fingers.

Swift had gasped at the loss - a sharp, rapid intake of breath that had put Ruby in mind of a new mother on a maternity ward, protesting an interfering midwife's removal of the child from her breast.

"I'll *get* you the money," she'd said, affronted. "Just not in cash. I'm not some sort of... *gangster*, handing over a briefcase full of used twenties whenever she buys something. I pay tax, for God's sake. A purchase like this will need declaring."

"You can *declare* it how you like. But it's cash or nothing."

Ruby was good at the job; always had been. She hadn't blinked; hadn't given an inch of ground.

And finally, Swift had caved.

"Alright," she'd conceded, after an eternity. "Alright, then. Cash."

Ruby had grinned, black-flecked canines showing through her thin, cracked lips in the one-bulb light of the cellar.

"Good," she'd said. "There's a Lloyds, a NatWest and a TSB on the high street - you should be able to get there 'fore they shut, if you head off now." She'd placed the faux-Glenallan back into its wooden lockbox, with a little of the reverence Swift had bestowed on it. "And don't you worry - I'll have *this* ready for you, soon as you come back."

Swift was gone for almost two hours: longer by far than Ruby had anticipated. And while Ruby hadn't been nervous, exactly - because she was sure, absolutely sure that they'd got her on the hook - she did confess later to having been a touch less relaxed than she normally would have been, waiting around for a mark to deliver a payoff; a feeling she'd attributed, at the time, to the wider sense of unease she'd been living with since the month before.

To her surprise, whatever low-level disquiet she *had* felt hadn't dissipated when Swift had finally reappeared at the house, a brand-new patent leather briefcase in her hand and the faintest trace of a smile on her face that had reminded Ruby, for reasons she couldn't quite get at, of the glassy-eyed leer of a Punch and Judy puppet.

"You comin' in, then?" Ruby had asked her.

"In a minute," Swift had replied, her eyes flickering off to the right and lacquered fingers tightening around the handle of the briefcase. "I just want to make sure... Before I hand this over, this money, I want to make *absolutely* sure of what I'm getting. So, to be clear: I give it to you, and you'll give me the Glenallan? The 1937 Glenallan you showed me down in your cellar?"

It was wrong, Ruby had understood then; all wrong. The strange specificity of Swift's words, recited as if for the benefit of an audience; the way she was gripping the case, like a woman terrified to let go; the darting eyes Ruby should have recognised sooner for what they were.

A tell.

"I ain't so sure now," she'd said, hesitantly - simultaneously hypothesising what might have happened to Swift, what she might have *done* in the time she'd been away from the house, and sketching out the beginnings of a plan to extricate herself from the situation before it escalated and she ended up in the back of a police car, or worse. "Had a bit of a headache come on, might need to go and have a lie-down. Perhaps come back tomorrow instead?"

At this, Swift's pupils had scanned not right but left - as if, Ruby had realised, she was looking at something, or *someone*, just out of Ruby's line of sight. Searching out answers from a stage-prompt. Seeking reassurance.

There'd been a rustle of feet and movement, to the side of the open door.

"It's alright, Patricia," Ruby had heard. "There's no need to keep pretending. I think she's worked out she's been rumbled, don't you?"

And there, all of a sudden, pushing Swift aside and marching forward until she'd been face to face with Ruby in the doorway, was Hannah D'Amboise - a triumphant smirk spreading from her mouth to the flints of her eyes like runoff from an oil slick.

SOHO, LONDON

1977

don't care who you are," Dolly said, letting the Cockney creep back into her voice, sharpening the edges of the accent that three decades of California sunshine had sanded away, "I ain't agreeing to nothing 'til your boss decides to ask me to my face. It's the organ grinder I deal with, not the bleedin' monkey."

Out of the corner of her eye, she saw the boy - Lucian, he was calling himself now, though he'd been plain old Luke, once upon a time - draw himself closer to her on the cushioned bench; getting ready to spring up at the bloke like a jack-in-the-box, if it came to it.

"I *told* you," the bloke in front of them said, his own voice like two boulders descending from the upper slopes of a mountain, "I'm the one you got. The boss don't do face to face meetings, not for this sort of caper. That's what *I'm* here for. So it's me you go through - take it or leave it."

He was a giant of a man, too big by far for the tight suede sports coat and drainpipe trousers that currently constrained him. He belonged bare-chested in the ring, or out on the cobbles in a pair of hand bandages, or stood on guard by the velvet rope of a West End nightclub. Not squeezed into a corner booth at a Chinese restaurant on Greek Street, playing middleman for a guv'nor too scared or too concerned about what the rest of the world thought of him to get his own hands dirty.

His name was Lomax; first name Rocky or Ricky, something like that. But who *he* was didn't matter, he'd told them early on in the meeting. What mattered - what it'd do them well to pay attention to - was who he worked for. Who the boss was, that'd send his minion out to commission a hit like this on his behalf.

Marchant. James Marchant.

Lomax had said it like they'd know immediately who he was; like the sound of the two words together would send shockwaves through them. In truth, neither Dolly nor Lucian - or so she'd judged, from the look on the boy's face at hearing the name - had any idea. Though if this Marchant, whoever he turned out to be, could afford to keep a block of granite like Lomax on the payroll, and had pockets deep enough to accommodate the considerable fees Dolly and Lucian charged for the performance of their duties, then he was probably a man worth knowing. Knowing *about*, at any rate.

"Think we'll have to leave it, then," Dolly said, sliding herself across the cushion and out of the bench and freeing Lucian up to do the same.

It wasn't a bluff. They'd had a good year, made some solid investments, and they could walk away from Lomax and his guv'nor, she knew, without it making even a dent in their nest-egg. But Lomax reacted like it was; like she'd been wrestling with him, sparring, and had got him in a choke-hold so tight it left him no choice but to tap out on the mat.

"Hold up," he said, not standing but extending his arm towards them and flattening his palm outwards, like he was stopping traffic. He sounded hot and bothered, too - worried that they'd leave, and he'd never see them again. "Hold up. I'll ring him, alright? Wait here, and I'll go and ring him. Tell him what you said and see if I can get him to come out."

Interesting, she thought, as Lomax wrenched himself loose from the booth and strode - she could see through the glass of the restaurant window - across to the red phone box on the stretch of pavement where Greek Street met Old Compton Street. *This Marchant... he must really want us for the job.*

She made a note to herself to press Lomax on *why*, when he came back. She - and now Lucian too - had a reputation, back in Los Angeles, and she didn't think she'd be flattering herself too excessively if she said that she, especially, was the first in her particular field that certain influential people would reach out to, whenever they needed her type of work doing, and doing well.

But she hadn't realised this reputation had stretched any further East than Nevada. She'd stayed away from London for a long time before the promise of this job and its very hefty payday - not to mention the first-class flights and five-star accommodations Lomax had arranged for them - had brought her back home. Stayed away by design. She might've still had family there, if you could still call them that when you'd hadn't said a word to them for thirty years or more; and alright, yes, she'd made a point of keeping a very distant eye on her sister, seeing how things worked out for her. But she had no ties to the place anymore; no clutching roots.

Whoever had told this Marchant about her, about her and Lucian and what they had to offer... they'd heard it from someone in California. Must have done.

And if he'd been looking that far afield for talent and avoiding the plethora of domestic boys and girls peddling their wares on his doorstep... then he had to be more paranoid than most about word getting out that he was hiring.

Which meant that the job, whatever it was, was very big, very risky, or very, very sensitive.

Whatever Lomax said to his boss, it did the trick: Marchant agreed to meet them.

"Not here, though," Lomax had said, when he'd huffed and puffed his way back to the booth in the restaurant, smelling as if he'd chain-smoked the best part of a pack of fags while he'd been in the phone box. "Too public."

They'd driven out of Soho onto Oxford Street, the three of them packed uncomfortably into Lomax's little yellow Porsche - passing the Beaux-Arts columns of Selfridges and the dirty white carvings on the Marble Arch and a dozen other landmarks she hadn't seen since she was a kid as they moved out West towards Ealing, to the empty house in Acton where Marchant had insisted they meet.

"It's one of his rentals," Lomax told them, somewhat elliptically, as they passed the Westway over Paddington - then had lit yet another fag, blown a stream of smoke through the crack in his window and kept his mouth shut for the rest of the journey.

The house was a shabby thirties semi not far from the Hanger Lane roundabout, free of furniture and fittings and looking to Dolly as if it hadn't seen a tenant for months, possibly years. There was nowhere to sit, so they stood while they waited for the man himself to make an appearance, every bulging muscle in Lucian's body tense as piano wire and her own jaw starting to clench with impatience.

There were no apologies from Marchant when he eventually arrived - braking his MG to a juddering stop on the driveway and stamping through the unlocked front door with the petulant, slightly sulky air of a spoilt child forced against his will to attend a gathering of distant relatives.

He was a decent-looking bloke, with his blue eyes and long Roman snout and thick dark hair parted off to the side, though no more her type than Lomax: too full of himself, too disdainful. She'd have known he was rich, even if she'd no more than passed him on the street: everything about him was tailored, manicured, precise in a way that only money could buy. Even the cologne he had on smelled expensive: Parisian, rather than something bought off a trader down the market.

"You called?" he said, the nasal twang to the not-really-a-question so smug it made her want to loosen his teeth with the point of her elbow.

"Wanted to see who we were dealing with, before we signed on the dotted line," she told him, keeping her cool. "I expect you know a bit about that yourself, man like you?"

She looked him dead in the eye as she spoke, neither smiling nor scowling but fixing him with the sort of stare that Lucian had told her, in one of his rare jovial moments, made it clear she couldn't've cared less if the person she was looking at lived or died - and that if she had to kill them herself, then so be it.

He met her gaze for all of half a second, then looked away - perhaps realising, she thought, that he'd bitten off more than he could chew in trying to intimidate her.

"Fine," he said, sighing, his bravado folding like a deck of cards. "If you must. Here I am, then. Were there questions you wanted to ask me, or did you simply want to confirm my existence to your satisfaction?"

Now she smiled, just a little bit; let out the smallest flash of the grin Lucian had once said reminded him of the giant barracudas he used to fish for with his stepdad.

"We got a few questions for you, yeah," she answered. "Don't we, Lucian?"

This was the boy's cue. She liked to get him doing the talking these days, once she'd set out their stall. It made him feel useful, feel part of the proceedings; stopped him getting restive.

Getting resentful.

"Who is he, this guy you want us to do for you?" he asked, still sounding like a choirboy impersonating Brando despite his best efforts. "And why us? Seems a lot of trouble to go to, flying us all the way out here for something you could've got done cheaper, closer to home."

"How much information do you need, to be able to do your job?" Marchant replied - speaking not to Lucian but to Dolly.

"A name," she said, hoping the boy's nose hadn't been put too far out of joint by the obvious dismissal. She'd have to remedy it later, if it had been. "An address. Bit of a sense of his comings and goings, if you've got 'em."

"And an answer to that last question, if you don't mind," Lucian added, asserting himself.

Marchant sighed again.

"His name is Saul Bellman," he said. "Ricky here can give you the address. I'm not entirely sure of his day-to-day movements, but I daresay we can find out for you, if it's absolutely necessary that you know them."

Bellman, she thought. *Bellman*. She'd heard that name before, somewhere - and recently, too.

Then it hit her.

"Bellman," she said slowly, drawing out the syllables - remembering the very cursory bit of background she'd read on Marchant on the flight out of LAX, the handful of newspaper cuttings Lucian had managed to get hold of. "Ain't that your wife's name, Bellman? Her maiden name, I should say."

She could actually *hear* Lomax's surprise; the quick, sharp intake of breath from his wheezing lungs. Marchant, though, was that bit more composed - as if he'd expected them to know everything about him, about his wife and kids and background.

"It is, yes," he told her. "And since I assume discretion is rather essential in your line of work, and since you may very well know already anyway - Saul Bellman is her father. My father-in-law."

It wasn't much of a revelation. A man wanting his father-in-law out of the way, it seemed to her, was an entirely valid justification for engaging her services; one she'd come across more than once before.

Lucian was greener, though; still apt to be taken aback by some of the things he heard and saw. He didn't *say* anything - he knew better than to do *that*, in front of a client - but Marchant had shocked him, she could tell.

"Good," Dolly said. "Should make things easier for us on the access front, if he's someone close to you."

"It can't look like... what it is," Marchant said, with just a touch more urgency. "You'll need to frame it as an accident. Natural causes, ideally, if that's an option. He's a big man, not in the best of health. I can't see anyone arguing with the coroner, if he were to come down with a heart attack."

She looked to Lucian - more so he'd feel included than because she had any need of his take on the situation - and he shrugged.

"We can do that, I guess," he said.

"There can't be any suggestion at all of foul play," Marchant added. "I hope we're clear on that. No suggestion whatsoever. I can't have anyone asking questions. And as to *your* question, earlier..." He hesitated. "There are certain things Ricky and I are able to deal with *in-house*, so to speak. And certain other things that require us to do not much more than bring in... outside contractors. Local ones."

"Occasionally, though, we find ourselves in need of a more... specialist approach. And I can't imagine it will surprise you to learn that we were hesitant to call on one of our London contacts. They're good men, decently competent for the most part, but they're not renowned for their circumspection. Unlike *you*, that is."

He looked, again, directly at Dolly.

"Didn't realise our good names had travelled quite so far over the ocean," she said.

"I assume that's *false* modesty, but just in case: it has. *Your* name certainly came up more than once, when Ricky here started making his initial enquiries across the pond for someone who might be willing to travel. And it helps, of course, that you're a Londoner yourself, even if you *have* been somewhat displaced. Saul knows this city and half the people in it like the back of his hand. Your knowledge of the geography of the place is a definite advantage. I'm not sure I'd trust an *American* alone to get things done here with quite the same finesse. No offence intended," he added, finally throwing a glance Lucian's way.

"Whatever, man," Lucian answered, more bored now than sullen and aggrieved - though Dolly thought it might have a been an act.

"This Bellman," Dolly said - wanting, now she'd heard what she'd been after, to have *this* part of the conversation over with, so she and the boy could talk money with the organ grinder's monkey and get on with the job they'd been brought over to do in the first place. "Your wife's old man. What's wrong with him, health-wise? Just his heart?"

"That we know of. Though it wouldn't surprise me if there were other things, too - things he's kept from Liz. He's looking more and more like Henry VIII these days."

"And what do you mean exactly when you say *natural causes*? D'you actually want us to *give* him a heart attack, or you alright with something like an accidental overdose, if it looks the part?"

Marchant took a moment to consider this, his handsome face striking the contemplative pose of a Hellenic statue.

"You know," he said, when he'd thought enough to have reached a conclusion, "I'm not sure I care, one way or the other. As long as it's clean and there are no repercussions... from my perspective, you can do with him whatever you like."

CHELSEA, LONDON

April 1998

D id you have to hit me *quite* there?" Hannah complained, pressing a folded sheet of toilet roll against one bleeding nostril and pinching disconsolately at the bridge of her nose. "I'll have a black eye for *weeks*. You couldn't have gone for the ribs or the abdomen? Somewhere it wouldn't show?"

"Cry me a fucking river, bitch," Karen growled back at her - hovering protectively over Kat, who sat hypnotised at the kitchen table, her slightly misted gaze fixed on the swelling beginning to rise around her knuckles, as if she couldn't quite bring herself to believe what she'd done.

El could very well believe it, though. She'd only been surprised that Karen hadn't taken a swing at Hannah, too.

It wasn't lost on her, the irony of all seven of them gathered together again in a West London kitchen - albeit one with more shades of fuchsia and a good deal more chintz than there'd ever been in Rose's place in Notting Hill. Nor that the atmosphere between them now was only marginally less strained - and their tempers scarcely less seething - than they'd been two years earlier. Two years earlier, when Hannah stood beside her pistol-wielding father as he held them hostage, Karen tied up on the tiles with a broken jaw - and Kat had lain unconscious in a hospital bed in Islington with a traumatic brain injury and a piece of her skull missing.

There was something of the Western gunfight standoff about the arrangement of their bodies in the room now, El thought: Sita positioned next to Ruby by the sink, in an uncanny echo of the way the two of them had stood in the moments before Ruby had sunk one of Rose's kitchen knives into the meat of Marchant's neck; Karen standing sentry over Kat; Rose standing rigid in the doorway, El now beside her with a steadying hand on her hip. And Hannah - Hannah in the epicentre of the action, all six pairs of their eyes locked on her, watching her every move.

"We're all here," Ruby said, the pent-up venom rendering her speech so guttural El could hardly make out what she was saying, "just like you wanted. So what now? What are you after? 'Cause whatever it is, we ain't inclined to give it to you."

Hannah withdrew the bloody tissue from under her nose, sniffed unnecessarily loudly, and turned her attention to Ruby.

She looked at once both exactly as El remembered her, and entirely different. Her physical characteristics were much the same: her body still tall and angular, almost gaunt, though now covered by a dark suit and black leather trench coat instead of head-to-toe Gucci, Prada and Chanel. Her hair was cut, still, into the same thick Anna Wintour bob, now dyed a solid copper red very nearly the same shade as Rose's; her cheekbones still jutted like daggers from the pale skin of her face. But her demeanour, the set of her shoulders and the way she carried herself - these were less familiar.

For much of the brief time El had known her, Hannah D'Amboise had been a mouse: shy, timid, only ever really speaking when spoken to, swallowing down her never-ending grief at what she'd characterised as the loss of her husband and unborn child. Only at the end of their acquaintance, that afternoon in Rose's kitchen, had what El had come to think of as the *real*

Hannah shown herself: the murderous, sociopathic cuckoo in the nest whose obsession with the father who'd abandoned her even before she was born had inspired her to win their trust, so that she could better betray them later.

El thought she could see it on Hannah's face, now she knew that it was there, that it had been there all along: the arrogance, the cruelty, the contempt. The abject disdain for anything and anyone she couldn't use, in some way, to her own advantage.

Her utter loathing for the six of them.

"You may want to reserve judgement on what you will and won't *give*," she told Ruby. "At least until you've heard my proposition. The sad truth of it is, you *need* me. She's coming for you, you see. And without me in your corner... you really don't stand a chance."

"It's alright, Patricia," Hannah had said earlier, at the front door, stepping in between Swift and Ruby. "We've got enough to go on. You needn't keep pretending."

"What the bleedin' hell is *this*?" Ruby had snarled, stepping forward herself until she and Hannah were eye to eye, practically nose to nose. "And what do you think *you're* doing, turning up here?"

Hannah had pulled something from the front of her trench coat: an already open leather wallet embossed with a Metropolitan Police stamp, into which had been slotted a warrant card so convincing Ruby herself had wondered, just for a second, whether it might be real.

"My job, Mrs Redfearn," Hannah had replied, in a bored-sounding, jobsworth drone Ruby had reckoned she must have borrowed from one of the actors off *The Bill*. "Lucky for Miss Swift here, we've been keeping tabs on you for a while. And I'm sorry to have to tell you, but - *you're nicked.*"

("If I'd had a bit more about me when it happened," Ruby told El later, "I'd've pissed myself laughing at that. It weren't *The Bill* she'd be watching - it was the bloody *Sweeney*").

"*Nicked*, am I?" Ruby had snapped back at her, baring her blackened teeth. "How'd you reckon *that*, then?"

"Do you... still need me, Detective?" Swift had asked Hannah, unusually timorous.

Neither Ruby nor Hannah had bothered to look at her as she'd spoken; had continued instead to bore holes into one another with the aggressive intensity of a pair of warring lionesses on the savannah.

"No," Hannah had said, when she'd eventually broken eye contact. "You've been very helpful, but I can take it from here. Someone from the station will be in touch to let you know when to come in and give your statement."

"Great. Thank you, that's... great."

Swift had begun to sidle away, then stopped herself, apparently remembering something she hadn't done, but was obliged to do.

"The case," she'd added, gesturing down at the black briefcase still in her hand. "Do you still...?"

"Yes, please," Hannah had told her, holding out a hand of her own. Swift passed her the briefcase - with, Ruby had considered, no small degree of reluctance, her fingers tightening to claws around the handle before she finally released her hold.

"And I'll...?" Swift had continued.

"Get it back? Yes. *Obviously*. But I'll need one of my team to take it back to the station to be processed before we can release it. *As we talked about*."

Swift, Ruby had thought, had seemed conflicted: instinctive deference to authorities more powerful than her ramming up against an equally instinctive reluctance to part with a case stuffed full - or so Ruby had guessed - of a king's ransom's worth of her own money.

"And someone from the station will...?"

"Call you with the details of how to reclaim it once we've finished with it, *yes*," Hannah had answered, impatiently.

She'd turned back to face Ruby; behaving, to all intents and purposes, as if Swift had removed herself from the equation already.

"Great," Swift had said, somewhat weakly. "Great. I'll go, then."

And, no longer able to pretend she hadn't been summarily dismissed, she'd scurried away from the house - leaving Ruby and Hannah still staring at one another in molten silence on the doorstep.

"What *she*?" Karen spat, the words fired Hannah's way like hollow-point bullets. "What are you even fucking talking about, *she*?"

"*You* know," Hannah told Ruby. "You *must* do. Surely."

"Only thing *I* know," Ruby answered, the veins in her neck visible even through her layers of body makeup, "is I want back what you took off me. Off all of us."

Hannah groaned, a low exasperated exhalation; bent down to the briefcase she'd been keeping next to her, laid it down flat on the floor and kicked it over towards Ruby.

"God," she said, "it's always *money* with you people, isn't it? Well, fine. Have it your way."

"What's in it?" El asked her, staring at the briefcase but making no move to pick it up or open it or look inside. None of them did, she noticed.

"An early birthday present. Or a down-payment - whatever you want to call it. I can't get you your money back, not immediately. I don't have the capability, let alone... well. I suppose we'll come to that. But since you're all so *obsessed* with getting your just rewards... here. Have at it."

"There's cash in there?" said Karen, suspiciously.

"A hundred thousand. Everything that appalling self-help woman was gearing up to give you for that bottle of cold iced tea in the cellar. Or is it muddy water? I really have idea how you go about these things. Anyway, it's all there."

Still, not one of them made a move towards the case.

"You didn't answer the question," Sita said, cool but calm. "Who is this *she* you suppose is coming for us? And what possible interest could *you* have in seeing us forewarned?"

"Believe it or not," said Hannah, "I want to help you. Help myself too, of course. But it so happens that at the moment, helping *you* is the best way of achieving that last end. Who'd have thought it?"

"I *don't* believe it," Ruby scowled. "Not one damn bit of it."

"You ought to. All that money you lost, your precious pots of gold? I'm the only chance you have of getting it back. And of staying alive, I might add."

"You're saying someone intends to hurt us?" Rose asked. "Someone other than you, I mean."

"*No*, sister dear, I'm saying someone intends to *kill* you. All of you. And if you don't start listening to me and *do* something about it, they almost certainly *will* kill you."

"And you're swooping in to save us, are you?" This was from Kat, still transfixed by her own sore knuckle at the kitchen table. "You'll have to excuse me if I find that a little bit tough to swallow."

Hannah issued a long, dismissive snort from her injured nostrils.

"Good heavens, are you *still* hung up on that little knock to the skull you took? People change, you know. And they're never just one-note performers. What's that Whitman quote? *I contain multitudes*. I'm capable of doing more than just hitting people over the head with blunt instruments. Just as I'm sure there's more to old Ruby here than stabbing perfect strangers in the throat with a carving knife."

By the sink, Ruby winced, the exaggerated wrinkles of her face shifting into something like regret at the memory.

"Look," Hannah continued, more placatingly. "You've lost everything. It's been taken from you, and you're sore from it - I understand that. But as bad as you think things have been, they're only going to get worse if you don't act. She's gunning for you now. *Really* gunning for you."

"*Who?*" Karen was yelling now, her own hands curling into fists that El had no doubt she'd be using, if Hannah tried her patience any further. "Who the fuck are you talking about?"

Hannah looked to Ruby; waited until Ruby was looking back at her before she spoke again.

"Are you going to tell them," she said, "or shall I?"

"Tell 'em *what*?" Ruby said, her own voice raised to a shout. "What is it you think *I* know that them lot don't?"

Hannah seemed for a moment genuinely bewildered.

"You mean to say you don't *know*?" she said, incredulous.

"No, I don't bleedin' *know*. And I'm about *this* close to punchin' your lights out myself if you don't spit it out."

Hannah smiled; shook her head, ruefully.

"You know, Ruby," she said, "everyone always says how *clever* you are, how *good* you are at covering all the angles and factoring in the possibilities... I really thought you'd worked it out. But we've all been overestimating you, apparently. Your sister - she's the one I'm talking about. Your *sister* is the one who's coming after you."

BETHNAL GREEN, LONDON
April 1941

She could never remember the exact moment she stopped speaking - whether it was straight after Uncle Jim had come and got her from the house in Camden, when he'd told her about her Mum and Dad and the bomb that hit The Happy Angler, or whether it was later, once the news had properly sunk in.

No-one noticed, at first: Uncle Jim was out doing whatever it was he did for a living every hour of the day, and Dolly had kept her cards close to her chest for as long as Ruby could remember, so it wasn't a surprise she didn't want to talk to her baby sister about whatever it was she'd seen happen at the pub that night.

("She's in shock," Uncle Jim had said, when the ARP warden had brought Dolly home, caked in soot and wrapped in blankets and half deaf from the force of the blast, and they'd got her washed and settled down in bed with a hot cup of tea. "Let her be. She'll tell us what she's got to tell us, when she's ready."

She never did tell them, though - not then, and not after).

It wasn't as if she or Dolly had lessons to go to, or teachers checking up on them. Half the kids they knew had been evacuated; what had *been* their school on Starcross Street had been bombed out not long after the war started and never rebuilt, and the one closest to Uncle Jim in Bethnal Green was shuttered up, so there were precious few people about for her to talk to anyway. Ruby spent most of her days reading, and making up stories for herself, and listening to the old men barter with the slick-haired spivs down Loot Alley for bags of sugar and bottles of gin. And Dolly hadn't been what you'd call chatty herself, even before.

When Uncle Jim *did* work out Ruby had been keeping schtum, he tried to bring her out of herself by getting her to come out with him, "on the job" - though she hadn't known what he'd meant by that, not then. But she'd shook her head *no*, and gone back to reading the battered copy of *Ozma of Oz* she'd found on a park bench outside a church in Russell Square, and he'd let it go.

The second time he tried, a couple of weeks on from his first attempt, it wasn't *her* he wanted to talk about.

"Any chance you know what's up with that sister of yours?" he asked, settling himself down in the chair next to hers.

She shrugged and looked down at the carpet. She knew why he was asking: she might not have had much to say, the last couple of months, but she had two good eyes and two good ears on her, and she knew *something* was up with Dolly. Knew she'd been sneaking 'round even more than usual, stopping out all night then coming back to Uncle Jim's with more colour than she had any right to in her cheeks and grinning like the cat that got the cream.

She was out robbing, Ruby reckoned: doing over corner shops or houses while the streetlights were off and there was no-one about outside to catch her doing it. It explained how pleased with herself she'd seemed lately, in spite of everything - in spite of what the pair of them had lost. And all the odds and ends she'd been collecting in her jewellery box under the bed, the one she thought Ruby didn't know about: the pearl earrings and gold necklaces and little silver brooches that looked like they might have been nicked from the dressing room of a Duchess.

"*Something* ain't right, I know that much," Uncle Jim continued. "I don't know what she's got herself into, but I seen what she brought back in the house with her last night, what she trod on the kitchen floor 'fore she cleaned it up. It was blood, girl. Blood, all over the soles of her boots. And not just a bit of blood, neither. Looked like she'd been pacing up and down a slaughterhouse."

"Blood?" Ruby said, before she even knew she was saying the word out loud.

If Uncle Jim was surprised that she'd chosen there and then to break her silence, he didn't show it.

"That's right. Blood. You tellin' me you don't know nothing about it?"

"No," she whispered - wondering if *he* knew about the jewellery box, if *he'd* put the pieces together and worked out what Dolly had been doing, the same way she had. If the whole conversation was his way of getting her to admit it.

"Right, then," he said, getting up from the chair as abruptly as he'd sat down. "Suppose I'll have to have a word with her myself, then, won't I?"

Except he didn't get the chance.

Ruby sat up all that night in the living room, waiting for Dolly to come back - waiting for Uncle Jim to ask her the same questions he'd asked Ruby, for Dolly to confess where she'd been going and what she'd been doing and who she'd been stealing from. But Dolly - she never *did* come home. Not that night, nor the next, nor any of the long nights after.

CHELSEA, LONDON

April 1998

What's she want?" Ruby asked - her head down and expression entirely unreadable.

"What was that?" Hannah said.

"I *said*: what is it Dolly wants?"

Hannah frowned.

"Dolly? Is that what you called her?"

"What I *called* her?" Ruby raised her head, looking directly at Hannah. Her eyes were bloodshot, El saw - in a way that suggested she'd been crying, or that she'd got herself so worked up she'd managed to burst a blood vessel. "It's her bleedin' *name*."

"Not now it isn't. Her name's Thea - or that's the name she's been using, anyway. Since at least the eighties, was my understanding. Thea Madera."

Ruby took a moment to absorb this - then whistled, softly, through her teeth.

"Thea Madera," she said, under her breath. "Thea *Madera*. Christ."

She hesitated again, rolling her eyes heavenwards - castigating herself, or her sister, or the universe itself, El wasn't sure.

"Her name," she added, more loudly, "her full name, the one she was given... it's Dorothea. Dorothea Wood. Thea for short, I s'pose, though none of us called her that and she never used it for herself, least the way I remember it. And *Madera* - that's *wood* in Spanish, ain't it? So Dolly Wood, Thea Madera... they're *the same name*, just about. Dolly, she ain't *changed* her name – she's just messed about with it. Turned herself into a bleedin' *word game*."

She let her eyes drop again, her body sagging against the sink top.

"A sister?" Sita said quietly. "You never mentioned a sister."

She sounded sad, El thought; *hurt*, even. And maybe that was understandable. The two old women lied to the rest of the world constantly; had done for as long as El had known them. But she'd been under the impression that they very rarely lied to each other, or held back very many secrets *from* one another. Ruby, El knew, was one of the very few people Sita trusted with her life.

"No," Ruby replied, just as quietly. "No, don't suppose I did. Left not long after my Mum and Dad died, didn't she? I was nine. 'Course, she'd only just turned thirteen herself then, not that she let *that* stop her. She just sort of... upped and went one night. Went out and never come home. Ain't seen hide nor hair of her since. Truth be told, I'd more or less convinced myself that *she* were dead an' all."

"She just... *left*?" Rose said, horrified. "At *thirteen*?"

She's thinking of Sophie, El realised. Sophie, walking out the door and never coming back. Or worse, being *taken,* and never seen again.

"She weren't exactly a kid," Ruby told her. "The things she'd been up to, just before she legged it... Well, I'm pretty sure she could look after herself, put it that way."

Karen raised a hand, as if seeking permission to speak, then very deliberately cleared her throat.

"Sorry if I'm coming off insensitive for asking," she said, sounding not remotely apologetic, "but I'm not seeing what this - no offence, Ruby -

antique bit of family gossip has got to do with why this Thea bird's coming gunning for us now. Especially if she's not seen you in fucking forever. Or what *that* bitch is doing tangled up in any of it." She pointed a disparaging finger Hannah's way. "*Or*, come to think of it, what's she's doing here now, sounding the alarm about it."

"Are you looking for enlightenment?" Hannah asked her, mock-sweetly. "Or did you just want to get that off your chest?"

Karen really *was* going to punch her soon, El thought.

"If you have something to tell us," Rose said, sounding to El somewhere between furious and exasperated, "then *say it*. Say it or go."

Hannah tutted.

"Honestly," she said, "you're no fun at all, are you? But fine. I suppose I *do* owe you *some* sort of explanation. Are you all sitting comfortably? No? Well, no matter. I'll just have to begin anyway."

She'd banked on Charlie Soames and his vendetta being the hammer-blow to bring them down - to get them all locked up, at the very least.

It had been a bitter disappointment, seeing *that* plan fail; more disappointing still to see them revel in their little triumph at Karen's wedding to that skinny ginger boy who could have been the third Proclaimer.

Fortunately, because Hannah wasn't a *complete* idiot, she'd had a back-up: a trump card she'd been holding back, should the very worst transpire.

Her father, she'd gathered from all those years of watching and waiting in the wings, had relied on his fixer to do the majority of his dirty work - that *Minotaur* Lomax, who'd spilled his deathbed guts to Rose for a pitiful sack of blood money. It was Lomax her father had charged with cleaning up what messes there were to clean; with making disappear what problems there were to resolve.

But occasionally, he'd needed more than Lomax alone could provide. And at times like *those*, he'd call on Madera.

Reliable information on *her* - and on her brawny bullock of a henchman, and the scattering of other specialists in her inner circle - had been painfully hard to extract, but worth its weight in gold. And when Hannah had paid off the many, many informants and investigators and former police detectives who'd fed her the disparate snapshots she'd pieced together herself into a cohesive picture, she'd been left with three invaluable pieces of information: who Thea Madera was, what specifically she'd done for Hannah's father, and where she might be found.

Hannah's efforts to make contact with Madera had taken, her - ironically, given Ruby and Co.'s recent pilgrimage to San Francisco - to California: not to the Bay Area but to LAX, and from there to a Mediterranean micro-compound in the Santa Monica Mountains, so shaded by the hill and rock and Big Leaf Maple trees around it that Hannah would undoubtedly have driven straight past it, had she not known exactly where it was.

Its gates were high and intimidating, its security ferocious, and Hannah had been in no doubt that Madera, or perhaps one of her minions, would have happily shot her dead on first sight, had she tried to make her way in surreptitiously. There was nothing for it, she'd told herself, but to be upfront in her intentions: to press the buzzer at the entrance, state her case, and hope Madera found it sufficiently compelling.

Madera had come down to the gates herself to investigate the unexpected visitor, which had taken Hannah aback; with the money the woman must have made over the course of a lifetime of doing what she did for the people she did it for, she could surely have afforded a retinue of staff. But that wasn't the real shock.

Looking at Madera had been like looking right at Ruby Redfearn -

though, perhaps, a Ruby Redfearn who'd known the benefit of a West Coast tan, a well-paid stylist and a very good moisturiser.

She was very slightly taller, Hannah had noticed as the woman came closer, and somewhat slimmer, her apple-shaped dimensions flattered by a well-cut summer dress and decent heels. Her hair was streaked honey blonde, expertly coloured - not grey and silver, as Redfearn's was when the old harpy was off the clock - and the grooves age had carved so starkly around Redfearn's mouth and forehead were, for the most part, absent, though Madera must have been somewhere close to seventy.

But the eyes were the same: a bright, clever azulejo blue, so sharp you could believe they might cut into you if you stared at them too long.

And the *way* she'd looked at Hannah from the other side of the gate; that curious, appraising, faintly threatening stare she'd issued through the gilded bars... it had been so terribly, *terribly* familiar.

"There something I can help you with?" she'd said - and the voice had *sounded* local, on the surface, but there was something below it, a pace to the delivery of the words that had seemed to belie the veracity of the accent.

And that - that had been enough for Hannah to be certain of who the woman was to Redfearn, who the woman *must* have been, even if she hadn't been sure what to do with the knowledge.

"I'm James Marchant's daughter," she'd said, defaulting to the only line she'd thought stood a hope of persuading Madera to let her inside.

Madera had shifted her posture into something more aggressive.

"What about him?" she'd replied, and had Hannah been imagining it, or was the accent slipping just a little, letting just a sliver more of what *had* to be Cockney show through, like a glimpse of old paint brought to light by peeling wallpaper? "He's on the run. Saw it on the news."

"He's dead. Murdered."

The smallest note of surprise had registered on Madera's face, then was gone as quickly as it had come.

"You sure about that?" she'd said. "Because the way I heard it, he stole a bunch of money from his own company and took off into the night."

"You heard wrong. I was there when he died. I saw who killed him." She'd paused - partly for effect, and partly to gauge whether the story she was telling was landing the way she'd needed it to. "That's why I came. The people who did it - they've been talking. To the police. Not directly," she'd added quickly, to preclude any irritating misunderstandings that might lead to her, for example, taking a bullet in the chest from a disgruntled hit-woman. "They haven't been arrested, and frankly I doubt they ever will be. But they've been tipping off the Met. That's what we call our police, in London."

She'd been all but certain that the clarification was unnecessary, but hadn't been able to resist needling her, this Redfearn doppelgänger - pressing her buttons for a reaction.

"I'm familiar with them, thank you," Madera had all but growled back.

"Alright, then. Well, as I said: the people who killed my father, they're talking to the Met. Drip-feeding them intel. And I'm afraid to say, your name came up."

The look of surprise had returned to Madera's face.

"My *name*?" she'd said, and had Hannah not already suspected what she'd suspected, then the emphasis - the stress not on *my*, but on *name*, as if there might have been a question mark over *what* name that could have been - would have been enough to tip her off.

"Yes," Hannah had confirmed, moving in to close the deal. "So how about you let me inside, and I'll tell you all about it?"

"You *put her onto us*?" Karen said, through gritted teeth. "This woman's coming after us because *you told her to*? And now you're here, not only admitting to it but telling us you want to *team up* so she doesn't off us? You got some brass-neck, I'll say that for you. 'Cause if you think for one fucking second..."

"She's a killer?" Ruby interrupted, her eyes turned to Hannah's. "Our Dolly, that's what she does now? Offs people for money, for men like Marchant?"

She sounded... not horrified, exactly, El thought, nor even disbelieving, but mournful. Like she'd expected the worst but was crestfallen nonetheless to discover that the worst really *had* come to pass.

"Yes," Hannah said. Then: "Sorry."

Madera had opened the gates, but wouldn't let Hannah in the house - showing her, instead, to a grass and patio piazza around the back of the property, where a vast rectangular swimming pool jostled for space with cacti and white wicker recliners and a covered wooden barrel that Hannah had guessed to be a hot tub.

The old woman had taken a seat at the glass-topped table beside the pool but hadn't invited Hannah to join her. Hadn't said a word.

"I suppose I should start at the beginning," Hannah began, pulling out another of the garden chairs and settling herself into it regardless.

"Who are they?" Madera had said, entirely disinterested in Hannah's pleasantries, "and what have they been saying to the police about me?"

The accent had *really* wavered, then; had threatened to abandon the States altogether in favour of a return to the East End. It had to have been deliberate, Hannah reasoned; a woman like Madera wouldn't make such an amateur slip-up.

She wants *me to know where she's from*, Hannah had told herself. *Does she think it'll intimidate me, knowing she's from my... what is it they call it, manor?*

She really is *just like her sister, if she does.*

Because it had to *be* sisters, she'd thought. The resemblance between Madera and Redfearn had to be familial, and close-familial at that. They might even have been twins; twins ran in Redfearn's family, after all. Those peas-in-a-pod sons of hers were proof of that.

The question was: would disclosing Redfearn as the ringleader of the offending party, the way she'd planned to - as the rat who was even at that moment singing like a canary down at Scotland Yard - help Hannah's cause, or hinder it?

Would Madera be *more* or less *inclined* to act on Hannah's information - and act in the swift and above all *decisive* way Hannah had hoped she would - if it was her own sister she'd have to act against?

"They're con artists," Hannah had answered, erring on the side of caution. "Grifters. They went after my father - that's how I know them."

"And they've been saying *what* about me to the old Bill?"

She'd been pure London then; no trace of LA about her at all.

Hannah had counted to ten - replaying the lie she'd been formulating since she'd made the decision to fly out to the States before committing to it by repeating it aloud.

"The con they were working on my father," she'd said, keeping her tone steady and her eyes on Madera, "it took them to Ricky Lomax. I assume you came across him, at some stage?"

"*Lomax*? He's dead too, ain't he? Thought that cancer of his got him."

"It did. But one of *them* got to him first - got him to talk. On camera, no less. And he, I'm afraid, was rather forthcoming about *you*. About the... work you did, for my father."

Hannah, in truth, had had no sense at all of how many jobs Madera had taken on at her father's behest: it might have been two, or it might have been twenty. None of her sources had been able to lay claim to that particular piece of information. The best she could do, she'd thought, was bluff it, if she were asked to expound on any of the finer points of *that* claim.

Madera hadn't asked, though. Instead, her own gaze lingering not on Hannah but on the cool sapphire surface of the swimming pool, she'd said:

"What's in it for you, telling me this? What is it *you* want out of it?"

For *this* question, at least, Hannah had prepared an answer - one that, unlike the others she'd given thus far, wasn't entirely a lie.

"I want them dead," she'd said, with perfect honesty. "All of them - every one of those bitches who took my father away. And I thought perhaps, if I told you what they've been up to, you might feel the same."

CHELSEA, LONDON

April 1998

Y ou sold us out," Karen said wearily. "You sold us out to a fucking hitwoman. I don't even know why I'm surprised."

"It's certainly in character," Rose agreed. "But actually, my question isn't at all dissimilar to the one this Madera woman asked of you. Why are you telling us this, and what do you expect to happen as a consequence? Inciting a professional killer to track us down and murder us isn't at all the incentive to welcome you back into the fold with open arms you seem to think it is."

"Would I be telling you at all if I didn't want to help you?" Hannah told her, as if delivering the definitive rebuttal.

"What you're telling us," Rose replied, "if I've understood you correctly, is that you want to help extricate us from a situation *you created in the first place.* One that, had you not gone out to L.A. with the *express* purpose of having us done away with, wouldn't, in fact, exist."

"But I'm here *now*, aren't I? Here and ready to help. That has to count for *something*, surely?"

"And why *are* you here?" Ruby said, her voice as cracked and strained as

El imagined it had been when she'd been talking with Patricia Swift. "Cause *I'd* like to know, same as Rose. Same as our Dolly did."

Hannah had at least the perspicacity to look embarrassed, though El had no faith whatsoever in her sincerity.

"I may have overestimated my own indispensability to the course of action I encouraged her to undertake," she said, sounding faintly sheepish.

"What does *that* mean, then?" Ruby demanded.

"I pissed her off," Hannah said, more flatly. "And now, I'm sorry to say, she wants *me* dead, too."

They hadn't told the police *everything*, Hannah had assured Madera, that day beside the pool. Some of what Ricky Lomax had disclosed to them - they were holding it back, as insurance. They hadn't *named* Madera, not yet; nor had they passed along the details of the services she'd rendered for Marchant.

"But it's only a matter of time," she'd added. "Which is why it's so imperative that we act *now*. Before it's too late."

"*We*?" Madera had said, her face still half-turned away from Hannah's. A face, Hannah couldn't help but think, so very like Ruby Redfearn's, even in profile.

"*You*, then. If you, you know... decide you want to do something about it."

Still Madera had kept her own counsel, leaving Hannah to fill the silence.

"You won't find them like the other... problems you're used to dealing with," she'd gone on. "They're resourceful. Well connected. And they've got money - more than enough to make themselves disappear, if they catch wind that they might be in the firing line."

Madera had said nothing. Hannah might as well have been a piece of furniture herself - or an irritating bird, a parrot or a seagull, squawking into the breeze on the edges of Madera's hearing but easy enough to tune out, with a small effort of will.

"They have video tapes of Lomax," she'd said, a torrent of half-truths and almost-lies escaping from her mouth at a rate of knots. "Confessions. Their inside woman – she has them, at a cottage she keeps outside of London. You'll need to destroy them, the tapes. The house too, perhaps, if that's easier."

"And you'll need to find a way to cripple them financially, before you make a move. It'll take time, planning – you mustn't rush it. By all accounts, they're drip-feeding the police the information... so you *have* time. A little of it, anyway. You'll have to drain their accounts somehow, so they can't just... I don't know, hunker down in Bolivia on false passports for the rest of their days. They've all got them - false passports, I mean. They change their names as often as some people get a haircut, and they've got any number of contacts on tap to help them do it. For a price, I should say. That's why it's so important that you get to their money, you see - if you don't, they'll find a way to buy themselves out of trouble. Perhaps you know someone who might be able to do that? Take away their assets?"

She *did* have, and Hannah had known it. The details she'd been given were scant, but she'd remembered the basics: that among the small team of associates Madera and her muscle-man lieutenant recruited to pull off their larger-scale projects was a technical specialist, a young computer wizard who went by Pasadena in the digital realms he frequented. His real name might have been Huang, or it might have been Zhang - he'd used both in the past, according to Hannah's sources, though either or both might have been pseudonyms. He'd purportedly worked in security for several of the larger Silicon Valley start-ups before leaving to go freelance, and thereafter even further off the map than he'd been previously.

Hannah had wondered idly, at the time, how he and Karen Baxter might have got along, had they known one another. Whether their paths might ever have crossed, on the internet if not out in the real world.

"Know a lot about what I ought to be doing, don't you?" Madera had said - as if she were addressing the water, rather than Hannah.

"I just want to make sure you have all the information," Hannah had told her, choosing her words carefully. "So you can decide for yourself what to do with it."

"You're not exactly helping your own cause here," Rose said, adjusting her own stance into something very slightly more aggressive. El hadn't seen her adopt it often - usually in defence of Sophie, and thankfully never directed at *her* - but she recognised it for what it was. If Hannah didn't start offering them something useful, and soon, it might be Rose, and not Karen, who tried to punch her lights out.

"I'm getting there," Hannah said. "And if you stop interrupting me every five seconds, perhaps I'll get there sooner - have you considered *that*?"

"Who are they, then, these people?" Madera had asked - finally turning to look at Hannah as she spoke to her. "I notice you've not told me their names."

Hannah had known the question would be coming; it was unavoidable. And she'd come out to the mountains fully prepared to throw them all to the lions: not just Redfearn and Sita and El bloody Gardener and Hannah's own sanctimonious mess of a sister, but Redfearn's sons, the ginger boy who'd put a ring on Karen Baxter, even the whining child Rose had managed to spawn with her dead gay husband... every one of them, and more.

Madera's connection to Redfearn, though - it threw a spanner in the works, potentially. She'd have to navigate things cautiously; very cautiously.

"The main one is El Gardener," she'd replied. "She's the inside woman I mentioned - the one they sent in to swindle my father. There's a technical person - a little thief named Karen Baxter. Rose Winchester - she's the one who brought them all together in the first place. And Kat Morgan - she's mostly a sort of prostitute, I believe."

"That all of them, is it? A grifter, a thief, a call-girl and whatever this Rose is?"

Hannah had thought carefully before she spoke again.

"Not quite. There's an older woman, Sita - I don't have a clue about her surname, I'm not sure anyone does. And another one, too. The sort of... mastermind of the group, I suppose you'd call her."

"And *she* have a name, does she?"

Hannah had swallowed.

"It's Redfearn," she'd said. "Ruby Redfearn."

There wasn't time to hold her back. Rose was flying forward before El had even registered she'd gone, long before El's own reflexes had kicked into gear.

The first punch Rose landed - a fist to the stomach with the full weight of her body behind it - had Hannah doubled over. The second struck her just below the jaw and sent her sprawling onto her shoulders on the kitchen floor, the fall generating an audible crack that had El suppressing a wince.

"You'd give her my daughter?" Rose screamed, standing over her - getting ready, El thought, to deliver a kick to her ribs. "My *daughter*? And El - you'd give her *El*?"

None of the others lifted a finger to stop her, El noticed. Ruby stayed propped up by the sink, as blank-faced as El had ever seen her, with Sita -

her initial surprise and disappointment now apparently abated - resting a comforting hand on her upper arm. Karen was watching the fight unfold with what struck El as the detached interest of a spectator at a boxing match, and Kat... Kat was smiling, a feral glint in her eye that suggested more than a little vicarious pleasure taken in seeing Hannah beaten bloody.

It's on me, El thought. *If I don't stop this, no-one else is going to.*

She took five wary steps towards Rose, a defensive forearm already half-raised in preparation; fully expecting Rose to lash out before her rage dissipated and she remembered who El was, and that she wasn't another enemy to fight. When she was close enough, she placed one, very tentative hand of her own on Rose's lower back, below the fabric of her shirt; let it sit there, putting no pressure at all on the skin, until she felt Rose's muscles begin to relax under her fingers.

"It's okay," she said gently - stepping in closer, letting her hand move from Rose's back to her waist, as much to dissuade her from kicking out or throwing another punch as to offer support. "You can stop. It's okay."

"She's a monster," Rose whispered, sounding to El as if she'd run a marathon. "She's like him. Just exactly like him."

The *him* was Marchant, El knew. It couldn't have been anyone else.

"I know she is," El said. A thick lock of hair had come free from the onyx clip Rose used to keep it out of her face; El smoothed it down, tucked it back behind Rose's ear. "I know. But it won't help to keep hurting her."

"You should listen to your girlfriend," Hannah said from the floor, a line of blood trickling from her cut lips down onto the tiles. "She's not wrong."

"Do you *want* to get your teeth knocked out?" El told her. "Because I guarantee that's what'll happen, if you keep talking."

Hannah wiped the blood from her mouth with the sleeve of her trench coat; began, warily, to pull herself up from the floor.

"No," Ruby said - so abruptly, every one of them turned her way.

"No?" El asked her.

"No. She needs to finish. We might not like it - we ain't *gonna* like it - but we need to know, don't we? What she knows, what she's passed along to our Dolly. What Dolly's got planned."

"I'm glad at least *one* of you is thinking sensibly," Hannah said, rubbing a spread palm against her injured stomach.

"Don't fucking push it," Karen warned her. "Wanting to hear what it is you've got to say's the only thing stopping *me* from laying you out right now."

Hannah looked as if she was getting ready to launch into a comeback; then appeared - wisely, El considered - to think better of it.

"Finish your story," said Ruby, gravely. "Now."

Hannah had left Madera's house in the mountains that day almost certain that her plan had worked: that even with her own sister in the mix, Madera was primed to clean up the mess Hannah's father's death had left behind.

She hadn't seemed to react at all to Hannah's use of Ruby Redfearn's name; had neither blinked nor flinched, leaving Hannah to conclude that the Redfearn sisters - the *Madera* sisters, perhaps? - had a relationship more akin to hers and Rose's than any closer familial bond.

Which would surely make things easier. For everyone, with the possible exception of Redfearn herself.

They'd agreed to meet again the following day, back at Madera's house. Madera needed, she'd said, to consult with an associate, who might in turn have questions for Hannah - Lucian Carruthers, Hannah had assumed. Every report she'd been given had identified him as Madera's right-hand man; the one whom she'd worked with the longest.

She hadn't asked Hannah if she'd mind coming back; had simply told her where to be, and when, as if she knew there was no possibility at all of Hannah refusing. Which would have been altogether infuriating, had Hannah not had a larger goal in sight.

In fact, twenty-four hours had proven too long for Madera to wait to see her a second time.

She'd been having dinner in the restaurant at her hotel - a frustratingly over-done Kobe steak and an absurdly elaborate pomegranate salad - when the pair of them had joined her at her table: Madera in the seat across from her, an inappropriately romantic candle flaring between them, and Carruthers actually *next* to Hannah, encroaching onto her space by dint of the sheer size of his quads and deltoids and biceps.

He'd been larger in person than she'd expected, bigger even than Lomax - an absolute Atlas of a man. But terribly young looking, though she'd guessed him to be not all that much younger than she was: baby-faced, his pudgy child's features mounted on the body of a professional heavyweight wrestler. What remained of his straight, dark hair grew past his ears, but had thinned to almost nothing at the crown and temples, and there was a smattering of acne across his tanned cheeks - in both cases, Hannah had suspected, as a result of the steroids he must surely have been pumping into himself at the gym. He hadn't seemed, at least from the hunch of his posture and the expressionlessness of his raisin eyes and cherub's mouth, as if he intended to come across as intimidating, but she'd felt the very fact of him beside her as an intimidation, nonetheless.

"This *is* a surprise," she'd said, keeping her voice even, casual.

She'd doubted they had plans to harm her - not there and then, in public. This wasn't *The Godfather.*

But equally - she hadn't told them where she was staying, had she? Had been very careful to not so much as hint at which part of the city she'd be heading back to, in her conversations with Madera.

So *that* was a worry.

"When was this?" Ruby interrupted her. "When did all this happen?"

She was trying to keep the timeline clear in her head, El thought: to establish how long Madera had known about them. How long they'd had a target on their collective backs.

"February," Hannah answered, running the tip of one nail gingerly along her cut bottom lip. "You noticed your money gone not long after that, I'm guessing?"

"It wasn't just *money* we lost," El said quietly - thinking of her cottage; of the smoking, stinking rubble that was all that was left of the things she'd spent a lifetime accumulating.

Rose, calmer now, slipped an arm of her own around El's waist; pulled her in closer.

Hannah rolled her eyes at them.

"Remember what I said, about wanting to deck you?" Karen told her. "I'm not seeing much that's dampening that impulse."

Hannah rolled her eyes again, defiantly. But continued her story.

"We had a few questions," Madera had replied - her accent back to the same bland Transatlantic drone she'd adopted when she'd first met Hannah by the gates of her house in the mountains, the one that could have been from anywhere or nowhere. "*Lucian* had a few questions."

The leviathan beside her shifted in his seat, the metal slats straining audibly under the weight of him.

"Oh?" Hannah had said.

"So, I made some calls, right after you and Thea talked earlier," Carruthers began - *his* voice an entirely inoffensive, even slightly mellifluous variant on California Surfer, rather than the rumbling bass his appearance had led her to expect. "Spoke to a couple friends in London."

Where is he going with this? she'd wondered. *Who could he* possibly *have spoken to, and about* her?

"And these friends," he'd continued, "they put in a couple more calls to some friends of *theirs*... And from what *those* guys said... it seems like maybe you know the women you talked to Thea about a little better than you let on? Like, maybe you *worked* with them before?"

"On a con, by all accounts," Madera had added. "Interesting, you not mentioning that when you came by to see me."

Hannah had frozen in place, her glass of too-warm Chardonnay hovering between hand and mouth.

They thought she'd thrown in with Redfearn and the other women, she'd realised; had heard enough of what she'd been up to two years earlier, from whichever only half-reliable sources they'd tapped into, to believe that, rather than infiltrating Redfearn's little gang in the interests of helping her father subdue them, Hannah had *actually been one of them.* Had worked *with* them, not against them.

Which meant that Madera, in all likelihood, believed that Hannah was trying to hoodwink her, somehow; to lay a trap for her by feeding her misinformation, or omitting key points that might radically alter the shape and implications of the tale Hannah *had* told her.

Which was, in turn, a somewhat uncomfortable - and in all probability, very dangerous - position for Hannah to have found herself in.

"It's not what you think," she'd said, immediately regretting her choice of words. *It's not what you think?* What was she, a cheating husband trying to allay the concerns of a suspicious wife with a pocketful of Travelodge receipts? She wouldn't have believed *herself,* with a line like that.

"No?"

It had been Madera who'd answered. Carruthers had only sat there, wet mouth pursed in consternation and muscles flexing and loosening in tiny - she assumed involuntary - motions, as if he'd been performing a set of Kegel exercises under the tablecloth.

"No. I *pretended* to work with them, very briefly - perhaps that was what your friend's friend was referring to? But only for my father's benefit. I was never, you know... *one* of them."

"You sure about that?" Madera had said. "You sure they didn't just - let's say, for example - cut you out of a job, and now you want to get your own back by getting rid of them?"

It hadn't sounded like a threat - it had been almost conversational, in fact, the way she'd framed the question. If Hannah had been an outsider, listening in, she might almost have believed Madera had asked it in nothing more than the spirit of legitimate curiosity.

Almost, but not quite.

"Positive," Hannah had said brightly, working to project both absolute sincerity and a firm conviction that both Madera and Carruthers were, *of course*, reasonable people more than capable of parsing the reality of a given situation from unverified scuttlebutt. "It's a misunderstanding, obviously. I'm just glad you brought it to me so we could get it cleared up. Now, can I tempt you to a glass of wine?"

She'd waved the all but full bottle of Chardonnay at them, smiling with such maniacal good humour that her cheeks had spasmed, and had scarcely waited for Madera to grace her with an indifferent nod before she'd filled the empty glasses by their placemats up to the brim.

"Cheers!" she'd toasted them, still grinning like a lunatic as she'd downed the remainder of her own wine.

They didn't believe her; that much had been clear. But perhaps, she'd told herself, it didn't matter? If they'd bothered to ask around after *her*, then the odds were good that they'd looked into Redfearn and the others already. That they'd found that what she'd told Madera - about *them*, at least - checked out.

It would have been a moment's work for Carruthers to confirm that there really *was* a Gerry Adler at the Met; would have taken only a little more informal digging for him to ascertain that Adler was - as Hannah had assured Madera he was - a close friend of Sita's. Hell, Carruthers and Madera might even have had their tech man determine that it really *was* Karen Baxter who'd delivered that first incriminating video of Ricky Lomax to the police, in the wake of her father's disappearance.

And if they *had* looked, and they *had* found enough to convince themselves that they were liable to be dropped in the shit at any moment... then they almost certainly *would* want Redfearn and the others out of the picture, regardless of what they believed to be Hannah's motivations for *wanting* them gone.

The train of thought had reassured Hannah; not completely, but enough that she'd been able to relax sufficiently to enjoy another glass of the inadequate wine, more or less secure in the knowledge that she wasn't about to be stabbed to death with a butter knife over her salad.

Until the moment when, three sips later, the residual fear had hit her bladder, and she'd needed, quite urgently, to pee.

She'd been ninety percent sure that, if she were to get up and leave the table for the bathroom, neither Madera nor Carruthers would follow her; that she'd be free to empty her bladder troubled by neither physical violence nor the immediate threat of it.

That missing ten percent, however, had been enough to keep her in her seat, her own pelvic floor muscles clenching, until she could take no more, and had had no choice but to excuse herself and race away from the table to the facilities.

The restaurant had been bookended between the hotel lobby and its cocktail bar, and sandwiched on either side by what had been, until the tobacco ban imposed on California workplaces that year, twin smoking lounges, partitioned off from the restaurant by opaque Japanese slide-panels - a fact imparted unto her five minutes after she'd arrived at the hotel from the airport by a disgruntled concierge none too happy to see her reaching into her purse for a packet of Marlboro Lights.

This layout, she'd suspected, would likely have afforded Carruthers - though not Madera, across the table from him - a clear view of her as she performed her rapid crabwalk *to* the restrooms. What neither he nor Madera could have known, though - and what Hannah herself had learned only after two consecutive nights of dining in the place - was that those restrooms were accessible through *two* doors: the second opening out onto not the lobby, as the one she'd *entered through* had, but the left-hand smoking lounge. An area which had run, very conveniently for Hannah's purposes, parallel to the table at which she'd left Madera and Carruthers sipping at their Chardonnay.

And perhaps it might be sensible, she'd told herself as she'd entered the restroom through the *first* door, to take advantage of that particular architectural quirk.

She'd peed; dislodged the day's gathered clumps of mascara from the corner of her eyes with a fingernail and then - with no concrete plan in mind but a moment or two of eavesdropping - left the restroom via the *second* door, spilling out into the narrow stretch of maroon carpet and ashtray-smelling leather armchairs concealed behind the Japanese panels.

Then she'd had only to manoeuvre herself, surreptitiously, to the appropriate section of panel, place an equally surreptitious ear to the divider, and listen.

She'd been close enough to the table to catch the conversation playing out between Madera and Carruthers in her absence - though not, thankfully, close enough for *them* to be aware of her breath catching and discharging at the things she'd heard.

"She still in that bathroom?" Madera had said.

"Guess so," Carruthers had told her. "Haven't seen her come out."

"What do you think, then?"

"Do I think she's lying, you mean?"

"Oh, I *know* she's lying. Just can't quite put my finger on what *about* yet. She's not quite *right*, is she? Not right in the head at all. You can see it, just from looking at her. Not... how would you put it? *Stable.* It's true what she said, though, about that Gardener girl and the rest of them - I'll give her that. I spoke to Henry Anderson myself this afternoon. You know him?"

"The forger guy's son? Sure. Think I met him when we went to Golders Green that time. Or was it Little Venice? No offence, but it all kinda looks the same to me once you get out of the West End."

"It was Willesden. Anyway, I spoke to him, and she's not lying about *that*, at least. Gardener and... the rest of them: it looks as if they *did* do something to Marchant, before he vanished off the face of the Earth. And they're definitely talking to *someone* at Scotland Yard."

Had it been Hannah's imagination, or had Madera stumbled slightly over *the rest of them*?

"What do you want to do about it?" Carruthers had asked.

There'd been a small pause; just long enough for one of the two - she'd thought probably Carruthers - to loudly chew and swallow something Hannah had guessed to be a piece of bread.

"She'll need getting rid of," Madera had concluded, when Carruthers - it had to have been Carruthers - had concluded his mastication. "Women like that, *unstable* women - they can bring a world of trouble to your doorstep, if you let them. It'll have to wait until we've done the other ones - Gardener and all that lot. We definitely can't have *them* up and about if they're running their mouths off. But afterwards... yeah. She'll need to go."

"What then?" Ruby said, levelly.

"Then?" Hannah raised a palm to her mouth to disperse yet more of the blood but succeeded only in smearing a streak of it across her cheek. "*Then* I put on my big girl pants, went back into the bathroom and let them see me walking back to the table. Where I sat down, finished my steak and made pleasant conversation about nothing until they finished their drinks and left."

"*Then* what?" Karen pressed her. "Not even a psycho bitch like you'd just hang around waiting to see what happened after *that*."

Hannah grimaced.

"You know," she replied, "I'm going to end up with a complex, if people don't stop questioning my sanity. And no - as it happens, I didn't just *hang around waiting* to be murdered. I paid my bill, went back up to my room, packed my suitcase and got on the first flight out of L.A. that would sell me a ticket."

"In February," Ruby said, seeming to El very deep in thought. "Two months ago, that was. And you're only just here now, telling us this. So what were you doing in them two months, while our Dolly and her lot were robbing us blind?"

"It's obvious, innit?" Karen told her. "She's been sharking around looking for other ways out of the hole she's dug herself into. We're not Plan B - we're her last resort."

El couldn't disagree. Perhaps she'd have done the same in Hannah's position, though she struggled to imagine herself ever *being* in Hannah's position - laid low somewhere that wasn't Britain or the States, stockpiling all the cash and paperwork she could get her hands on, trying to pull together something like a plan to make herself disappear, permanently and untraceably.

Though evidently for Hannah, this strategy hadn't paid dividends. Why else would she be with them now, after everything?

"I prefer *only option*," Hannah said tartly. "But you're right, obviously. It's you lot or a bullet in the head. And I've always been a pragmatist, as I'm sure you remember."

"And what do you think it is we'll do to look out for you, now you're here?" Ruby asked her. "Last time we let you anywhere near us, you tried to have us bumped off. You just about killed young Kat over there. And this whole thing *started*, if I've understood right, 'cause you tried to have us bumped off *again*. You ain't one of us. And you certainly ain't welcome."

Rose tensed again in El's arms; El tightened her grip around her waist, pre-emptively.

"You need me," Hannah said, so matter-of-factly *El* could have hit her. "I know things - about your sister and her crew, about the way they operate. I may, ironically, be *your* best chance of putting an end to her. Of keeping yourselves alive."

"How do you reckon that, then? Think you know a way to stop her, do you?"

Hannah shook her head in a mocking facsimile of disappointment.

"*Stop* her? Really - have you even been *listening* to what I've said? You can't *stop* her. She's a bloody *machine* - her whole *life* has been about putting people in the ground, even people who don't want to be found and go to very great lengths to keep themselves hidden. People cleverer than all of *you*, I hasten to add. No - what you *need* to do is eliminate her altogether, if you don't want to spend the rest of what lives you'll have hiding out and looking over your shoulders. You need to *kill her*. For all our sakes."

LUDGATE HILL, LONDON

April 1998

Rohan Rasmussen's London *pied-à-terre* was nothing at all like the luxurious apartment his mother had left behind in Kensington.

If Sita's former home had been a case-study in opulence, a Versailles-esque explosion of rococo furniture and neoclassicist artwork, then Rohan's investment property in the City was a scene from a zen garden - a minimalist, monochromatic set of rooms with the consciously cultivated characterlessness of a modern hotel room.

Or had been, until the weight of Sita's accumulated possessions had landed on it with the force of a farmhouse on a wicked witch.

"Sorry about the mess," Sita said, making her way along what seemed like the only navigable path through the wooden crates and cardboard boxes that vied for floorspace with the loveseats, gilded mirrors and chests of drawers she'd brought with her in the move - a tea set, milk and sugar bowl balanced precariously on the Florentine tray she was carrying. "There's rather a lot to unpack."

"Really, it's fine," El told her, rising from the waist-high pile of books she'd been perching on and taking the tray from Sita's hands. "You should see how *we're* living. I'm not sure there was much space in that flat even *before* Harriet let us stay."

Sita settled herself on the edge of a dressing table and sighed.

"And how *is* Harriet?" she asked. "Rose mentioned there'd been some... tension between you."

Did she? El thought.

She'd been telling herself that the strained atmosphere that seemed to settle over the flat whenever she and Harriet were in it together was perceptible only to the two of them; that neither Rose nor Sophie had picked up on it.

Evidently, she'd been wrong.

"It's fine," she said, far more cheerfully than the situation had left her feeling. "It's just what happens when you're cooped up with someone too long with nowhere to go." She bit, absently, at the skin around the nail bed of her left thumb - a nervous habit she'd developed, for the first time in her life, over the preceding weeks. "I didn't tell Rose I was coming," she added. "That was what you wanted, wasn't it?"

It had been uncomfortable, lying to Rose about her whereabouts that afternoon - not least since Sophie, after cornering her by the front door of the flat as she was leaving, had made it clear that both she and Rose *knew* that El's excuse about going down to Oxford Street to do some shopping had been a fabrication, but had mutually decided not to press the issue.

("You're broke, and you hate shopping," Sophie had said, more exasperated than any fourteen year-old child had any right to sound. "I mean, come *on*. You weren't even *trying*").

Sita, however, had insisted that El's visit be kept secret from the others: not only Rose but Karen and Kat, too. And, to El's surprise, Ruby.

"I'm sorry to have to ask, darling," Sita replied, pouring hot tea from the pot into the cups and drowning it in milk. "It's terribly cloak-and-dagger, isn't it? But I thought it might be best, given Auntie Ruby's... state of mind."

She had a point. In the three days that had passed since Hannah

D'Amboise had hurled herself back into their lives and ushered in an entirely new raft of problems for them, Ruby's behaviour had been decidedly odd.

She'd been far too quiet, for one thing. Sharp as she was, and while she was never less than five steps ahead of everyone else - including El, at times, as infuriating as *that* could be - Ruby was rarely given to introspection, much less to brooding. But there was no better word than *brooding* for the way she'd been acting, since Hannah had left them at the Chelsea house - to let them *think things over*, as she'd put it, before they decided how to proceed.

("I'd think quickly, though," she'd said, throwing the final rejoinder their way as she'd stepped out onto the pavement outside, still cradling her injured and by then visibly swollen jaw in one hand. "It's a terrible cliché, I know, but you really are in terrible danger, the lot of you. Which means that *I* am. And I really do *hate* that").

What Ruby had said when she *had* spoken, moreover, had not gone over well with the rest of them.

"We'll have to do it," she'd told them, once Hannah had gone. "I don't like it any more than I expect you lot will, but she's right: we need her, if we're gonna find a way around this."

"*Need* her?" Karen had replied - more shocked than angry, at least then. "What would we *need* her for? Even if it's true, what she's saying - and it probably isn't, 'cause she's a lying bitch - then we don't need *her* around to sort it out, do we? If we really *are* in the shit, then we can get ourselves out of it a lot quicker without the fucking spawn of Satan along for the ride."

"I'm afraid I've got to agree with Karen." This had been Rose, breaking free of El's grip and walking over to Ruby, her tone placatory but resolute. "We can't trust her. She's a murderer; a sociopath, if you want my honest opinion.

She'll say and do anything, if it serves her own agenda. And we've no reason to believe that what she's saying now is any more reliable than any of the other yarns she's spun us in the past. Perhaps she *has* crossed paths with your sister, I don't know - and perhaps she *has* managed to piss her off sufficiently to cause problems for herself. But there's every chance that all of this is just her trying to use us to get her own back, somehow. For all we know, she took the money and torched El's cottage herself as a convincer."

"No." Ruby had shaken her head. "No. You don't know our Dolly. All that, what that Hannah just said - I can believe it. Believe it of Dolly, anyhow."

"And she was *how* old when you saw her last?" Karen had challenged her. "Thirteen? Going on sixty years ago?"

"She's my sister. Some things you just know."

"Alright," Sita had said. "Let's say she's telling the truth about that - about your sister. Let's say she *is* some sort of... assassin for hire. We can't be sure that any of the rest of it - that business with Marchant, for example - isn't just something that Hannah plucked out of the air to reel us in, can we?"

This had given Ruby pause. Sita rarely disagreed with her in front of the others, at least about anything strategic or logistical. As much as they bickered - and they bickered almost constantly - they were rarely less than a united front, when it came to the important stuff.

"What do you suggest, then?" Ruby had asked. "We can't just leave it and pretend she was never here. The money's still gone, ain't it? And if she *is* right, if she *ain't* lying, then it'll be more than just capital we stand to lose."

"That we do what we always do, before we commit to a plan. We *do our research*. At least *some* of what she said must be verifiable, surely? Madera's connection to Marchant, at the very least?"

Sita hadn't called her *Dolly*, El had noticed.

"Karen," she'd added, turning temporarily away from Ruby, "might you be able to put in some phone calls yourself this afternoon, if I make some of my own? Ask some questions? Perhaps even use that computer of yours to unearth any detail that might be... more difficult to find elsewhere?"

"Yeah," Karen had said, grudgingly, "alright. That's all I'm doing, though: looking."

"That's fine. *More* than fine. Now, do you have it with you, the computer?"

"I've got a laptop in my bag. Not sure how much use it'll be if I'm not online, though."

"As luck would have it, I happen to know that this particular house is... how might you put it? *Connected.* One needs to be on the internet, apparently, if one wants to make a living out of writing romance. It's all *chatrooms* and *dating websites* these days."

"That mean you want me to look *now*?"

"If you wouldn't mind? I suspect we'd all prefer to know where we stand *now*, while we're all together, rather than wait it out in our respective boltholes. Then we'll be equipped to actually *make* a decision."

Kat, who'd been so quiet for so much of the afternoon, had looked sharply up at them, her gaze finally leaving her own two hands.

"And then what?" she'd said. "Let's say Karen goes off and does her digging, and it turns out this Madera *is* after us 'cause she thinks we've got the police onto her... what are you saying we should do about it? Just throw in with the bitch and tell her everything's forgiven if she'll help us out? 'Cause I've got to say," she lowered her gaze to her legs, to the walking stick propped up beside her chair, "I'm not sure I'm feeling quite so forgiving as you lot seem to be."

"Rose isn't happy," El said. "She'll go along with it, I think. But she doesn't like it."

"*I* don't like it," Sita replied. "And I do hate to sound so ominous, but I have a terribly bad feeling about the whole business. A *terribly* bad feeling."

"She's not lying,' Karen had told them - obviously disgruntled by the conclusion she'd been forced to draw, once she and Sita had made their calls and done their digging. "Not about Marchant and Madera, anyway. Madera *did* do some work for him, by all accounts - the heavy stuff, the sort of shit he couldn't pass along to anyone else. And I hate to say it, but it looks like that bitch Hannah really *was* in L.A. a couple of months back. Stayed three nights at a five-star place in West Hollywood - reserved the suite for a week, but bought herself a last-minute ticket back to Heathrow and left after three nights. Flew Economy, as well, which *really* isn't her bag, so you'd best believe she took off in a hurry."

"And Gerry Adler confirmed, I'm afraid," Sita had added, "that he'd heard a rumour of an American man asking after him. He wouldn't say who told him, and I'm not sure at all that he's been given very many more details than he gave to me - though I swear, that whole *department* of his has the structural integrity of a leaking bucket - but it does rather seem as if this Lucian Carruthers might have been poking his nose around Scotland Yard, after all."

Ruby had winced.

"That's it, then, ain't it?" she'd murmured. "We're gonna have to bring her in, somehow - Hannah, I mean. At least until we work out what to do about our Dolly."

There'd been a scraping of metal and a thump of rubber on tile as Kat had picked up her walking stick and pulled herself up from her chair, leaning into the cane for support.

"I'm going to assume," she'd said, slowly, "that that last bit was just you doing your thinking out loud, and *not* you saying you want to bring her back into the fold."

"I don't see no other way 'round this one," Ruby had answered her, voice as soft and distant as it had been when Hannah had begun to tell her story. "If our Dolly's really after us, we're gonna need every scrap of information we can get on her and whatever crew she's running. Even if we don't much like where it comes from."

"Think so, do you? 'Cause you know, I'm not so sure we *do*. Maybe it's the brain damage talking, but it seems to me that there might be potential for it to be a little bit of an own goal, relying on the word of an *actual fucking psychopath*."

"What she says she's got on Madera," Karen had said, with more than a hint of an apology. "All the stuff she paid people to find - it'd take me weeks to get to it. Longer even, maybe. And it doesn't sound like we've *got* that sort of time, you know what I mean? Plus, she's actually *met* Madera, actually *talked* to her up close - her *and* this Carruthers bloke. Met her recently, I should say," she'd added, her eyes darting towards Ruby's.

"Think I give a shit about that, do you, after what that cow did to me? She comes running back here, tail between her legs, and says there's some great scary Terminator who *might* be after us, and it's enough to get you lot tripping over yourselves to break out the welcome mat... meanwhile, you all seem to have forgotten that *she tried to fucking kill me herself*, not so long ago. Right now, you can say what you like, but there's a big fuck-off question mark over this Madera and what she might be after. Whereas I *know* what Hannah is, see. 'Cause I was there, wasn't I, when she put a hole through my head. So at this moment, if you asked me which of them I'd be more worried about, if it came right down to it... it's *her*. Hannah."

Ruby had listened in silence to everything Kat had said. But when she spoke, El at least had known that she was finished arguing the toss.

"It's happening," she'd said. "I'm sorry, I know you don't agree with it, and *you* know this ain't how I like to play things... but it's happening. It's *got* to happen. 'Cause like I said: I know our Dolly. And if she's the same now as she was back then - the same, but *better at it* - then really, I promise you: we're gonna need every tiny little bit of help we can get."

"What do you want to do about it, then?" El asked. "I'm guessing you want to do *something*, or you wouldn't have told me to come out here like this."

Sita looked positively pained.

"I wish I knew, darling," she said. "To be perfectly honest, a part of me had hoped that *you* might have some thoughts of your own on how we might proceed. As things stands, I'm a little concerned we may be flying headlong into some rather serious trouble."

"Ruby hasn't told you what she wants to do, if we manage to track down Madera?"

"She hasn't told me *anything*. All she'll say is that *we need to find her*. What she imagines we'll do once we've *found* her... it's something of a mystery."

"You think she agrees with Hannah? About, you know... having to kill her?"

Sita shook her head.

"No," she said, emphatically. "Perhaps she's decided it's in all of our interests to intimate to that woman that she does. But your Auntie Ruby - she isn't a killer. Whatever else you may think of her, I can absolutely assure you that she doesn't have it in her."

El thought back to the scene in Rose's kitchen, the year before last: Marchant dead on the floor, a bloody trench dug from the place where his throat had been, and Ruby crouching over him, a knife in her hand.

"She doesn't have it in her," Sita repeated - performing the mind-reading trick she and Ruby so often practised in El's company. "Whatever she might have done before... it wasn't premeditated. Oh, she'll defend herself when she has to - and defend the people around her, for that matter. She'd mow down a thousand James Marchants before she'd see harm come to you or Rose or the boys. But she'd never knowingly *plan* a death. It isn't her way. Especially not when..."

"When it's her sister's death she'd be planning?" El guessed.

"Quite. Yes."

El finished her tea; took a few seconds to frame the question - the *statement* - she'd been dying to pose for the last three days.

"You didn't know she had a sister," she said carefully. "She never told you."

"No," Sita replied. "No, she never did."

"And her mum and dad? Did you know about them?"

"About what happened to them in the war - the way they died? Yes, of course. We haven't spoken of it often - it isn't something one dwells on, the loss of a parent - but I knew."

El, who'd lost her own mother when she was barely older than Ruby had been the night hers had failed to come home, found she had little to say in response.

We're orphans, she told herself. *The whole lot of us, bar Karen. Me, and Rose, and Kat. Even Hannah.*

Not a single, solitary parent between us.

And now Ruby, too. Ruby, all along.

Is it any wonder we managed to find each other? That we manage to keep *finding each other?*

"What do you *think* she thinks?" she asked eventually. "About finding her again - her sister. Thea. Dolly. Whoever she is."

Sita took El's cup from her hand and replaced it on the tray, along with her own.

"I've known your Auntie Ruby a very long time. A very, *very* long time."

"And?"

"And in *all* that time, I've never known her to be *in need* of anything - emotionally speaking. Some people, when they've suffered a loss... it's as if something of them is missing. As if there's a hollow - an echoing space, somewhere inside them."

People like me, El thought. Or people like I used to be, maybe. Before Ruby and Sita. Before Rose.

"Auntie Ruby, though," Sita continued, "she isn't one of them. Never *has been* one of them. If she hadn't told me herself, I'm not sure I'd ever have guessed that she'd lost a parent, let alone both of them in one fell swoop."

"Okay."

"What I'm trying to get at it is: I don't know *what* she thinks, about this lost sister. She's... well, a black box, frankly. A closed book. And between us: I'm finding that almost as frightening, under the circumstances, as the threat of Madera herself."

WEST HAMPSTEAD, LONDON

April 1998

There are four of them," Hannah said, sinking back into Ruby's armchair like it was her own - indifferent, if not oblivious, to the mix of disapproval and outright loathing emanating from the others in the room. "That's including Madera herself, by the way. It's a very small circle of associates she keeps - she doesn't seem to trust very many people at all. Can't *imagine* why."

"Who?" Rose asked, making no effort to disguise her revulsion. El had been only semi-convinced, before they left Harriet's for Ruby's flat that morning, that she'd decide not to come; that the prospect of spending a sustained period of time occupying the same space as Hannah would prove too off-putting for her, even with so much at stake.

That Rose *had* come, El thought, was probably a greater testament to her wanting to protect Sophie from any move Madera might make against them than to her belief that Ruby had made the right call, bringing Hannah in on whatever plan she was concocting. A plan, El couldn't fail to observe, that Ruby had yet to share with the rest of them.

Kat, unsurprisingly, had declined the invitation to attend.

("Just tell me what she says if it's worth knowing, yeah?" she'd said, when

El had caught up with her the previous day. "I can't be doing it - sitting there with that bitch like we're mates, like it's all water under the bridge. I don't know *what* the hell she's thinking, Ruby. I get that you love her, and she's a bit of a surrogate mam for some of you lot, but come on - even *you've* got to see that this is mental, surely?")

"Who?" Hannah smiled sweetly at Rose, her freshly bruised face reshaping itself into an impression of genuine confusion. It was pretty convincing, El thought; she might even have believed it, had she not known Hannah better.

"Madera's associates," Rose snarled, her anger so thinly veiled that El wondered whether she might need to intervene again, in the event of another fist-fight erupting. "*Who are they?*"

"Oh, *them*. I see." Hannah settled even further back into the chair, curling her bare feet under her body - the way Ruby herself tended to, in that same position. "I've told you about Carruthers, haven't I?"

"You've told us you met him, and that he was a big bastard," Ruby said - sounding more even-tempered than Rose but still distant, distracted, as if only a part of her was there with them in the room. "But that's about it."

"Right. Now, the important caveat about Carruthers - about *all* of them, actually - is that the information I was given was very, very piecemeal. And a lot of is unverified. I'd go as far as to say *unverifiable,* in some cases. But I believe it's true."

"Oh, well, if *you* think it's true...," Karen started - swiftly curtailing the remainder of the sentence before Ruby could tell her to pipe down.

"*Anyway,*" Hannah continued, glaring at Karen through swollen eyes, "I'm fairly sure Lucian Carruthers isn't his real name. Unlikely though it sounds, there are no records of anyone of that name having been born, in California or anywhere on the West Coast, between 1955 and 1965 - which, given his current age, would be just about his bracket. Now, it's possible that he was born elsewhere and simply *moved* to California later - but I've heard the man speak, and he sounds like one of the Beach Boys. More to the point:

it's not just the birth records that are missing. From what my investigators tell me, there was no Lucian Carruthers anywhere in California until the mid-seventies - when he would have been eighteen or so. Not at school, not at the doctor or the dentist or anywhere else you might have expected a boy to put up. There's nothing; not so much as a library card. *Lucian Carruthers*, to all intents and purposes, only sprang into existence in 1976, when he turned up at the DMV with a social security number to apply for a driving licence."

"What's interesting, though, is that while there wasn't a Lucian Carruthers anywhere in California in the sixties or early seventies, there *was* a boy named Luke Carter. Born and raised in Santa Monica, just outside of L.A. - not far, incidentally, from where Thea Madera was living at the time. An entirely unremarkable child, by all accounts, as if *that* means anything - at least until he went missing in the spring of 1973, just after he'd turned fifteen. Ran away from home one day, never to be seen again. Just like someone else we know, eh, Ruby?"

"Lot of kids run away," Ruby said flatly. "Lot of kids never come back. Ain't sure you should read too much into it, if that's all you got."

"And perhaps I wouldn't, if that was all. But I've seen photos of Luke Carter - the ones his family gave to the police. And others too - some more private ones my contact out there was able to get hold of. More to the point, I've *met* Carruthers - had a chance to look at him in close quarters. And I'm sure, absolutely sure that he and Luke Carter are the same person."

"And that means *what*, for our purposes?" Rose interjected.

"For God's sake, will *any* of you people let me finish? Listen: if I had to hazard a guess, I'd say that, sometime in the early seventies, when he was a teenager, Luke Carter and Madera crossed paths - and something happened that made him want to follow her wherever she was going. As an apprentice, perhaps? A sort of fledgling murderer? We know *Lucian Carruthers* has been working with her since at least '77 - my guy talked to at least half a dozen people who remember meeting them both, back then. Which *means*, sister mine, that he's probably as loyal to Madera as all of *you* are to Ruby here. It *means* that he's not just her right-hand man - he's her acolyte. And if she's giving him orders, then you won't get past him - or get him to give up on the idea of killing you all - through any sort of traditional incentive. You can't bribe him or con him into giving her up."

Ruby crossed her arms; shook her head, apparently rejecting Hannah's conclusion.

"Everyone's got levers. Everyone. It's just about finding 'em, that's all."

"*Is* it?" Hannah raised her hands - the previously manicured nails now chipped and bitten, El saw - in an *if you say so gesture*. "Anyway - that's him. Carruthers."

"And the rest?" said Karen. "There are four of them, you said."

"Yes. I believe I've mentioned the tech person already - Pasadena? As I said, we're very light on details on who *he* is. We know he's identified himself by several names before: James Huang, Leo Zhang and Jacob Li are the three we're certain of, but there are probably more, and I wouldn't count on any of them being his birth name. He worked in IT security, or so he's claimed before - but we only have the word of the people he's spoken to online to corroborate that. People in chatrooms, IRC channels - you know, *your* sort of thing."

"*My* sort of thing?" Karen's hands were balling into fists, her palms apparently itching to reach out and slap Hannah across the face, or worse, and El found herself wondering yet again just how it was that the woman always succeeded in getting so completely under their skin.

"Yes. You know - the internet and things. *Geek stuff*, isn't that what they call it? In any case, the important thing about Pasadena *now* is that he seems to be completely off the grid. It's probably safe to assume that he's still hooked up to a computer somewhere, talking to strangers in cyberspace and doing whatever he does for Madera and Carruthers. But he's effectively untraceable. From a distance, anyway. Tracking him down, I suspect, will be a question of *literally* finding him: working out where he is, where his *body* is, and actually going there."

"And where do you think that might be?" Rose enquired - seemingly calmer than she'd been, though El could see the effort she was exerting just to stay on an even keel.

"Search *me,* darling. Though if you want my opinion, I'd say we're apt to find him wherever Madera and Carruthers are. She strikes me as a woman inclined to keep her collaborators close, for the duration of a job."

The word *job*, in that context - the call-back to the *sort* of job Madera took on - sent a chill through El; reminded her of the very real danger they were in, the very imminent threat of attack every one of them faced. And not *just* them: their family, their friends, their network. Dexter and Michael. Karen's Fergus.

Sophie.

In the whirlwind of strangeness that had engulfed her more or less since the moment she'd slid her card into the cashpoint and found the balance of her accounts at zero - losing the money, losing her home, fusing her life with Rose and Sophie's not in a penthouse apartment overlooking Hyde Park but in Harriet Marchant's overstuffed living room – she'd failed, El realised, to fully reflect on the implications of what Hannah had told them. On the possibility, the *probability* that a group of strangers not only wanted them dead, but were entirely capable of *making* them so, at the moment of their choosing.

Making Rose dead. Making *Sophie* dead.

El wasn't the maternal type; she'd always known as much. But even if she wasn't *exactly* a mother to Sophie, even if she'd never feel the same unbreakable attachment to the kid that Rose did... she felt protective of her. Responsible *for* her. And the thought of something happening to her, of someone like Madera taking a shot at her for no reason beyond her connection to El and Rose and Ruby... it was close to unbearable.

More that that: if what she felt was even a fraction of what *Ruby* felt, knowing that her own sister was the one coming for her family, blood *and* found... well, maybe it made sense after all that Ruby had been so quick to listen to Hannah, to make that particular deal with the devil.

"And then, of course," Hannah went on, "there's the girl. That bloody circus freak."

"Circus freak?" El said, concerned she might have missed an important part of the conversation while she'd been lost in stomach-churning reverie.

"I'm sorry, is that not the politically correct term? Contortionist, then. Tumbler? Whatever else you'd call a person capable of pulling their feet behind their ears without so much as a warm-up stretch."

"She got a name, this girl?" Ruby asked.

"She does. And happily, in this case, we actually know it. It's Lawton - Kerry Lawton."

"And she was in the circus, was she?"

"She was an *acrobat*, if you can believe it. Rather an accomplished one, apparently. She played the casinos in Las Vegas in her heyday - trapeze, aerial straps, tightrope... real Cirque Du Soleil stuff. Martial arts, too: Wushu, Capoeira... if there's a high kick and a backflip in there anywhere, then chances are it's a discipline she's mastered."

"But now she works with our Dolly."

"Exclusively, by all accounts. She stopped performing at twenty-eight - which *sounds* young, I realise, but apparently isn't all that uncommon for people who do that sort of thing. They're like gymnasts - they start early, but it's more or less over for them by the time they're thirty, so it's not all that surprising she was looking for a career change. Though quite how she got into breaking and entering, I don't know..."

"She's a thief?"

"A *cat burglar*, of all things. I can't tell you how long she's been with Madera, or how often Madera uses her - it might be every fortnight or three times a year - but she *does* use her, whenever there's a... let's say a *complicated logistical element* to one of her commissions. Lawton's very, *very* good with break-ins, as you might imagine. And not just the *getting in*, either. If there's a lock to be picked or an alarm to be disabled, she's the one you want to handle it. *She's* rather like you, too, come to think of it," she quipped, raising her eyebrows at Karen. "Or would be, anyway, if you performed your own stunts."

"Carruthers, Pasadena and this Lawton," Rose said. "That's three. The fourth is Madera?"

"It is." Hannah yawned; covered her bruised mouth with her hand.

She's knackered, El thought. *Absolutely exhausted. Oh, she'll try to pass it off as boredom or nonchalance... but she's not been sleeping.*

And I'll bet it's fear that's been keeping her awake.

"What did you find out about her?" Ruby asked. "About our Dolly?"

"Do you really want to know?"

"Ain't that the whole point of you being here, to fill us in on who's coming after us? Damn right I want to know. I want to know bleedin' everything you've got to give."

"Have it your way. But don't say I didn't warn you, if you don't like what you hear. I'm only the messenger."

"Just the messenger who *rained all this shit down on us in the first place*," Karen reminded her. "None of us'd even be on Madera's radar if you hadn't gone shooting your gob off, trying to get her worked up."

"Let her speak," Ruby told Karen. "You need to be listening to this. We all do."

"*Thank* you," Hannah said, glowering at Karen. Then, to Ruby, she continued:

"As to Madera - I suppose I ought to start at the beginning. Or at what I *thought* was the beginning, before I knew who she was. Who she was to you, that is."

"Now, the furthest back my people were able to go, when they were trying to trace her, was 1946 - which would have been, what? Five years after she left you?"

Ruby nodded, her face a carefully composed blank.

"It *seems* as if she was living in Paris then. She was certainly *working* there, doing much the same as she does now, though in a rather more rudimentary way. And not alone, I should stress. The Frenchmen my investigators spoke to on their travels were uniformly old, and I daresay their short-term memories leave something to be desired these days, but they were all *very* clear that Madera was shacking up with another... what would you call it? Contract killer? Another contract killer like her. An older man, and English - Benjamin or Benedict, something like that. Quite an unappealing chap, apparently. Very large teeth. Every one of the Frenchmen seemed to think Madera could have done better for herself, if she'd wanted to."

"She wasn't calling herself Thea Madera then, in case you were wondering. I don't know how long she clung on to Dolly, but she was going by Lillian then - Lily. No one seemed to know a last name, if she even used one."

"We assume she left Paris sometime in the early fifties, because the next time she turned up anywhere - turned up anywhere we could find any sort of record of - she'd already made the move to the States, to California. She spent much of that decade, according to my people, selling herself as a sort of triggerman for some of the bigger Hollywood players - studio heads and producers, the occasional actor with a grudge to settle. It seems as if that's how she made most of her money, to begin with - before she really took an interest in investing. Her investments now, incidentally, are *very* significant; somewhere between thirty and forty million, was our best guess. And that's *pounds*, not dollars."

"She was in South America for at least some of the sixties - Chile, Argentina and Colombia, we think, although the details of her movements in that particular period are sketchy, even in comparison to the other bits we've pieced together. Personally, I wouldn't be at all surprised if she was *working* out there: there are at least a couple of anecdotal accounts that put her in a town or a city around the same time as a politician who got his throat cut or a young revolutionary who ran his motorbike off the edge of a cliff. It doesn't sound like *she* was very political, herself," Hannah added, as if to quell any concerns Ruby might have had on that score. "I mean, I don't think she was, you know... a Communist, or anything like that. I think she very likely just went where the opportunities were - where she could find clients who could afford her."

"Oh, *good*," said Karen, sarcasm dripping from every pore. "As long as it was only the *money* she was in it for, not the *politics*."

"*Then*," Hannah went on pointedly, "we're into the seventies, where she stumbles onto Carruthers, and the two of *them* begin to work together. That's when Madera starts to really... grow the business, you might say. To take on American clients outside of the studios - bankers, and businessmen, and so on. And then, back in London, in the early eighties..."

"She meets your old man," Ruby concluded.

"Yes."

"And starts doing jobs for *him*."

"On and off... yes."

A long, leaden silence fell over the room - all of them lost, or so El suspected, in their own very specific memories of James Marchant, and their own speculations around the character of the sort of person he might go to, when a job was in need of more cold-eyed, ruthless finesse than even he and Ricky Lomax could muster.

"We ain't gonna kill 'em," Ruby said eventually.

"Then they'll kill you," Hannah replied. "All of you. And then me, for good measure."

"There's other ways of doing things. We'll find 'em."

"Yes? Do tell, then. I'm quite literally *dying* to hear what they might be."

"I ain't figured it out yet. But I will. *We* will. Same way we always do. You think this is the first time we've ever had our feet held over the fire? This Carruthers, and the circus girl, and what's his name, *Pasadena*... they're just people. People with buttons you can push, if you know how. I'm telling you now, we'll *find a way.*"

"And your sister? I notice you didn't mention *her*, there."

Ruby's eyes narrowed to slits.

"You needn't worry about her," she said, in a leonine growl that seemed to rise up from somewhere deep in her chest. "You just help us deal with Carruthers and the rest of 'em, alright? Our Dolly... you can leave her to me."

PAHRUMP, NEVADA

September 1995

Kevin Lewis, manager and proprietor of the Sugar Love Mountain Ranch brothel, was - from all that Dolly had seen of him - a wholly unprepossessing gentleman.

Snaggle-toothed, beer-bellied and sporting an extravagantly coiffed blond mullet, he was, as she understood it, both a sex addict and a compulsive gambler. The former addiction presented few problems for him in his day-to-day life - his ownership of the Ranch granting him, in effect, free and unfettered access to the bodies of the girls in his employment.

The latter, however, had a tendency to land him in hot water.

His most recent exploits in the cardrooms had placed him in the path of one Santino Randazzo, himself an amateur poker-player - and, unluckily for Lewis, the younger brother of one of the more prominent mob-bosses in the Las Vegas area. Lewis hadn't known who Randazzo was, or so Dolly assumed, when he tried to cheat him with a (by all accounts, poorly executed) card-up-the-sleeve trick; if he *had* known, and had gone ahead with the ruse anyway, then Dolly could only credit him with both more guts and fewer brain-cells than appearances suggested.

Randazzo had been alerted to the attempted con, of course. And, though he'd let Lewis leave the table after the game, he'd been far from happy.

"Kill him," he'd ranted at Dolly, when he'd summoned her and Lucian to his penthouse suite at one of the bigger hotels on the Strip - holding court for half an hour in his silk pyjamas like the ghost of Howard Hughes. "Squash that little fucker like a bug. I want him *ended*, you understand me? Ended!"

They'd taken the job, because it didn't do to say no to a Randazzo - even a second-tier one like Santino. But neither she nor Lucian were anticipating taking much satisfaction from the kill.

Sugar Love Mountain was open twenty-four hours a day, seven days a week. But Lewis, they knew, tended to work the night shift until 5am and retire thereafter to the cabin he kept on site, where he'd stay sleeping until at least two o'clock in the afternoon.

They'd decided on 9am, therefore, as the best time to make their approach - by which point, they'd reasoned, he would have passed into unconsciousness.

He kept the doors to his cabin unlocked: partly, Dolly suspected, because the Ranch was so far out in the middle of nowhere that even the most committed burglar would think twice before crossing the desert to get there, and partly because the madam who ran the place in Lewis' absence - a Mae West type with a sharp eye, a lot of tight corsetry and an enviable collection of firearms - wouldn't have thought twice before unloading every round in the chamber of her revolver into the vitals of any would-be interloper.

But they went in through the back window anyway: Lucian pulling up the wide glass pane in his giant's hands without so much as a drop of sweat falling from him even in the heat of the morning sun, and the pair of them slipping through the gap he'd created, unfurling themselves softly on the ugly moss-green carpet of Lewis' study.

And saw that there was someone there already.

Not Lewis, though: a girl, young and white and skinny as a garden rake, gloves like theirs on her hands and a grey-green wad of hundred-dollar bills in one fist so thick it would have been incriminating even if she *hadn't* been standing by the open wall-safe she'd very clearly just raided.

A thief, Dolly thought. *A thief, doing him over just as we've come by to do him in. What are the odds?*

Lucian reached for his weapon to put the girl down, but she was - to Dolly's astonishment - too quick for him: darting across the room and hurling herself through the gap in the window in an acrobatic roll, landing upright on the balls of her feet with the grace of a swan and sprinting away with cheetah speed across the sand outside.

He turned to follow her, gun out and ready, but Dolly stopped him.

Not now, she told him, very nearly silently. *She's got what she wanted - she won't be back while we're here. We can deal with her later.*

He nodded, acquiescing - though she could tell he wasn't best pleased - and they pressed on, further into the cabin.

It was a straightforward hit. Lewis was sleeping, curled up in a foetal position in his underwear, drool gluing his face to the sheets: three clean shots to the head through a pillow and it was done, Santino Randazzo's little problem solved.

She bought Lucian breakfast, afterwards: drove them both to an all-day restaurant she knew and liked in Henderson and ordered him scrambled eggs and pancakes and three refills of the fruit smoothies he seemed to always be drinking.

"You're annoyed we let her go," she said, pouring herself a coffee. "The girl."

"A little," he said, through a mouthful of eggs. "Maybe."

"You want to go after her? Girl like that shouldn't be too hard to find, if we ask around."

He chewed, swallowed the eggs and replaced them immediately with a square of buttered blueberry pancake.

"Maybe," he said. Then: "She was good. Fast."

Dolly nodded, wondering where he was going with the observation. He was a closed book sometimes, she found; inscrutable, even to her.

"That she was," she added, wary. "Light on her feet, too."

He finished the bite of pancake, Adam's apple bobbing in his bull neck, and washed it down with yet more of the smoothie.

"Do you ever wonder," he began, a contemplative look in his eyes, "whether it might be good for us, to bring someone like her in on things? Someone who could get us in and out of places fast, when we need to?"

Ah, Dolly thought - remembering how she'd felt herself before she'd found *him*. How she'd really begun to *feel* the lack of an extra pair of hands when she was on the job.

That's it, then. He wants a helper.

"Might be," she told him, blowing steam across the rim of her coffee mug. "Let's have a think about it, shall we?"

GOLDERS GREEN, LONDON

May 1998

It wasn't the most elaborate of birthday dinners. But it was the best El had been able to do and, with the acquisition of *Weeping Skeleton* on hold - and with it, Colin and Lauren Robinsons' dreams of securing for Horatio the most coveted rosette the Northamptonshire dog world had to offer - she was determined that Rose should enjoy it.

And as insalubrious and unromantic a venue as it was, Aphrodite's was at least familiar. A run-down Greek taverna around the corner from the Golders Green Underground, it had served innumerable times over the years as a meeting-place for El and Ruby, and occasionally Sita, while in the throes of a job, and in the absence of any more convenient location. All three of them knew the owner, an Australian entrepreneur by the name of Lachlan Andreou, and were sufficiently well-acquainted with all five of his ubiquitously sullen waiters and bar staff that finding a table to eat at or an empty stool on which to down a complimentary ouzo was rarely a problem, even when the place was at its busiest.

Today, it was entirely empty, save for El and Rose and Andreou himself, who - in the spirit of longstanding almost-friendship and the promise of a favour repaid at an unspecified point in the future - had offered El the exclusive use of the restaurant between 2 and 5pm and a three-course meal on the house, with a bottle of his finest Moschofilero thrown in.

Both the front and back doors were locked and bolted, at her insistence; the Closed sign had been hung in the window to deter any would-be diners. El happened to know, moreover, that Andreou kept a very powerful, wholly unregistered twelve-gauge shotgun behind the bar; and, more comfortingly still, that he knew exactly how to handle it.

Eating there was a less secure move than doing as Ruby had recommended and staying put in the Holloway Road flat with the windows shut. And perhaps, El considered, it was a stupid one: accessing the restaurant from the outside would have been difficult, but not impossible, and however quickly Andreou might have been able to move to retrieve and aim his weapon, there was no doubt in her mind that Madera and Carruthers could be quicker.

But it was Rose's birthday, and Sophie was safe under the watchful, protective and possibly - as El suspected but hadn't been able to confirm - similarly well-armed wings of Harriet and RD Laing... and they'd had to do *something*, hadn't they? Something even a little more pleasurable than spending another afternoon on that sofa, *waiting*, surrounded by toppling towers of hard rock detritus and the pungent scent of cat?

Although... perhaps the waiting, at least, would be over soon. If everything went to plan.

"Thank you," Rose told her, reaching for a final piece of baklava. "This was lovely."

"I'm sorry it's not, you know... more," El replied, lighting a cigarette and inhaling deeply, regretfully.

Rose picked up her knife; cut the baklava in two and put half on El's dessert plate.

"It's funny," she said, watching El over the rim of her wine glass, "but the more I think about it, the more I wonder whether Ruby might have been onto something about you, after all. You really *do* worry too much."

"Do I?"

"You do. I just told you, very clearly, how much I enjoyed this - you doing this for me, arranging it all. I actually used the word *lovely*. And yet your immediate reaction, on hearing this, is to apologise. To tell me how inadequate you find it."

El froze, a jet of smoke escaping her mouth; felt suddenly, unexpectedly ambushed.

"I love you," Rose continued, matter-of-factly, cleaving the remaining baklava into four still-smaller pieces. "It's possible I don't tell you enough, I realise. But I do. I really do. And if I've somehow *done* something to make you anxious that this isn't the case or given you reason to believe you ought to be anything other than absolutely secure in my commitment to you or to our relationship... then *I'm* sorry."

She took one of the slivers of baklava between her fingers and ate it, thoughtfully.

"I'm sorry," El repeated, when she could speak again.

Rose frowned at her - not unkindly but quizzically, as if El had begun out of the blue to speak in Sumerian.

"Not *sorry* sorry," El added. Rose's frown deepened. "I mean... fuck. I'm not sure I even know what I mean. Sorry."

At this, most feeble attempt at an explanation, Rose smiled.

"You don't have to be sorry," she said. "Not for *this*," she gestured around at the restaurant, "which has been - as I may have mentioned - the loveliest birthday I could have hoped for. And certainly not for anything else. I know these are strange times - God knows, I know - but I couldn't have wished for anyone better to have suffered through them with me. Okay?"

"Okay," El mumbled, dropping her eyes and taking another, deeper drag on the cigarette.

Rose's smile turned sardonic.

"You perhaps haven't noticed, but I've been a little all over the place these last few months. These last couple of years, actually. Tense. Stressed. Absolutely terrified, actually - of something happening to Sophie, obviously. But then also, lately, you know... to you."

"To me," El said, monosyllabic in her awkwardness.

"To you, yes. And how's this for irony? The more terrified I've become of it... the more I've needed you. And so now, as I'm sitting here literally frightened for your life and my life and my daughter's life... I find I need you a great deal. So much so, in fact, that I'm not sure at this stage what I'd do without you. And I realise also, now I say it, what a lot of pressure that is to place on someone I've been with for barely six months, so perhaps we could skim over that part?" She paused, El thought to catch her breath as much as for emphasis. "The point I'm trying rather circuitously to make is: if the worries you have are founded even slightly on the belief that I'm likely to turn around one day soon and tell you that I've had enough or, I don't know... somehow got you out of my system... then I can assure you, absolutely and wholeheartedly, that they're baseless."

El, struck entirely mute by Rose's speech, could only nod, and extend a hand towards her across the table, stubbing out the ashy residue of her cigarette with the hand that remained.

"Good to know," she said after a while, covering her nerves with a phantom cough. Then: "I love you too."

Andreou drove them back to Holloway Road, as arranged; his armoured 4x4 - purchased in the heat of an internecine, multi-factional war between North West London restaurant owners now cooled to a detente - giving El at least a little reassurance as they sped through Highgate and on into Archway.

Harriet and Sophie, they found when they arrived at the flat, had decorated in anticipation of their - or rather, Rose's - return: adding a floating, multi-coloured cluster of helium balloons to the already-full-to-bursting living room, and throwing paper streamers over some of the larger pieces of memorabilia. A home-made Victoria sponge was waiting for them on the coffee table, its forty-two candles already burning.

"This is wonderful," Rose enthused, once the candles had been extinguished, all four of them had squeezed together on the sofa and Harriet had gone at the cake with a metal spatula. "Just wonderful. But when did you find the time to make it? And shouldn't you be getting ready?"

The latter question she directed at Harriet, who looked - even by El's sartorial yardstick - somewhat underdressed for the task she'd agreed to perform, in her faded jeans and ripped Soundgarden t-shirt.

"It doesn't take long to whip up," Harriet said, finishing up the thin sliver of sponge she'd served herself. "And I don't know what you mean. I *am* ready."

Was it possible, El wondered, that she *wasn't* being disingenuous? That - even with a PhD in social psychology and a decade in applied research under her belt, in prisons and psychiatric institutions no less - she genuinely believed that her outfit fit the bill?

"I thought perhaps something slightly less... casual?" Rose offered, with such caution El could almost hear the eggshells cracking underfoot.

"This is fine, I promise you," Harriet assured her. "Something like this... it will go *far* more smoothly, if I present as myself. I'm not like El here," she dipped her head, disparagingly, El's way. "I'm not a *con artist*. For me to play this at all convincingly, I'll need to stay as close to myself as I possibly can. And if I *were* me, rather than the three-dimensional honey trap construct *El* would, I daresay, conjure up at a moment's notice, then *these* are the clothes I would be wearing. QED."

Her irritation at the slight notwithstanding, El had to concede - grudgingly - that the argument had merit. Harriet *wasn't* a professional; she *didn't* routinely masquerade as someone she wasn't, especially not when the stakes were as high for everyone involved as they were here.

Being herself, with just enough of a deviation from the standard template to make the task itself possible, was probably her best shot at pulling it off.

"Is there a dress code?" El asked.

The bar Harriet would be going to - the one they'd discovered, mostly through Karen's skill in following the electronic breadcrumbs left by an American credit card used repeatedly on British soil, had been frequented by the mark almost every night she'd been in London - was small, discreet and prohibitively expensive: its clientele mostly wealthy, occasionally very wealthy, and exclusively female. El had been herself a handful of times, though always in the course of a job rather than as a way to meet women; Rose, despite fitting the club's target profile to a tee, claimed never to have walked through its heavily guarded doors.

Harriet - who, as far as El knew, was straight, or at least so uniformly uninterested in *everyone* for the issue to be moot - hadn't known the place existed at all.

"If there *is* one," Harriet said, with a generous helping of the maybe-inadvertent condescension El was fast becoming inured to, "I shall find a way around it. I'll pay them extra at the door, if I have to. That usually does the trick."

It wasn't a boast, this allusion to the enormity of her personal fortune. Harriet's relationship to her own wealth - the wealth inherited from her father - was, at best, ambivalent; underpinned by an emotionally loaded combination of guilt, resentment and discomfort at being saddled with the Marchant name and legacy. According to Rose, she rarely touched the money she'd been left, and certainly wasn't given to spending any of it on herself. The mountain of memorabilia she'd amassed - the ornaments, the signed posters, the guitars - had been paid for in their entirety out of her own pocket, drawing on nothing but the university salary she earned for herself.

But still, El - having lost everything she'd ever had - found it stuck in her throat anyway, just a little.

She's just nervous, she told herself. *She's new to this, and anxious, and her anxiety is coming off as rudeness. That's all it is.*

They'd brought Harriet in on the job just once before: a year earlier, when Charlie Soames had put the thumbscrews on them and they'd had to look further afield for support. She'd been brilliant, then; hadn't dropped the ball once, and had managed not only to aid them in bringing their own Soames problem to a resolution, but to convince Soames' long-abused wife - and eventually his son, too - to free themselves from the grip of the man's control.

She'd agreed to get involved for Rose and Sophie then, too, El remembered. To protect them; to stop harm coming to them.

This time, when Rose and El had sat her down and explained the specific nature of the threat to them all, when they'd outlined the plan Ruby had formulated and begged her to help them implement it, Harriet had said yes immediately. Hadn't blinked; hadn't hesitated, in spite of the danger it might bring to her door, too.

Though that, of course, had been *before* they'd told her exactly what helping would entail, in this particular set of circumstances...

"Thank you for doing this," Rose said, smiling weakly at her sister.

"I'd say *any time*," Harriet replied, smiling back - kinder and more sincere, now the words were directed at Rose, "but I suspect this may be a *once and done* for me. I really don't know that I'll make a very *good* honey trap."

"You'll be brilliant," Sophie told her. "Just try to come off a bit mysterious and withholding. A little bit, you know... *oh, but we mustn't*. Women like that."

El wasn't sure what disturbed her more: the kid's enthusiasm for the con, since Rose had decided to stop keeping her in the dark and instead to tell her everything *they* knew about what was going on, or that the kid now - seemingly from nowhere - considered herself an authority on *what women wanted*.

'What the *hell* has Ruby been teaching you?" Rose asked her - her face overcome with exactly the look of consternation El imagined she'd briefly worn herself, on hearing Sophie's pronouncement.

"Honestly, Mum," Sophie said, once again managing to sound both exasperated and patronising, "I keep telling you: it's *Sita*, not Ruby. Ruby's not taught me anything in *ages*. Not for, like, a *month*."

"Well, whichever one of them it is, I'm not sure at all that I like them advising you on... on..."

A blush began to form on Rose's cheeks; deepened, then spread outwards, up and down, until her skin was the colour of pink grapefruit.

"How to meet girls?" Sophie offered, mock-innocently.

"Jesus," El muttered, under her breath - making a mental note to speak very seriously to Sita, once the Madera business was sorted.

"Didn't know you were such a prude," the kid said, grinning. "That *either* of you were. You don't need to worry, anyway. She wasn't telling *me* how to do it - she was telling me how *she* does it. I don't *want* to meet girls. Or boys, come to that."

"Hear, hear," agreed Harriet, her own lips now stretched into a grin. "In any case, Sophie - it's very good advice, and I for one appreciate it, even if these two don't."

"You don't have to *encourage* her," Rose chided.

Harriet stood up from the sofa, straightened her t-shirt, ran a hand through her hair and smoothed down the front of her jeans.

"It *is* good advice," she said. "And *you* should be happy about it, too. The more *mysterious* I appear, the less likely I am to give us all away. Really, in an ideal world, I'd say absolutely nothing at all. Just *stand* there at the bar like an enigmatic statue until she takes my hand and leads me back to her hotel room."

"Jesus!" El repeated, more loudly.

"Don't worry, I've heard her say worse," Sophie told her. "*Much* worse."

"And yet somehow, I find myself not remotely comforted," Rose replied, still blushing furiously.

"*Anyway.*" Harriet paused; ran her tongue over her teeth, apparently in the spirit of removing any errant cake crumbs that might have been caught there. "Time I was off. Wish me luck."

"Vaya con Dios," Sophie said.

Rose looked from her daughter to her sister and then, helplessly bewildered, to El, who could only shrug.

"Much appreciated," said Harriet, making for the door. "Here's hoping I can sweep her off her feet, eh? For all our sakes."

KINGSTON, LONDON

May 1998

While Harriet was steeling herself to hit the bar scene, Karen and Fergus, El knew, were preparing themselves for a different but no less daunting challenge.

"Fucking kills me to say it," Karen had answered, when Ruby had asked her how feasible it would be for her to execute the idea they'd been kicking around, "but I don't think I can do it. Not on my own. I'd need help. A lot of help."

"What sort of help are we talking?"

Karen had mulled this over.

"Bodies," she'd said eventually. "Two more than me, at least. One to work the system remotely and another to come with me and do the business with the alarms while I… you know. A very *particular* sort of someone, that last one."

With this, it had been Ruby's turn to ponder the options.

"Your Fergus," she'd begun after a while. "Know anyone like that, does he?"

Karen had looked down, thoughtfully, at her own hands; at the tips of her fingers.

"You know what?" she'd said. "I reckon he might."

The induction of Fergus himself into their ever-growing crew for this particular stage of the job had been, as Karen had put it, a no-brainer. He knew already how his wife and her friends earned their money, so no uncomfortable revelations or explanations had been necessary; he was every bit as adept with technology as Karen - though his interests led him by and large in other directions - and could therefore be trusted to do what needed to be done at Karen's laptop, even while she was otherwise engaged. Perhaps most importantly, he was so absolutely devoted to her that there had been almost no chance of him refusing to participate.

It was through Fergus' intervention, moreover, that Karen had been able to recruit the *second* body she'd sought.

"His name's Jeremiah," she'd told El. "He's Fergus' best mate from uni. You've probably met him - he's the one who did the ceremony at the wedding."

El had remembered, though somewhat vaguely, a pale but heavily tattooed white boy in a suit at the altar of the chapel, reading from a sheaf of printed notes as he pronounced Karen and Fergus husband and wife in a reedy Estuary accent. And something else, too; something about his skin, his knuckles...

"The one with the implants," she'd said. "The LED lights on his hands."

"*In* his hands," Karen had corrected her. "They're subdermal. *Under* the skin, not on it."

Like Fergus, she'd explained, Jeremiah was a grinder: a biohacker, dedicated to improving the performance and aesthetic of his body through modification, and specifically the introduction of the lights, magnetics, microchips and other technological paraphernalia that both men believed would make them, in a succession of small and incremental ways, very slightly more than human.

"Does he have horns, too?" El had asked – her imagination conjuring another set of spikes like Fergus', another pair of metal nubs protruding from another pink-white forehead.

"No." Karen had snorted. "I told you - the horns don't *do* anything.

They're cosmetic - he just likes the look of them. I love the boy, I do, but seriously - he might as well have gone out and got himself breast implants, for all the use they are."

What Jeremiah *did* have, and what he'd offered to share with Karen - once he'd committed to the job - was an extensive knowledge of anti-surveillance makeup.

"For security cameras," Karen had said. "CCTV. You know they're starting to link it up to automatic facial recognition systems now? Don't ask me how I know, and don't pass it on, but I've got it on very good authority that at least one local council near here's planning on rolling it out, end of this year. It's fucking scary. You get caught on camera somewhere hooked up to a database of faces, and all of a sudden everyone knows *exactly* where you are and where they can find you. Not just the police, either."

"And the makeup... hides your face?"

"Sort of. Facial recognition algorithms look for patterns in images - like we talked about last year, yeah?"

She'd meant the con they'd run in San Francisco, El had known; the one that had necessitated that Karen create a facial recognition software package of her own, albeit one that was more or less entirely non-functional.

"Sure."

"Well, same principle. What the makeup does is disrupt the pixels in the images, so you - or the database, probably - can't tell one face from another. Or, if the makeup's *really* good, from a different sort of image altogether. That's the problem, when the technology's as rudimentary as it is at the minute - the algorithm can't see something and *intuit*, the way a person would if they saw a face."

"And you're using this makeup to stop the cameras recognising you?"

"If they're there... yeah. This Pasadena bloke... odds are, he's paranoid as fuck. I would be, if I were him. And if he's paranoid *and* he's clever, then he won't be relying on any existing CCTV network - he'll rig up his own, around the perimeter of his gaff, and hook it up to every fucking database going. So, assuming the cameras *are* there... we'll need to find a way around them."

"And you couldn't just wear a balaclava? Or, I don't know... a coat with the hood up, or something?"

Karen had sighed and shaken her head, the gesture a pitch-perfect replica of the one Sophie so often deployed when El or Rose or both of them said something so irredeemably foolish she felt it barely worthy of a response.

"And look like we're about to rob the place?" she'd said. "Yeah - great idea *that'd* be. No, what you *want* is us looking like we're out for a walk, or we got lost on our way somewhere. We go *properly* wild with the makeup, and chuck on a bit of glitter or whatever, and if anyone's looking - if *he's* looking, Pasadena - then he'll think we're on our way to a fancy dress party. And by the time we're close enough to him that he might be starting to get suspicious, we can knock out whatever cameras are left ourselves. You know - manually. By hand."

His proficiency with camouflage makeup, though, wasn't the only skill Jeremiah would be bringing to the table.

"Biometrics," Karen had related, later on - the day before Rose's birthday, when Karen and Fergus and Jeremiah had been preparing to get their own efforts underway.

"Biometrics?"

"Yeah. Trust me, if this Pasadena's anything like me, and I reckon he is - there'll be some sort of biometric security in place at the house, at the very least on the doors. Fingerprint recognition on the locks, maybe. Jeremiah can get us 'round it."

"How?"

Karen had looked, suddenly, very shifty.

"You'll keep it to yourself, if I tell you? Like, *really* to yourself?"

"Sure."

She'd paused; taken a swig of the isotonic drink she'd been sipping from.

"He can clone them," she'd said. "Fingerprints. As long as he can get hold of a copy of them - and they're everywhere in the States, Americans fingerprint bloody *everyone*, all the time - then he can clone them. He uses... I'm not even sure *what* material it is, to be honest with you, he's never even told Fergus. Some sort of cured resin, maybe. He hacks the fingerprints, downloads them, uses a 3D printer to etch them onto the material... and what he ends up with, you can stick on top of your own fingertips like an extra layer of skin. Like... you know those plasters you get for blisters and verrucas? Like that. Or like a contact lens, but for your fingers."

"Bloody hell."

"Tell me about it. That sort of technology... it's properly innovative stuff, even by my standards. Christ knows how he got it. Or how he *built* it, knowing him. He's not..."

"Wait a second," El had interrupted her, remembering how Hannah had described Pasadena. "*How* would Jeremiah get them, the fingerprints? I thought nobody even knew this Pasadena guy's real name, let alone had access to any of his records."

The shifty look had morphed, almost immediately, into a broad, impish grin.

"That was then," Karen had answered, obviously delighted with herself. "Different story now, innit?"

"You found him? Found out who he is?"

The grin had widened further.

"Oh, yeah. He *is* a clever fucker, don't get me wrong. But me and Fergus... turns out, we're cleverer."

Pasadena, she'd told El - alias James Huang, Leo Zhang, Jacob Li and a dozen other online pseudonyms - had been born thirty years earlier in Burlingame, Northern California, not far at all from what would become Silicon Valley. His birth name - and the one still listed on his passport and tax returns, to Karen's surprise - was Stuart Ma. He'd studied computer science at

MIT, then had started, though hadn't completed, graduate work at CalTech in Pasadena - the source, Karen had speculated, of his nickname. He *had* been an IT security consultant, she'd discovered - though only briefly, leaving the role after six months to, in effect, disappear into the digital ether.

"Nobody else seems to have rumbled who he actually is, which is interesting," Karen had said. "And when I say *interesting*, what I *mean* is useful. Really fucking useful."

"Yeah?"

"Oh, yeah. You know how Ruby's always talking about finding people's levers?"

El had nodded.

"I think - I *think* - we might have one of his."

Fergus, they'd agreed, would stay behind at the house in Kingston - working remotely in their basement Batcave, while Karen and Jeremiah headed out into the encroaching night.

For this particular stay in the U.K., Pasadena had landed on the most rural part of London he'd likely been able to rent: a remote farmhouse built on a patch of countryside not far from Osterley Park, surrounded on one side by woodland and on the other by a disused field.

They drove most of the way out there, crossing south to west in Jeremiah's Beetle before pulling in to a car park close to the Osterley Underground and tackling the remaining mile on foot, white leather holdalls on their backs and Pierrot clown costumes complementing the dazzle camouflage slathered across their faces. This appearance attracted only a small amount of attention from the commuters milling around the station; almost certainly, Karen claimed later, because she'd been right, and everyone who saw them had leapt immediately to the conclusion that they were indeed on their way to a fancy dress party. What else, after all, could two young people possibly have been doing in the west London suburbs on a Tuesday evening, dressed like auditionees from an am-dram revival of the *Commedia dell'arte*?

She'd been right about the security too, she told El. By whatever means, Pasadena had arranged for the installation of a sophisticated array of private CCTV cameras around his property - their lenses keeping watch not only on the farmhouse, but on the adjacent field, the woodland and the stretches of road that circled both. For the benefit of the latter cameras, she and Jeremiah had put on a show: laughing and staggering and exchanging friendly shoulder-punches in the manner of the drunk party-goers Pasadena, if he was watching the footage, would likely believe them to be. The *other* cameras - the ones around the farmhouse - required somewhat more sophisticated tactics.

"He'll jam them," Karen had said, meaning Jeremiah. "He's got this... let's call it a signal-blocker, shall we, for argument's sake? It's not an even slightly accurate description, but it's a good enough analogy if you don't want me to spend all day explaining how wireless signals work."

"Wireless?" El had responded - feeling every bit as out of her depth as she always did, whenever Karen got technical.

"I'm not talking about an *actual* radio, before you ask. Not in the way *you'd* mean it. Wireless... it's a way of transmitting camera signals over a network, instead of along a cable. Over a radio band - hence the name. If Pasadena's not been in town long, he's not gonna have had a chance to dig up the ground and lay a load of cables, is he? So his cameras, and there'll *be* cameras... they'll have to be wireless. He'll have to set up his own network and relay the footage over it. The commercially available stuff, what bit of it there is... it doesn't run fast. The images it sends are more or less unwatchable, they're so jerky. But if the bloke knows what he's doing, he'll have a tinker. Find a way to make it run faster, so he can get *his* cameras working wirelessly."

"And Jeremiah's going to block the signal?"

"He'd better. He'd fucking *better*. Or we're *all* fucked."

Fortunately for all concerned, except possibly Pasadena himself, the signal-blocking had gone smoothly: Jeremiah's jammer, a handheld black box that called to mind the fruit of a union between a cigarette packet and a hedgehog, apparently proving powerful enough to disrupt the farmhouse's security cameras with ease.

The backdoor lock - biometric, as Karen had predicted - had given them even less trouble: a single scan of the duplicate fingerprint that sheathed Jeremiah's index finger like a tiny condom proving sufficient to grant them access to the farmhouse's interior.

All they had to do, after that, was deal with Pasadena face-to-face.

MAYFAIR, LONDON

May 1998

Madera was in London; she had to be, if Carruthers and Pasadena and the acrobat girl had bedded down already.

Unlike her colleagues, though, Madera appeared to have paid cash for everything she'd bought since arriving in the city - and had left, or so Karen insisted, not so much as a traceable receipt for a cup of coffee in her wake.

Which made finding her nigh-on impossible.

In the end, after sweet-talking the porters, concierges and night receptionists of every high-end hotel she could think of and coming up empty, Kat settled on a change of tack – one which seemed to satisfy Ruby, once she'd run the idea past her.

Clearly, Kat couldn't go to Madera. But maybe, just maybe, she could get Madera to come to her.

Now, Madera hadn't sounded, from that bitch Hannah's description, like someone who'd suffer anything less than five-star quarters - so unless she owned property of her own in the capital, and was holed up *there* for the duration, her accommodation options were pretty finite. Which meant that at least one of the hotel staff she'd spoken to must have been lying; likely because Madera had paid them handsomely enough to keep their silence, even in face of Kat's most merciless charm offensive.

But there were other questions she could ask. Other clues she could drop.

She'd visited ninety-three hotels that first time, a whirligig of flying visits that had taken her the better part of three days. Three very uncomfortable days: her hips aching and her legs seizing and cramping whenever she dared to put weight on *them* and not her walking stick, worried sick that someone - maybe Carruthers, maybe Madera herself - was going to take a shot at her from a high window or run her through with a knife whenever she was outside in the open.

She was more selective, the second time around; restricting her interrogations only to those staff members – twenty-two of them, in total - who'd struck her as awkward or evasive or prevaricating at first blush. All of them had been hiding *something*, she was sure - though she knew from experience that a little prevarication was sometimes par for the course, in high-end hospitality circles. She just had to hope that *one* of them was hiding Madera.

To the twenty-two - seven women and fifteen men, every one of them working the front desk - she relayed the same request:

She wasn't going to ask again, she told them, if they had a guest named Thea Madera staying with them. Their business relied on discretion, and assumed names were so commonplace they were virtually an industry standard; she appreciated that. But if they *did* happen to have an older woman staying with them who fit Madera's description - late sixties, honey blonde hair, *very* bright blue eyes, unplaceable accent and probably travelling on a US passport - would they be kind enough to pass along a message to her?

Alright, all twenty-two of them answered, all equally non-committal - neither confirming nor denying the presence of any such woman in their establishment. What's the message?

Tell her, Kat said, that Dolly Wood is looking for her.

Dollywood? several of them queried - one or two raising a sceptical eyebrow at the moniker.

Dolly Wood, she reiterated calmly. Two words. Nothing to do with Tennessee or country music, I promise.

A couple of them very nearly smiled at this, tiny cracks appearing in the smooth veneer of their professionalism.

Here's where she'll be, Kat added, passing across one of the twenty-odd sheets of paper she'd prepared earlier, each one filled with the handwritten details of the time and date and venue she'd decided on: 11am the following day, at a busy Belgian cafe on an equally busy section of The Strand.

And with that, she left.

The cafe was as busy as she'd hoped it would be, when she arrived the next morning: bursting to capacity with tourists, students, men in suits on coffee breaks. It was ten fifteen, a good forty-five minutes earlier than the time she'd given in her note; a necessary evil, she thought, if she was going to get the drop on Madera.

It still wasn't early *enough*, though.

She'd been seated for barely the time it had taken her to order a cappuccino - at a very small table in the furthest corner of the cafe, her back against the wall to circumvent any ambush from behind - when Madera appeared in front of her, looming like a bloody vulture and eclipsing Kat's view of the tourists, the baristas, the *exit*.

"You're Katherine Morgan," she said, taking a seat of her own opposite Kat.

The voice... wasn't what Kat had expected. It was full-on Cockney, for a start; it could've been Ruby talking, not her sister.

How Madera *looked*, though - that was the real revelation.

Lying, murderous bitch though she was, Hannah hadn't been wrong about the similarity: from a distance, Madera could have *been* Ruby, if you ignored the hair and the slightly straighter, stiffer posture.

She dressed better - Ruby's shirts and sunglasses and denim jackets traded up for a navy A-line dress and a matching belt and earrings studded with what Kat was pretty sure were real sapphires. And her skin, unlike Ruby's, was clear and free enough of wrinkles to have Kat suspecting she'd pulled on more than just expensive cold cream to achieve the effect.

But God, it was *uncanny*, the resemblance. You couldn't look at her and not know, immediately and with absolute certainty, who she was. Kat would've guessed it from a mile away.

"And you're Thea Madera," she replied, with all the artificial confidence she could muster. "Or do you prefer Dolly?"

A smile like a needle run over the surface of a block of ice spread across Madera's unlined faced.

"Dealer's choice," she said evenly. "I've answered to a lot of things. Same as you, I'd imagine."

You can do this, Kat told herself. *Don't let her scare you.*

I mean, yes, alright - she's absolutely fucking terrifying, sat there like the plagues of Egypt about to rain down on you. Yes, she could probably tear your throat out with nothing but her teeth and nails, if she fancied it.

But she hasn't yet, has she? Because she's curious. She wants to know why you got her here. What it is you've got to say for yourself.

Not for the first time in the last couple of years, nor even the hundredth, she found herself cursing the day she ever let Ruby Redfearn reel her into the Marchant job. The night she let Hannah fucking D'Amboise drive her out into the middle of nowhere and shatter her skull and the mind inside into so many pieces that she'd never be able to put herself together again, not really. Cursing *herself* for letting that bitch turn her into Humpty fucking Dumpty.

It's her *fault*, she thought. *If anyone's to blame for this, it's that waste of skin who calls herself a human being.*

She's the one who's making you do this. You wouldn't be here at all if it weren't for her, would you?

It's all her.

And the rest of them... well, that can't be helped, can it? You can't make an omelette without breaking eggs.

You of all people should fucking know that.

"You'll be wanting to know what I want, I expect," she said.

Madera sat very slightly back in her chair; pressed her hands together and considered Kat appraisingly over her steepled fingers.

"Want to tell me, do you?"

Kat swallowed.

Just do it. Fucking do *it, and it'll be done.*

"I've got a proposal for you. A proposition, if you like."

"A proposal."

It wasn't a question; wasn't a request for more information. She already knew Kat wanted to talk; that she *would* talk.

All Madera had to do was sit and wait.

"Yeah." Kat's mouth was bone-dry now, her tongue so thick and desiccated it was a miracle the words came out at all. "I want to make a deal. With you."

Madera didn't react; remained as still and unblinking as a salamander on a rock.

"Interesting," she said eventually. "Alright, then - I'm listening. You go on and tell me about this deal."

El had thought, at first, that Ruby and Sita would arrange to have Carruthers arrested, to remove him from the equation; that Sita would have a discreet word in Gerry Adler's always-attentive ear about the threat Carruthers posed to them, and that Adler - driven as much by a desire to play Sita's knight in shining armour as by his commitment to banging up a serial murderer - would swoop in on some fabricated pretext or other and make the arrest.

Ruby, though, had disabused her of that notion the moment El had mentioned it.

"Wouldn't work," she'd said. "I don't doubt Adler'd do it if she asked him - he's got stars in his eyes for her, always has done. But *arresting* Carruthers wouldn't solve nothing on its own. You'd have to find a way to make sure he *stayed* locked up longer than just a day or two. And the sort of cash him and our Dolly've got knocking around, the bloke'd have some thousand-pound-an-hour brief in a fancy tie bailing him out in about the time it'd take one of us to nip down the shops for a pint of milk."

"I'm afraid your Auntie Ruby may be right, darling," Sita had added. "Gerry is certainly... obliging, but I doubt even *he* has the clout to keep Carruthers in a jail cell for very long without due cause. And if Carruthers has survived this long doing... what he does, then he'll have sufficient wits about him not to allow himself to be baited into lashing out while the police are watching."

What they *ought* to do to Carruthers instead, Ruby had insisted, was what they always did. What they were good at.

They needed to con him. To pull his levers.

In fact, she'd gone on, she and Sita had a sense already of *how*: how they might get to him, what his Achilles' heel might be.

"He's a vain bastard," she'd said. "That Hannah said as much, didn't she? All them muscles, and the sharp suits and that. And he's got to be pretty arrogant, doing the jobs he does and getting away with 'em clean. Don't tell *me* a man like that goes 'round taking money for putting people six feet under every fortnight without a hefty slab of self-belief."

"You want us to play to his vanity?" El had asked.

"I want us to play to his *entitlement*. Been with our Dolly since he was a kid, hasn't he? Quarter of a century or more. And sounds like she's always kept him close, don't it? Right by her side, where she can keep her eyes on him and make sure he don't try to pull a fast one. Can't say I blame her, neither. It's what *I'd* do, if I were her and I didn't want a mutiny on my hands."

That, El had realised then - perhaps for the first time - was something she'd always appreciated about Ruby: the way she'd never tried to rein El in or keep her close, just for the sake of being able to control her. Even when El had been a kid; been Ruby's protege. Ruby had always let her go her own way, let her make her own mistakes and revel in her own triumphs. And, more to the point, had always been quick to welcome her back into the fold, whenever she'd come back - which she always, always did. Probably always would.

It was one of a thousand ways, she'd thought, that Ruby and her sister were nothing alike.

"You think he wants out? Out from under Madera, I mean," she corrected herself. "That he's looking to fly solo? Cut the apron strings and branch out on his own?"

"I don't think it's at all improbable," Sita had agreed. "In which case, separating him from Madera - *getting him out of the picture*, as I believe you put it - may be as simple as offering him a better deal than the one he thinks he's getting while he's shackled to *her*."

"A deal," Ruby had said, "that's just for him."

The client would have to be American; they all agreed as much. Even with the work Madera and Carruthers had done for Marchant in London, the two of them were an American operation, and a mostly West Coast one at that. An approach from another Brit would be too suspicious; altogether too convenient.

"What about Kate Zhou?" Sita had suggested. "She's from California, isn't she? And lord knows, the girl's a chameleon."

El had bitten back her disagreement; her instinct to argue for bringing someone other than *her* in on the con. Literally anyone else.

It would have been baseless, the implicit criticism, and she'd known it. She'd met Kate Zhou only once, spending less than half an hour in her company more than a year earlier, but the woman's reputation as a grifter and the respect Ruby and Sita had for her - not to mention the help she'd given them in pulling off the Soames job - should have been more than enough to persuade El to go along with the recommendation.

The fact was, she was jealous.

Kate had made it clear, during their brief sojourn in San Francisco, that she was interested in Rose. She'd gone as far as to take Rose out for dinner the evening before they'd left the city - a date that Rose had insisted later was entirely platonic, at least from her perspective.

("Though it *could* have been more, had things been different," Rose had said with a smile, one night in bed when El had raised the topic. "It wasn't as if you'd made your move then. I was barely sure by that point that *you* were interested at all").

Ruby had gone to stick the kettle on while she chewed over Sita's idea.

"Could work, I reckon," she'd announced on her return to the living room. "We'd have to get her over here pretty sharpish, mind."

"I'm sure she'd be happy to chip in," Sita had countered. "If we asked her nicely."

"And you'd be alright with that, would you?" Ruby had turned her attention to El, who could *feel* the sourness of her own expression, even in the absence of a reflective surface to confirm it.

Grow the fuck up, she'd chastised herself. *She's an ally, not a threat.*

Just relax. There's nothing to worry about.

"Fine," she'd answered, sounding entirely unconvincing. "Totally fine."

Among the very few things Carruthers liked to actually *spend* his money on, they'd discovered, were books - the older and rarer, the better.

He'd spent several thousand pounds on Charing Cross Road alone since landing in London, the outgoings spread across a handful of shops specialising in first editions and collectibles. He'd visited them most days, they'd seen, and always in the morning – with every one of the transactions Karen had unearthed processed somewhere between 11am and midday.

There was a strong chance therefore, they reasoned, that Kate would find him perusing the shelves of one of those shops, if she lingered long enough in the area.

She arrived at Heathrow, without fanfare, on the Sunday of the week

Ruby had called her to put in their request; took a few hours to sleep, shower and refuel in her hotel room, and then made her way from Belgravia to West Hampstead, where Ruby - after leading her on a whistle-stop tour of their predicament - briefed her on the plan.

The following day, at 11am on the dot, she was out on the Charing Cross Road, weaving in and out of the just-opened bookshops, eyes ostensibly trained on the glued, stitched stacks of paper and cloth and leather around her and peripheral vision fixed on the street outside, the bodies coming and going and passing through.

At 11.15, Carruthers entered the store she'd been browsing - cramming his outsized body through the narrow doorway and saluting the owner with an easy, familiar hello.

She waited five minutes; let him settle into place and slip his guard down. Then she moved; manoeuvred herself into position.

"Mr Carruthers," she said, appearing at his shoulder, looking to the casual observer as if she were doing nothing more remarkable than scanning the titles on the set of shelves they were facing.

The greeting didn't startle him - or didn't appear to.

"Think you've got the wrong person," he replied, not looking at her but picking a faded, dog-eared copy of The Brothers Karamazov off one of the shelves and thumbing it open.

"No," she told him. "Pretty sure I don't."

He angled his head to look at her; to take in the stranger who'd accosted him in what should have been his private domain.

They'd decided, for the purposes of the job, on a harder-nosed character than was usual for Kate: a former hedge fund manager named Cindy Chen, newly settled in Santa Cruz after abandoning her big-city career in investment to launch a start-up that specialised in creating ethical beauty products from scratch and selling them on, for an obscenely high mark-up, over the internet.

Physically, Chen and Kate were different enough to avoid raising alarm bells for Carruthers, should he - unlikely though it was - have happened upon Kate's name and face during the course of his background research into El and Ruby and the others.

As befitted her recent professional interests, Chen was beautifully groomed and prettily attired: the stylish androgyny of Kate's slicked-back hair and tailored suits exchanged for the high-femme glamour of a tight red dress, tartan jacket and enough makeup to satisfy even the most demanding drag queen.

She was also, necessarily, ruthless.

They'd thrown around several possible motivations for Chen's seeking out Carruthers: an abruptly broken engagement, a swindled inheritance, a love rival who refused to fade into the background. In the end, though, they'd gone for the most straightforward of the options: a business adversary, one Eliana Gregorians, whose product-distribution capabilities and ever-lowering prices were threatening to cut very starkly into Chen's bottom line.

Which wouldn't do at all.

"Like I said," Carruthers told her, when he'd looked her up and down and returned his gaze to the Dostoevsky in his hand, "you've got the wrong person."

"Mr Carruthers," she said, undeterred, "I have a job for you. And if you knew me at all, you'd appreciate that I don't normally travel quite this far out of state to do my hiring."

With that, finally, she had his attention.

"I need her gone," she continued, when they'd settled at her suggestion in a quiet and very empty Italian cafe on Litchfield Street and she'd relayed the story of her trouble with Gregorians. "Permanently off the scene. Can you do that?"

"With all due respect, Ms. Chen," he answered, taking an incongruously dainty sip of the double espresso she'd bought him, "I don't know you. I've never heard of you or your company. You could be anyone."

"Search for us, then," she answered, as if she'd been expecting just such a challenge. "Next time you're at a computer, search for us. Or I can give you the web address and you can go straight to the site."

It wasn't a bluff. Thanks to a little work on Karen's part that weekend, Chen's company, Good & Whole, had not only its own website - from which all manner of sustainably-sourced soaps, shampoos, lipsticks and foundations could be purchased with the use of a credit card - but IRS records of the company's tax declaration from the previous year and at least two dozen legitimate-seeming reviews of the Good & Whole product experience from a range of satisfied (and, for the sake of authenticity, several *un*satisfied) customers. Further back-room digging, should Carruthers wish to undertake any, would uncover a decade of Chen's personal tax records, an electronically-archived newsletter recounting her 1988 graduation (with Honors) from the MBA program at Harvard Business School, and - a detail of which Karen was particularly proud - a recently-created dating profile outlining Chen's interest in meeting professional males, of any ethnicity, measuring at least 5'10, weighing no more than two hundred pounds and based, ideally, within driving distance of the San Francisco Metropolitan Area.

"I'll do that," he said. "But Ms. Chen - anyone can make a website, if they know how."

She nodded.

"Yes, they can. And if we were back home and I was trying to convince you I'm serious and not a cop - which I'm guessing is what's got you worried - then I'd probably do something like pull open my dress to show you I'm not wearing a wire or say something so incriminating that even a deadbeat lawyer could get a judge to call it entrapment. But we're *not* back home, Mr Carruthers, and to tell you the truth, I sort of like this dress, so how about I just let you take a look inside my suitcase instead, and you can decide for yourself where you want the rest of the conversation to take us?"

She gestured down to the small, hot-pink travel case she'd been wheeling around with her since she'd got to Charing Cross Road, inviting him to open it.

He studied her, seeming to weigh her up, then bent his immense frame down towards the floor and began to unzip the fabric.

"Not too much," she warned him. "Trust me, we don't want everyone seeing what's in there."

He unzipped just one more inch and then, pulling apart the teeth of the zipper, peered inside. His eyes widened.

"Silver?" he asked her, voice pitched low.

"Yes. Twenty-eight bars, a thousand ounces - that's a little over ten thousand dollars' worth, if you don't keep track of the market. Not a lot, but as much as I could carry, and hopefully enough to assure you my intentions are sincere, even if they're not that honourable."

Altogether, the silver was worth slightly more than the figure she gave him, though she was pretty sure he wouldn't know that. Karen had been sad to see it go, and initially reluctant to part with it at all - but had eventually conceded, without enthusiasm, that the sacrifice was probably worth it, for the greater good.

Carruthers' eyes, still wide as saucers, raked over the ingots.

"How'd you get it here?" he asked her, awe overtaking his wariness.

"That's not for you to worry about, Mr Carruthers. Point is, I have it, and a lot more of it than *this*. You agree to help me, and you can take a little of it home yourself. How does a hundred thousand sound to you?"

"A hundred grand in *silver*?"

"It holds value better than cash, I assure you. And attracts a lot less outside interest."

He zipped the bag closed and straightened himself up in his chair.

"I'll have to talk to my partner," he said. "See if we can make it work."

"Ah."

She pursed her lips; clicked her tongue thoughtfully against the roof of her mouth.

"I say something wrong, Ms. Chen?"

She grimaced; sighed.

"I wouldn't say *wrong*, Mr Carruthers. But I guess I should've been clearer upfront: it's *you* I want for this job. *Only* you."

He hesitated before answering.

"I work with a partner, Ms. Chen. Always have."

"Yes. And I know all about her. Oh, don't look so surprised - you think I don't do background checks, for something like this? Of course I do. I'm not a goddamn idiot."

"You know about her, but you don't want to work with her? I find that hard to believe."

"Don't be offended, please. She has a good reputation - a *great* reputation. Comes highly recommended. But she's not getting any younger. She's, what - nearly seventy now? That's a little long in the tooth to be doing the kind of work you do. The kind of work that demands... precision. A steady hand."

"She's *still* great. I don't know what you heard, but..."

"Let me interrupt you here, Mr Carruthers, before you go on. I love that you're loyal to her - really, I do. But it isn't *her* I want. And that part of the deal really isn't negotiable."

He lapsed into silence.

"Do I get to think about it?" he asked.

She pulled her lips into another grimace - this one suggesting that she'd rather he *didn't*, but if he absolutely *had* to...

"I'm in town until tomorrow night," she told him. "If I don't hear from you before then, I'll assume it's a no and move on to another contractor."

"Tomorrow night?"

"Yes, Mr Carruthers - tomorrow night. Thirty-six hours, or thereabouts. Should give you the time you need to decide, shouldn't it? And when you've decided... you just let me know."

OSTERLEY PARK, LONDON

May 1998

I must say, it's been a while since I did *this*," Sita said, pushing a tree branch away from her face. It swung away from her and then, like an arboreal boomerang, yo-yoed back, its leaves rustling loudly as they hit her for a second time.

"Keep your voice down, would you?" Ruby hissed, parting another set of branches with her own, Kevlar-covered hands. "They'll hear you all the way out in bleedin' Ruislip, the way you're talking."

"*Forgive* me for trying to assuage our nerves with a little conversation."

"Shut it, both of you," Karen snarled quietly over her shoulder. There was something of the military squadron leader about her, in her dark camouflage gear; in the bulky bulletproof vest protecting her torso from hip to throat.

Do I look like that? El wondered, looking down at her own vest, her own black camo gear and boots.

Neither Sita nor Ruby did, she knew that much. Sita wore her vest like a fashion accessory, casually unzipped at the neck and carried off with so much panache that it might as well have been a gilet thrown on for walk in the countryside, while Ruby - short and round and bearing the weight of a loaded rucksack over her charcoal burglar's attire - might have been an old crone from a fairy-tale, peddling apples door-to-door to unsuspecting princesses.

Rose, El was unsurprised to see, fit the outfit like a glove, moving as easily in the body armour as she might have in a pair of jeans or a sundress.

It's because she's used to it, El reminded herself. *She'd have to be, wouldn't she, with all that breaking and entering and robbing she did as a kid?*

Apparently chastised, the two old women pressed on through the wood, El and Rose behind them and Karen leading the way, Hannah at her side.

("You keep her close," Ruby had warned Karen, before they set out. "She's a bloody rattlesnake, that one. Can't be trusted, not as far as you could throw her. So you don't take your eyes off her, alright? She'll have to come with us – we need as many warm bleedin' bodies as we can get. But she'll kick us in the teeth soon as look at us, if she thinks there's something in it for her. You'd do well not to forget it."

"Trust me," Karen had told her, "there's no danger of me forgetting. *No danger*").

Kat hadn't joined them, for this part of the job. El could forgive her for it, even if her absence did nothing to bolster their body-count advantage.

("It's not that I don't *want* to go," she'd told El. "I mean, I *don't* want to go, because what sort of fucking lunatic would want to go walking straight into the lion's den like that? But even if I *did* want to, I couldn't. I wouldn't last two minutes traipsing through a forest with my legs the way they are. One of you lot'd end up bloody *carrying* me to the finish line, the way I'm going").

Even through the encroaching foliage and with the dark closing in all around them, El could see the cameras, strung about - and in some cases, mounted on - the trunks and upper branches of the trees: sleek grey cylindrical things, as free of wires as Karen had suggested, and entirely unlike any CCTV system she'd seen before. Stuart Ma, she suspected - it seemed ridiculous to keep calling him Pasadena, now they knew his real name - wasn't just adept at using and manipulating new technology, but at inventing it, too. Coming up with his own solutions, when the affordances of existing hardware fell short.

"Stop worrying," Rose whispered, following El's gaze up into the red pinprick iris of the nearest camera. "They've been taken care of, remember?"

And they had been; Karen had assured her of it. Disabling them - every one of them, from the woods and fields to the farmhouse itself - was one of several things she and Jeremiah had arranged, on the first visit they'd paid Ma.

But still, their presence made her nervous. Their proximity.

Even Ruby softened her step as they approached the farmhouse; as they trod on tiptoe to the back and turned the handle of the unlocked door that led to the kitchen, as Ma had instructed.

"They won't hear you, if come in that way," he'd told Karen and Jeremiah, the night they'd dropped by to see him. "They're never in the kitchen. They're always here - in the games room. There's a drinks cabinet down here, look - right in the corner. Thea likes to drink, while they talk."

Karen's eyes had swept, disinterestedly, to the cabinet, then right back to Ma.

"Doesn't seem very *definite*, if you ask me, Stuart," she'd replied. "So how about this instead: we tell you when we're coming, and you make very fucking sure they're down here for it, enjoying a little snifter of something expensive out of one of the bottles you got in that cupboard. That sound good to you?"

Ma had stared at her, utterly terrified; then he'd nodded, taken his head in his hands and wept.

Locating Ma, once they were in the house, had been - as Karen described it - a piece of piss. They'd heard him from outside the kitchen: the rhythmic thud of the game he'd been playing - a beat 'em up, by the sound of it - reverberating up from the open door of the basement below.

He didn't notice they were there until long after they'd descended the stairs, so absorbed was he in defeating his pixelated opponent; didn't falter in his manipulation of his control pad until Karen had perched herself on the edge of the pool table behind him and Jeremiah had spun the swivel-chair he'd been sitting in around to face her.

"Alright?" she'd greeted him - the replica gun in her hand entirely for show, although she'd had a sense that *he* hadn't known that.

He'd tried to make a run for it, to spring up out of his chair and race for the door, but Jeremiah, who'd anticipated just this, held him down, the fingers of the boy's bony but surprisingly strong hands digging into the tender flesh of Ma's upper back.

Ma hadn't been able to speak at all at first - just gape and gawp at them in their hellish clown makeup, his mouth opening and closing as wordlessly as a fish's.

"You say something, there?" Karen had asked him, cupping a hand - the hand *not* holding the weapon - exaggeratedly to her ear.

"Take the money," he'd begged. "Please. It's in the safe in the master bedroom, I can get you the passcode. Whatever's in there, you can have it, all of it. Just please, please - leave the rest."

"The rest?" Jeremiah had said, curious.

"The hard drives. The laptops. Please."

Jeremiah had glanced at Karen for confirmation of what to do next - a look she'd rewarded with a wide, bright smile.

"Sweetheart," she'd told Ma, looking down at him from her baize-upholstered throne, "we're not after your gear. Or your money, come to that."

Ma had shrunk back into his seat and lowered his head, the bleached-blond strands of his boyband hair falling limply into his reddening eyes.

"What is it you want, then?" he'd asked, voice beginning to break.

And Karen's grin had widened.

Ma met them in the kitchen; ushered them through, closed the door behind them gently, and pressed a finger to his lips for silence.

He was *still* terrified, El saw: gnawing at his lip and wringing his hands, his pulse leaping out from his neck and his jaw grinding involuntarily back and forth, as if he'd taken more amphetamine than he was used to and washed the lot of it down with a Turkish coffee.

Karen raised an eyebrow at him, expectantly, and a tremor ran through him.

She tilted her head, the gesture somewhere between a question and an instruction.

He lowered *his* head in return, turned on the spot, and beckoned them to follow him further into the house.

"You don't know who I am, do you?" Karen had said, leaning in to close the distance between her and Ma. "Funny, I thought you'd be more observant than that, all the time I heard you've been spending eyeballing me. But then, I suppose I'm not normally done up like a David Bowie album cover, am I?"

She'd reached the gun-free hand into her pocket, pulling out a tissue-sized packet of wet wipes.

"Easily sorted," she'd added, and rubbed the wipe across her face - once, twice, half a dozen times, until enough of the makeup had gone for the features underneath it to be clearly discernible.

Recognition had dawned across *Ma's* face, then, and he'd let out a gasp before he'd been able to stop himself.

"And *now* he sees me!" she'd told Jeremiah, who'd twisted his own lips into a wry approximation of a smile.

She'd jumped down from the edge of the pool table and walked towards Ma, until she was standing over him.

"I can't stop her," Ma had said hoarsely, raising his chin to look at her. "I can't call her off."

"Her?" Jeremiah had asked.

"He means his boss," Karen had answered, when Ma didn't. "Madera. Isn't that right, *Pasadena*?"

Ma had said nothing, mashing his lips together like two halves of a clamshell.

"He's scared of her," she'd told Jeremiah. "More scared of her than of us, I reckon. And why wouldn't he be? She's Rosa fucking Klebb, and we're just some twats who walked in off the street. Except," she'd tapped the tip of Ma's nose very lightly with the muzzle of the gun, making him flinch, "he doesn't know what *we* know, does he? Or what we've got on him."

Something like panic had seemed to grip Ma, at that final statement.

("Once he'd twigged who I was," Karen said afterwards, "it couldn't've taken him long to work out what I might've done to him. And *how* I might've done it to him, if you know what I mean").

"What did you do?" Ma had croaked. "What the fuck did you *do*?"

She'd pointed down to the floor - to the white holdall she'd carried with her to the farmhouse.

"Grab the laptop out of there, would you, J?"

Jeremiah had blinked, just once, by way of assent, and opened the holdall, from which he'd produced a boxy grey PowerBook.

"Have a look at this," she'd told Ma, as Jeremiah had flipped up the computer's screen and placed it, with no small amount of reverence, on the flat denim planes of Ma's upper thighs.

Ma had peered into the soft blue glow, his eyes darting from left to right as he'd taken in the information displayed on the screen.

"That's not possible," he'd said, but with just enough of an edge of panic to indicate that even *he* wasn't wholly convinced by the words.

Jeremiah had clapped him, hard, on the shoulder.

"It's not just *possible*, mate. It's *done*. Karen here... she's done it."

"He's not kidding," Karen had agreed.

Ma had blinked at the laptop - over and over, an owl in thrall to a blast of strobe lighting.

What he'd been seeing, Karen said, was a distillation of the behind-the-scenes work she and Fergus - *especially* Fergus - had been doing since Hannah had rocked up at the house in Chelsea. The document was short, just five pages of text interspersed with the occasional passport-photo image, but from Ma's perspective, the most terrible kind of threat.

It was, in effect, a list: a chronologically ordered inventory of every pseudonym Ma had used since leaving university - and attendant details of the financials, addresses and registered possessions associated with each - alongside brief but incendiary summaries of the multiplicity of local, federal and international crimes he'd committed under cover of each identity. And, more damning still: allusions to a far larger trail of evidence connecting each identity back, irrefutably, to Ma himself.

It would have been enough, had it been passed along to Interpol or the FBI or the California Department of Justice - or indeed any other of the investigation and intelligence services interested in garnering verifiable, legally admissible intel on the person they'd known only as Pasadena - to keep him in a supermaximum-security penitentiary until the day he died.

Karen and Fergus, though, had been formulating a different use altogether for the data they'd gathered.

"And you're thinking," she'd told Ma, "that all this is looking pretty fucking bad for you, right? I mean, *I* would be. Thing is, though, Stuart - can I call you Stuart? I feel like we're *there* now, you and me. The thing *is*," she'd crouched down next to him, until the pseudo-gun was level with his heart, "it's actually *so much fucking worse* than it looks."

"What did you do?" Ma had repeated, stammering and swallowing, blinking eyes caught between the gun, the screen and Karen's beaming, makeup-smeared face.

"What did we do? We *deleted* you, Stuart. *All* of you, every trace. Every name, every social security number, every fake birth certificate and driving licence you've ever used. And I know you like sniffing around other people's money, so you'll get a kick out of this one - every bank account, as well. Everyone you've ever been, and everything they've ever had - gone. All gone. Pasadena - gone. And Stuart Ma - you can probably guess where I'm going with this, but... he's gone, too."

Ma had looked, Karen said, as if he was going to pass out. A stress-induced stroke hadn't seemed, from the abject horror written across every visible inch of him, like a complete impossibility, either.

"Now," she'd continued, judging that the moment to deliver the killing blow had come, "would you like me to tell you what you can do for us, to get him back?"

OSTERLEY PARK, LONDON

May 1998

They followed Ma through the house, El marvelling at how little sound their feet made on the carpet underfoot.

Had Ma had the place soundproofed? she wondered.

Had Madera *asked* him to have it soundproofed?

And if she had... what plans did she have for the house, that meant it *needed* to be soundproofed?

The inevitable conclusion of the thought was both logical and profoundly alarming. El shut it down before it could take root, or tried to - but still, the idea of the house as what she couldn't help but think of as *a killing room* persisted, dancing uninvited on the edges of her consciousness, and she shivered.

Everything okay? Rose mouthed at her, concerned.

Fine, she mouthed back, trying for a smile but falling short, the rigid muscles around her mouth straining with the effort.

Ma stopped moving halfway down the hall, raising his hand in a stalling gesture that brought the rest of them to a halt.

He leaned in towards Karen - the nervous blinking she'd described to El now in overdrive - and whispered something in her ear.

Kerry, El saw him say - the movements of his own mouth and cheeks so exaggerated that she'd have been able to understand him even if she hadn't been able to lipread. *I couldn't get ahold of her - I don't know where she is. She could be here any minute.*

No, Karen told him. *She won't be. She's been dealt with.*

At *that*, at least, El smiled.

In all the planning around blackmailing Ma and laying the bait for Carruthers, El had very nearly forgotten about Kerry Lawton - "that little circus girl," as Hannah persisted in calling her.

Thank God for Harriet, El thought. She might not have been the warmest of hosts, and she might not be all that happy to have El as a prospective sister-in-law... but she'd done a hell of a job.

The club had been heaving when she'd arrived. That was how Harriet had told it, anyway - given the woman's aversion to human company, El wouldn't have been surprised to discover that the place had held no-one but Harriet, the bartender, two other drinkers and a cat. Though if there *had* been a cat, perhaps Harriet would have mentioned it - to RD Laing, if not to her and Rose.

She'd bought herself a glass of orange juice, lit a clove cigarette with a box of matches she'd procured for the occasion - though she didn't smoke, and El was sure she'd complained to Rose in private before about *El's* habit - and taken herself off to the least-dark section of the establishment she could see, where she'd begun to read.

The book she'd bought with her was a novel - a novel about a circus, no less. It had been a strategic choice on Harriet's part, as had the cigarettes: a way of piquing Lawton's interest in what threatened to be a crowded marketplace.

"I'm an attractive enough woman," Harriet had said, investing the statement with no more vanity or boastfulness than she might have a comment on the weather outside, "but we don't know what she looks for in a partner, do we? And what I have to work with might not be enough to stand out from the pack. So it would serve us well to load the dice, as much as we're able."

Someone reading a book in a nightclub would, she'd reasoned, attract at least a little attention - would turn heads her way. Perhaps many of the women who looked would find her pretentious and would immediately look away – and if they did, that was fine. Because if they'd *looked*, they'd also have seen the book's *cover*: a vivid, Fauvist depiction of a female acrobat suspended in mid-air, her ankle wrapped around a trapeze.

"And the cigarettes?" Rose had asked. "Do cloves have some sort of... aphrodisiac property?"

"None that I'm aware of," Harriet had replied. "But if I've learned anything from those old detective films you two keep insisting I sit through, it's that no *femme fatale* worth her salt goes *anywhere* without a cigarette in her hand. And the flavoured ones are the only kind I can stomach."

Lawton had entered the club around 9pm. Harriet would, she said later, have guessed from the first look that the girl had been a performer - a dancer or a gymnast, if not an acrobat - even if she hadn't been briefed on her background. There was an unusual fluidity to her, a precision; the weaving of her tall, thin body in and out of the gathering crowds around the bar and tables seeming designed not to navigate the space so much as to cut through it with an invisible scalpel.

She'd been casually dressed, her clothes barely more elaborate than Harriet's: jeans, a fitted black t-shirt, long blonde hair pulled back into a ponytail. But it had been clear, from the darting of her eyes and the aura of restlessness that surrounded her as she walked the club, gaze briefly stopping to rake up and down the other bodies she saw there, that she'd been on the prowl.

It had taken her a few minutes to spot Harriet - still sipping at her orange juice and smoking her sickly-sweet cigarettes and leafing through her paperback. But once she'd seen her, and seen the book, she'd been sufficiently intrigued - as Harriet had predicted - to walk over to Harriet's table and sit down on the low banquette beside her.

"Good book?" she'd asked, her voice deep and gravelly and recognisably American - Western American English, as Harriet had mentally classified it.

"Not bad," Harriet had answered, not looking up at her. "I'm not sure the writer knows a lot about trapeze work, though. She keeps mixing up the catch trap and the fly bar."

"You know a lot about trapeze?"

Lawton had sounded amused, Harriet thought - tickled at the prospect of the unlikely-looking Englishwoman in front of her having any kind of familiarity with the acrobatic lexicon. But curious, too. Interested.

"A little," Harriet had told her, lying through her teeth. "I was Treasurer of my uni's Circus Society as an undergrad. Most of it was spinning and juggling - torch and poi and diabolo, that sort of thing. The occasional bit of unicycling. But I got rather into the aerial work, when we were able to do it. Hence, you know... *this.*"

She'd closed the book and held it up in one hand, so that Lawton could take a closer look. Lawton had ignored it, fixing her eyes instead on Harriet - weighing her up, taking stock (or so it had seemed to Harriet) of her value.

"You still practice?" she'd said eventually.

"No. I'd love to, but there never seems to be time. I've thought about private lessons, though. It'd be great to get back into... I was going to say *the swing of it*, but..."

She'd let her own eyes fall back to the book, ostensibly embarrassed by the inadvertent pun.

Lawton had smiled, slow and lazy.

"You know," she'd offered, pitch dropping to a drawl, "I know a little about aerial myself. Maybe I could show you sometime. If you want."

"I don't live far," Harriet had told her, following Lawton out of the club and onto the Albert Embankment. "It's Southwark - just across the bridge."

"Sounds good to me," Lawton had told her, linking her fingers in Harriet's.

Harriet had done her best, as she'd assured Rose and El later, not to flinch at the contact.

It had taken them no more than a few minutes to reach the flat: a suitably anonymous third-floor two-bed on Lavington Street that Harriet had rented for a night from a property company specialising in furnished homes-from-home for affluent commuters.

She'd led Lawton through the lobby, into the lift and - after several excruciating seconds in which she'd been convinced Lawton might try to pull her closer or, God forbid, *kiss* her - into the flat itself.

"Bedroom's down here," she'd told Lawton, gesturing to a closed door at the bottom of the hallway. "Go on through - I won't be a moment."

Lawton had nodded, walked the few steps to the end of the hall and, not bothering to turn on the light switch, stepped through into the bedroom.

Where she'd found Sita, sitting perfectly still on the edge of the bed.

WEST HAMPSTEAD, LONDON

April 1998

There's something terribly *familiar* about that girl," Sita said, examining the print-out copy of Lawton's passport that Karen had given them, in amongst the dozen other documents representing what information she'd managed to gather so far on Madera's associates. "I do wish I could put my finger on it. Remind me, darling - where did you say she was from?"

"Nevada, funnily enough," Karen replied. "Not the casino bit - unless you count the whole state as *the casino bit*, which maybe you should, I don't know. A place called Boulder City. Little town in the mountains, about twenty-odd miles outside of Vegas. I thought at first she'd just *moved* there, to be closer to the circus stuff, but no - turns out she's actually *from* there. Born and bred."

Sita squinted at the print-out, nose wrinkling in puzzled concentration.

"Reckon you know her from somewhere?" Ruby asked.

"I don't see how I *could*. I haven't been to Nevada in *years* - not since that debacle with the Randazzos and the canary diamonds, if you recall. She wouldn't have been more than a child, then."

"You sure?" El said. Sita had a hell of a memory for names and faces; it was one of the things - when used in conjunction with the charismatic affability that led so many of the people she met to persuade themselves they'd fallen a little in love with her - that made her so formidable on the job. If she thought she recognised someone, then the odds were good, in El's opinion, that she'd met that someone before, somewhere along the line.

"No." Sita looked again at the image on the page; studied it. "Not at all, in fact. It's that mouth, you know - that mouth, and those eyes. And the cheekbones. Honestly, if she were even a few years older, I'd almost have said..."

She stopped, mid-sentence.

"What?" said Ruby.

"Nothing," Sita told her, shaking her head. "Nothing."

"Pull the bleedin' other one. I know that look."

Sita looked up from the print-out, momentarily defiant - then, her defiance wilting in the heat of Ruby's glare, shrugged.

"I can't be certain. I'm *not* certain. But I believe - I believe I'd like to make a phone call. To John Hertzberg, among others."

"Hertzberg? Weren't he that mob lawyer, the one you took up with in Reno?"

At this, Sita threw *Ruby* a glare: one that El, fluent by now in the subtextual communication that flowed as ceaselessly between the two old women as psychic energy along a ley line, interpreted as *we will talk about this later.*

"Fine." Ruby threw her hands in the air, exasperated but apparently prepared to wait until the others had left for her answer. "Have it your way. Go and ring him. But for Christ's sake, don't go telling him where we're living these days. I ain't in the mood to have another one of your suitors swearin' undying love for you from behind the bushes like Cyrano de bloody Bergerac."

SOUTHWARK, LONDON

May 1998

This your idea of a set-up?" said Lawton, taking in Sita's silhouetted form on the bed. "Your friend Redfearn gonna pop out of the closet and shout *surprise!*?"

"No," Sita replied evenly. "Just me. Would you like to take a seat, Kerry? You may not be able to see it very clearly in this light, but I believe there's a chair in the corner by the desk."

Lawton didn't move.

"Guess you know who I am, then. Okay. Well... fair's fair, right? I mean, I've heard *a lot* about you and your friends, these last couple months."

"You won't sit down?"

"No." Lawton shifted position; withdrew something small and dark from the inside of her jacket and redistributed her weight, almost imperceptibly, onto the balls of her feet. "No, I think I'll stay where I am, if you don't mind."

"I'm an old woman, Kerry. I have arthritis and high blood pressure and bones that complain when I stand up too quickly. I assure you, I couldn't do a girl like you the least bit of physical harm, even if I wanted to. There's no sense at all in you attacking me."

"Who says I want to attack you?"

"There's a knife in your hand - a combat knife, if I'm not mistaken. What do they call it? A Ka-Bar. And I expect you have a few other weapons about you, too. It would certainly make sense to come prepared, in your line of work."

Lawton's weight shifted again. The handle of the knife, Sita noticed, remained clasped in her fist, the dark edges of the carbon steel blade catching what little light had filtered into the bedroom through the half-drawn blinds.

"What is it you need, Sita?" she asked. "'Cause as pleasant as it is making conversation with you... I kinda had a different end to this evening in mind."

"I know you can't call them off," Sita said, suddenly harder, sharper. "Madera and Carruthers - they're a law unto themselves, I realise that. But I *can* request that you remove yourself from the situation - that you step away and let them get on with whatever they feel they need to do to us. Which is what I'd like to ask you now - to go. Get out of London. Tomorrow, ideally, if not sooner."

Lawton very nearly choked on her laughter.

"That's your solution to your problem? *Requesting* I go away and leave you alone?"

"It's one solution. I also have a second."

"Which is what?"

"Calling Madera myself to let her know who you are, and why you've been working for her."

"Oh, this is *good*! Go on, then - tell me, I'm dying to know. Who *am* I?"

"Santino Randazzo's daughter. His daughter who, unless I'm *very* much mistaken, has been for quite some time now passing him the more salient details of Madera's targets. And of how he might capitalise on their passing."

Lawton moved quickly; preternaturally quickly. But still, the words were out of Sita's mouth before the girl could bridge the distance between them with the knife.

"Kill me tonight, and Madera will find out."

Lawton stopped dead, a foot away from Sita's body on the bed.

Sita stood, looking neither old nor frail but every bit as fearsome, in her way, as Lawton had as she'd pulled the knife.

"As you've said, Kerry - I have friends. Several of those friends know *exactly* where I am currently. They know *why* I happen to have found myself here. And they know, moreover, who *you* are. Should any harm come to me, any harm at all... any one of them would be willing to make that phone call to Madera. And it may be that I'm underestimating her capacity for forgiveness, but it occurs to me that *she* might be disinclined to offer you the sort of head start *I* just have before she acts on the information received."

A pleased but faintly flummoxed look had settled over Sita's face when she finally returned to the living room after making her phone calls to Nevada, that afternoon in Ruby's living room.

"Found out what you wanted, did you?" Ruby asked her, the curiosity emanating from her in waves.

"You could say that, yes," Sita said, sidling past El and Rose and collapsing into the most overstuffed of Ruby's armchairs.

"And? Spit it out, for God's sake. We've been on bleedin' tenterhooks in here."

Sita took a cigarette from her little gold case, lit it and inhaled, the resultant smoke exiting her nostrils in a rapid succession of thin, translucent quills.

"It's a rather peculiar thing, isn't it, serendipity?" she began. "One can believe oneself down to one's very final chip, and then the croupier spins the wheel *just so,* and suddenly one finds oneself a hundred thousand in the black. Quite remarkable, really."

"What the *hell* are you on about, woman? You're not making no sense."

The cigarette returned to Sita's lips, and she took another, longer drag.

"I believe," she said, "that I may have, quite inadvertently, stumbled upon a solution to at least *one* of our problems."

"And that is?" Rose prompted her, her own patience for Sita's performance - or so El thought - wearing thin.

"John Hertzberg - the man I spoke to just now. As Auntie Ruby mentioned: he's a lawyer. And the majority of his clients are... not altogether what you'd call *upstanding citizens*."

"Bleedin' mafia, is what she means," Ruby added. "Dons and capos and consiglieri and what have you. Syndicates. Crime families."

"That's one way to characterise them, certainly."

"So Lawton's... something to do with the mafia?" El asked.

"In a way, darling. It seems she may be the daughter of... oh, what would you call it? An underboss. The second-in-command of a crime family. And not just *any* crime family, at that - the biggest in Las Vegas."

Matteo Randazzo, she explained - though Ruby had evidently known already - was the godfather of the Randazzo family: an enormously powerful and vastly influential criminal organisation that controlled, through means both direct and insidious, the majority of business conducted in the Las Vegas Valley area. A self-taught polymath passionate about medieval philosophy and Modernist literature, he was, at least in Sita's estimation, a gentleman, despite the occasional act of retributive violence necessitated by his line of work. Whenever their paths had crossed - the time, for example, when he'd called on her help to retrieve a haul of jewellery stolen from his elderly mother by an unscrupulous travelling salesman - she'd enjoyed his company immensely.

His younger brother Santino, however, she'd found less captivating by far.

"The runt of the litter, he was," Ruby said. "Touch of the Fredo Corleone about him, if you know what I mean. None too bright, and not much cop at the physical stuff, neither, but always thought he should've had more of a slice of the pie than what he got given. Wouldn't've been nowhere, if it weren't for old Matteo."

The familial connection had won Santino a place at the table, however ill-deserved, and he'd served as his brother's second-in-command - though the majority of his days and nights he spent drinking, gambling, ingesting prodigious volumes of cocaine and sexually harassing the young female dancers, escorts and cocktail waitresses who worked the hotels and casinos of The Strip.

"Proper grabby little bastard, Santino," Ruby added. "Nasty, an' all. Sort who'd pinch your arse with one hand and slip a Mickey in your drink with the other, then threaten you with the sack or a visit from the Old Bill if you told him where to stick it."

"An unpleasant man," said Sita. "*Deeply* unpleasant. You'd never feel entirely comfortable leaving any of the girls alone with him, even when he was prepared to pay them for an hour or two of their time."

Despite this, though, Santino had a lover: a long-term girlfriend, whom he kept stashed away in a picturesque town along the Colorado River, not far from the Hoover Dam. She'd been an exotic dancer herself, performing five nights a week for a revolving-door crowd of tourists and inebriated convention-goers at a strip club behind The Sahara - though, as Matteo had told Sita one night in the hotel suite they'd adjourned to after dinner, giving up the dancing, and the income it gave her, had been one of the conditions Santino had placed on the girl, when he'd first set her up as his mistress.

"Such a beautiful girl," Sita said. "Very distinctive looks. Hers... wasn't a face one would forget in a hurry. Sapphire, she was calling herself then, though I daresay it wasn't the name she was given. Sapphire Lawton."

"Kerry Lawton's mother," El said, the disparate strands of the unwinding narrative beginning to thread together.

"Yes. And Santino Randazzo is her father. His name doesn't appear on her birth certificate, which rather tallies with what I remember of him - he certainly never struck me as a man who'd take easily to parental responsibility. But her father he is, nonetheless. John Hertzberg assures me of it."

"And he told you more than just that, I'm thinkin'," Ruby said, after they'd taken a moment to reflect on the revelation. "Judging from the look of you."

"He did. Though I don't believe he intended to." She paused. "It seems Santino has been stepping out of Matteo's shadow, of late - financially, at least. Making some rather canny investments - buying stock in certain organisations, and then dumping them at a profit just before their share price takes a tumble. It's almost as if he *sees* the dip coming - that was how John put it. Which is rather curious in itself, because if you'll recall," she looked Ruby in the eye, "he was *not* a man you'd trust to hold the purse strings."

"You reckon someone's giving him the inside track. And it's got something to do with that kid of his."

"It's all speculation, of course. I'll need to make a few more enquires. But it wouldn't surprise me in the slightest to learn that each of those particular falls in share price were precipitated by the death of someone at a senior executive level - a CEO, for example. Or that the deaths in question occurred in somewhat... unusual circumstances."

"He knows they're going to die," El said, thinking aloud. "Then he bets on them dying."

"Yes. More specifically: I believe he knows they're going to die because he knows that Madera and Carruthers have been commissioned to kill them. And I believe he knows *that* because his daughter has been tipping him off about their targets."

Ruby let out a long, slow whistle.

"Bit of a stroke of luck for Santino, having his girl take up with our Dolly," she said carefully.

"Perhaps. Or perhaps he helped to broker the relationship to begin with. It would have been a rather clever move, for someone of his intellectual calibre... but it may be that he found a way to plant Lawton in Madera's circle in the first place. That he's been using her as... what might you call it? His *mole*."

"I could kill you anyway," Lawton said. "Leave you choking on your own blood before I go hop on that flight."

Sita shrugged.

"You could. But unless you're able to teleport, I very much doubt you'd be able to reach those friends of mine in time to stop them passing the news along to Madera. They're listening to us now, incidentally." She pulled back a small section of the sari draped over her left shoulder, revealing the outline of the microphone Karen had taped to the inside of the fabric. "Would you care to say hello?"

Lawton's eyes flickered down to the microphone, then back to Sita.

"Bullshit," she said. "You got nothing."

She inched forward, the Ka-Bar in her hand extended like a cutlass.

Sita smiled.

"Try me, darling," she told her, stepping into what space remained between them until the tip of the blade met the soft flesh of her stomach. "Just *try me*."

OSTERLEY PARK, LONDON
May 1998

own the stairs, Ma mouthed to Karen - pointing, for emphasis, to the staircase leading from the ground-floor hallway to the basement games room.

Karen nodded back at him; pointed a finger of her own to the back door they'd come through.

I can go? he mouthed.

She nodded again. He didn't ask a third time; just turned around and made for the door with nothing but the clothes on his back.

Quite *where* he'd go, El wasn't sure: none of his erased identities had been restored, as far as she was aware, and if Fergus had done his job properly - and there was no doubt that he *had*, since he was doing it for Karen - then the guy's travel documents would be apt to raise a lot of red flags at passport control, if he even made it to the airport.

Wherever he ended up, though, she hoped he'd learned enough to disappear completely - to keep himself from showing up on their radar for the remainder of his days.

At the top of the stairs, Karen paused; ran a hand down her hip until it reached the holster strapped to her thigh and pulled out a handgun. A semi-automatic Glock, that was - unlike the other models she'd had occasion to use on the job over the years - not only real, but loaded with seventeen rounds of live ammunition.

The others followed suit, retrieving firearms of their own from the limbs on which the guns were holstered. All of them but Ruby.

Ruby, who'd declined - over the protests of all of them, even Hannah - to go up against Madera armed with anything at all.

They descended the stairs in silence, two-by-two, their feet as quiet on the carpeted steps as they'd been traversing the hallway above: Karen and Ruby at the front, El and Rose in the middle, Sita and Hannah at the rear.

The games room was long and wide, the length and breadth - or so it seemed to El, as the full scope of it came into view - of the farmhouse itself. Spotlights shone from the low-hanging ceiling, illuminating the pool table, the drinks cabinet and breakfast bar, the open fireplace beside the widescreen television hooked up to Ma's beloved video games console; the high-backed, oversized swivel chair in which, she imagined, Ma had spent many happy hours since arriving in London angled away from the stairs, facing the screen.

And Madera and Carruthers: one on either side of the pool table, *their* guns levelled at Ruby and Karen.

"She won't hurt me," Ruby had insisted, when El had pressed her - privately - on her refusal to carry a gun. "Our Dolly - whatever she's done, whatever choices she might've made... she wouldn't do that. Wouldn't look me in the face and pull no trigger."

El hadn't known what to say - Ruby's absolute conviction at odds with everything she knew about Madera and the way the woman operated.

"And Carruthers?" she'd asked. "No reason for him to hold back, is there?"

Ruby had hauled her backpack onto her shoulders.

"He'll be out the way before we need to worry about that," she'd said, pulling up the zipper on her bulletproof vest. "You mark my words."

When neither Madera nor Carruthers pulled their triggers immediately, El let herself relax - just a fraction, but enough to convince the panicked sinews of her hips and calves to propel her down the remaining stairs.

If she was going to kill us now, she told herself, with an illogical certainty, *then she'd have done it before Karen's foot touched the basement floor. We'd be dead already, all of us.*

She wants something from us. Wants to find out *something.*

Or maybe, a more treacherous voice in her head put in, *she just wants to talk a little first. Wants to catch up with her baby sister before she puts a bullet in her head. And then in yours.*

"We don't want no trouble, Doll," Ruby said, speaking softly. "That's not why we've come."

She stepped further into the room, disrupting the bottleneck of bodies that had formed behind her and making space for the other women to follow, until the six of them were spread out in a single-line formation, facing Madera and Carruthers and their guns like kids against a playground wall.

Or prisoners up against a firing squad, the treacherous voice added.

It was a curious experience, seeing both the sisters together: Madera's face a perfect replica of Ruby's, but cast - as Hannah had suggested - in smoother and more decadent materials.

Carruthers, by contrast, could have been cut from stone, the rock-hard protuberances of his muscles sheathed by a blue sports jacket and open-neck shirt. His expression, like Madera's, was impassive, as inscrutable as any El had seen, and his grip on the gun in his hand solid and unwavering.

He'd kill us, she thought. All of us, where we stand. Wouldn't even blink.

"You've been very talkative, for someone who isn't looking for trouble," Madera said, in the strange, clipped Katherine Hepburn-Transatlantic Hannah had described. "Spending a *lot* of time with the police, the way I heard it."

"No," Ruby said. "No, that ain't true. Is it?"

This last question she directed at Hannah, standing now at the end of the horizontal chain of bodies.

"I may have been… misinformed," Hannah told Madera, sounding chastened, almost timid. "The information I gave you may have been… not entirely accurate, after all."

"And how's that?" Madera asked her.

"She lied to you, Doll," Ruby said. "She wanted us out the picture 'cause of what we did to her old man, and she thought you'd get the job done for her, if she spun you the right yarn."

"Is that so?" Madera raised one, sculpted eyebrow. "You have a rebuttal, Mrs. D'Amboise?"

"Well…," Hannah began.

The shot rang out so suddenly, the noise of it alone knocked El sideways, sending her flying into Rose, who caught her before she fell to the ground.

Hannah cried out, once; staggered backwards, then crumpled to the carpet, eyes wide and leaking blood from the hole Carruthers' gun had made in the centre of her forehead.

Madera turned her head to him, her own gun still pointed at Ruby.

"What the hell do you think you're doing? I never said to shoot her."

"Did it need saying?" he answered, coolly.

"*Yes*, it needed saying. Needed *me* to say so."

He twisted the broad, corded flesh of his neck clockwise, until he was looking back at her.

"Maybe I'm capable of making a decision on my own, for once. You ever consider that?"

I could shoot, El thought. *Put a bullet in one of them now, while they're talking. And while I'm doing that, someone else could take a shot at the other one. We could put them both down, together.*

Except... however fast I could shoot, they're probably faster. They'd know, before I pulled the trigger. And they'd react, maybe even before they thought too hard about it.

And then I'd be nothing but meat on the floor, like Hannah.

She chanced a look at Rose, to her left; at Karen, beside Rose. Both of them were frozen to the spot, just like she was, both sets of their eyes trained on Carruthers and Madera.

They're thinking the same, she thought. *They want to risk it, to take the shot - but neither one of them believes they'd be able to do it soon enough.*

"Now's not the time for this, Lucian," Madera said.

"It never *is,* Thea. It never is." The finger he had pressed against the trigger of his pistol twitched, very slightly; the thumb he'd locked around the grip shifted, and the tendons in his wrist with it. "But it's something I've been wanting to talk to you about for a while."

He's going to quit, El thought. *To tell her he's leaving - that he wants to go off on his own, whether she wants him to or not.*

And if she doesn't... *what's left for him to do but blast his way upstairs and out the door?*

The bait they'd laid for him - that *Kate Zhou* had laid for him, with Karen's suitcase full of silver - seemed, suddenly, like a misstep. A very serious error of judgement.

"Later," Madera told him. "*After.*"

"No." He licked his lips; the thumb on the pistol grip shifted position again. "It's not gonna wait. I..."

Carruthers had been quick, when he'd shot Hannah; so quick he'd managed to catch them all off-guard. But Madera moved like lightning: unloading two rounds into his throat and another into his gut before he'd even squeezed his trigger.

He went down hard - the gargantuan weight of him crashing to the floor like a boulder, his own bright red, iron-reeking blood soaking his shirt and spurting in rapid, arterial spritzes from his throat and neck.

Her gun-hand steady and her eyes never leaving Ruby and Karen, Madera bent to a crouch, snatched his pistol out from his stained fingers and, bringing herself back upright, pointed *that* weapon, too, in their direction.

On the floor, immobile but with strength enough left to vocalise his agony, Carruthers screamed - whatever words he intended to speak emerging from his caved-in throat as nothing but a wet and gurgling incoherence.

He'll die, El thought. *Probably soon. But it won't be quick, and it definitely won't be painless.*

I doubt it ever is, when she kills.

"Still want to talk, do you, girl?" Madera asked Ruby - her voice changing even as she spoke, morphing into a mirror-image of her sister's.

"I ain't scared of you, Doll," Ruby told her. She took a step in towards Madera, then another, shaking off Karen as the younger woman moved to grab her by the biceps to stop her. "Never have been. Think I care what you did to that boy of yours, after what *he* done to God knows who many else?"

She glanced down at Carruthers, twitching and writhing in death-seizures where he'd fallen, the carpet around him stained purple and brown with his blood.

Rose looked too, El saw. First at Carruthers, and then across at Hannah, now entirely still.

She was her sister, El reminded herself, trying to read a reaction in Rose's face but finding nothing there but a cool, placid emptiness. *Whatever else she was, she was her sister.*

The sister who tried to have Sophie killed, the other voice reminded her. *Twice, if you remember. So I wouldn't shed too many tears for her, if I were you.*

"I reckon maybe you *should* be scared," Madera said, "after what you done."

"I didn't *do* nothing," Ruby replied. "Not one of us did. *Her*, there," she pointed the toes of one of her boots at Hannah's body, "she were lying to you. Trying to stitch us up."

"You sure about that, are you?"

There was no tell in that voice, El thought. No sense at all of what Madera thought; of what she'd do.

And the hand with the gun stayed just where it was, the muzzle of it barely a foot from Ruby's chest. Didn't waver, not by a millimetre.

"Think, Doll. Bleedin' *think* about it. Even if you reckon *I'm* trying to get one over on you now - think about *her* down there. You're not daft - you never were, even when we were kids. A girl like that, with her head screwed on that loose... you honestly tellin' me you trust a single word she told you?"

Madera hesitated.

"No," she said, after a moment. "No, I can't say I did. Which is why I did a little detective work of my own. Why I..."

"On Gerry Adler, you mean," Ruby interrupted. "You heard we knew him, heard we'd been talking to him... so you put it all together with what that Hannah told you, and thought you'd worked out we'd been grassing you up to the Bill. That about the size of it?"

"James Marchant. Killed *him*, didn't you?"

Rose *did* flinch, at this; and Sita too, El saw.

Ruby, though, was calm - still wholly in control of herself.

"Yeah, I did it." She shook her head, regretfully. "Wish I hadn't had to, but I did it. But I *ain't* a grass, Doll. And I reckon you know that."

Madera lowered the gun half an inch, until the muzzle pointed at her sister's stomach, and not her heart.

"You listening to this?" she said, raising her voice - speaking, it seemed to El, not to Ruby or the rest of them, but to someone else. Another person in the room.

Next to the fireplace, the high-backed chair opposite the television spun ninety degrees on its wheels.

And there was Kat: feet tucked under her body in a modified lotus position and a gun – another pistol, the barrel long as something carried by a cowboy in a Spaghetti Western - resting firmly in her hands.

"Yeah," she told Madera, nudging the gun left, until El and Rose were directly in her line of fire. "But I wouldn't go believing what they're telling you, if I were you. Take it from me - this lot, they'll say just about *anything*."

THE STRAND, LONDON

May 1998

Sitting opposite Madera, so close she might've felt the murdering old bag's breath on her face if she'd leaned in any further, Kat found herself unexpectedly lost for words.

"My sister sent you after me, I expect," Madera said, filling the silence. Her tone was conversational; casually inquiring.

Kat cleared her throat; tried again to speak.

"She did, yeah."

"Couldn't be bothered to come herself, though?"

"She wasn't sure how you'd react to seeing her, after all this time."

Madera paused, thoughtful.

"And she wants to cut a deal, does she?"

Kat nodded; knocked back a slug of her cappuccino, wishing to God she'd thought to lace it with something stronger.

"She's asked me to tell you... to *ask* you, really... to stop what you're doing, coming after us."

Just tell her the truth, Ruby had said. *That's all we got left to offer, ain't it? The truth.*

Madera bared her teeth in what she probably intended as a smile - the sort of smile, Kat thought, she probably gave her targets, just before she slid a blade between their ribs or snapped their hyoid bone with a length of chicken-wire.

"It's not the best offer I've had this year," she said. "She not much of a negotiator, our Ruby?"

"She wants you to know it's not true, whatever it is you've been told," Kat continued. "She wants you to know, we haven't been talking to anyone about you. Especially not to the police. That Hannah who came to see you, who told you that you needed to come over here after us... she doesn't actually *know* anything. She was just pulling your strings - trying to use you to get rid of us."

Because she's a lying fucking slag, she added to herself. *And if you were half as smart as you reckon, you'd've seen through her as soon as she set foot on that Hollywood patio of yours, and she'd be floating face-down in the swimming pool now like something out of Sunset Boulevard.*

"That all you got for me?" Madera asked her. "Your word - my sister's word - against hers?"

Kat shrugged, nervous.

"It's what Ruby told me to tell you. She said you'd see it yourself, if you stopped to think about it for a second. Said... and I'm sorry about this, these are *her* words, not mine... you'd have to be a bloody idiot to think that Hannah was a reliable witness."

Madera kept on smiling, fixing Kat with that infra-red stare of hers.

"Still wouldn't call that a *proposition*," she said. "More of an *insult*, I'd say."

Kat took two long breaths and another gulp of coffee to steady herself.

Now, she thought. *Do it now, while you've still got guts enough to speak.*

"The proposition I'm talking about," she said. "It's not Ruby's. It's mine."

A flicker of... *something* passed over Madera's face, then was gone; a deep-sea fish, catching a flash of sunlight on its tail before disappearing under the water.

"The thing is," Kat went on, abject terror subsumed - just - by the absolute necessity of what she was about to do, "Hannah *wasn't* lying to you. She *thought* she was - she's a pathological fucking liar, it's what she does. Odds are, she just told you the first thing that popped into her head that seemed like it'd get you riled up. But as it turns out, by sheer coincidence... she wasn't totally wrong."

Madera's smile faded.

"No? I thought you just told me she *was* wrong - that you *hadn't* been talking to anyone about me and mine."

This isn't your fault, Kat told herself. *If that fucking bitch Hannah hadn't gone out of her way to try to put you in the ground - again - then you wouldn't be here now. And the others - they know what she is, and they welcomed her back with opens arms anyway. Even after what she did to you.*

It's like that kids' fable, that - what's it called? The Scorpion And The Frog. The frog knows it shouldn't give the scorpion a ride on its back, because the scorpion's a fucking scorpion - stinging people's what it does, what it's built to do. Yet somehow... the frog goes ahead and does it anyway.

And then it gets stung and dies, like the fucking idiot it is.

Even though, if it'd had even half a brain to begin with... it would've run like the wind, the second it saw the scorpion coming.

So really, that frog - it's got no-one but itself to blame, has it?

"That's what she *told* me to tell you - your sister," Kat said, the simmering anger she'd been living with the last couple of months - hell, the last couple of *years* - rising to a boil. "It's the message she gave me to pass on to you. But it's not the truth of it."

"You been saying that a lot - *truth*. Almost like you're trying to sell me on a story of your own."

Kat looked down into her coffee cup, willing her nerve to hold.

"Maybe I am," she replied. "Lucky for me, what I'm telling you *is* the truth. Look into it yourself, if you don't believe me - I should think there's enough threads out there tying Ruby and that Sita back to Scotland Yard. Karen too, most likely. She's the one who put the police onto James Marchant in the first place, straight after Ruby did him in."

She took a final drink of the coffee, trying in vain to rehydrate the desert of her mouth.

"You said you had a proposition," said Madera. "Want to tell me what it is? I'm assuming you want more from this meeting than just the satisfaction of stabbing your friends in the back."

"Amnesty," Kat answered - quickly, getting the words out while she still could. "I want amnesty. A reprieve, or whatever you call it. I want you and *your* lot to stop coming after me."

"I'm sure you do. But I'm not sure why you think we would? All you've done since you've been here is give me more reasons to want rid of you. *All* of you, that sister of mine included. And I don't know if anyone's ever told you this, but you're meant to *keep hold* of your bargaining chips, not chuck 'em all down on the table the second you sit down."

"Yeah, well - haven't told you everything, have I? Just the... what'd you call it, 'round your neck of the woods? The *backstory*. I might've said what they've *done*, Ruby and that, but you've not heard me make a peep about what they're *doing*. What they're *gonna* do."

Now she was interested; Kat could see it. Could read the tiny tells Madera had been keeping, so far successfully, under wraps: the subtle raising of the eyebrows; the barely discernible widening of the pupils; the soundless opening of the mouth as the jaw dropped open, just a little.

"And what's that, then?" Madera asked - her voice, at least, undemonstrative.

"Not about to tell you *that*, am I? Not without us making a deal. No point me spilling my guts if one of your lot's gearing up to stick a knife in them."

"What makes you think I'd honour any deal we made, if that's what you think we're doing?"

"I don't. I trust you about as far as I trust that bloody psycho Hannah. But I *have* got a couple of chips left to bargain with, see? 'Cause the scheme Ruby and hers are cooking up... it's changing all the time. Every day, it seems like. Me telling you what I know about what they've got planned for you, as of *right now*... that might not be worth much to you, a week from now. So it's in your interests to keep me around, isn't it? If you want to know what they've got planned for you. And believe me, you *do* want to know. Assuming you want to still be alive and kicking this time next month."

Madera's smile returned, nastier than before.

"Appreciate your concern, but I ain't that worried."

"Well, you should be. She's smart, your sister. Got a lot of tricks up her sleeve. They all do, every one of them. You shouldn't underestimate her, if you know what's good for you."

"But you're smarter, is that it?"

"No. Not so sure that I am, actually. But I don't have to be smart, do I, to find out what they're up to? Just need to keep my head down and my ears open."

"And feed it back to me, when you hear it. That's your proposition?"

"Maybe. If it gets you off my back and keeps me out of harm's way."

Madera studied her across the table.

"I've read about you," she said, thoughtfully. "Your background. Why you joined up with them others, going after Marchant. I'd never have had you pegged as the disloyal type."

I expect you wouldn't have, Kat thought. *But that was* before, *wasn't it? Back when I'd be necking tea in the morning, not co-codamol. Before that fucking scorpion came along and persuaded us to give it a ride across the river.*

"Yeah, well," she answered quietly. "Things change, don't they? Sometimes all you can do is look out for yourself."

OSTERLEY PARK, LONDON

May 1998

Kat?" Ruby said - taking a step away from Madera and back towards the others, confusion deepening the wrinkles at her mouth and forehead. "What are you playing at, girl?"

"She came to see me, a few weeks back," Madera told her. "We had a nice little chat, the two of us."

"I know," said Ruby. "Who'd you think bleedin' *sent* her?"

Kat uncurled herself, slowly, from her sitting position.

"Yeah. About that." She rose, equally slowly, to standing, weapon still pointing at El and Rose. "Small confession to make: the conversation me and her had might not have panned out *exactly* the way I told you..."

She's sold us out, El realised, panic sending her thoughts into a terrified spiral. *She's sold us out to a murderer, just like Hannah did to Marchant.*

What did I tell her? What did we tell her, that she could've used?

"What have you done?" Ruby whispered. "Jesus Christ, girl - what the hell have you *done*?"

"Saved herself," Madera answered. "Sensible strategy, if you ask me." She cocked her head to the side, studying her sister. "You haven't changed, have you? Look at you, expecting *loyalty*. People don't work like that - I should've thought you of all people would've learned that by now. Cut 'em down the middle, and everyone's out for themselves."

Ruby paused; her face glazing over in what El recognised as concentration.

"She's told you the same as that Hannah," she said eventually. "That we been talking about you to the Old Bill."

"And very specific she was, too. I was a bit sceptical at first - you never can trust a defector, can you? But there's only so many times you can hear the same story before you start to think, *maybe there's a grain of truth to this business, after all*. She had it spot-on about you lot coming here tonight, an' all. And about that Pasadena running off, after your computer girl there got hold of his passwords and came up here to see him. Bleedin' little weasel *he* turned out to be. I'll have to have words with him myself, once we wrap up here."

She doesn't know about Lawton, El thought. *Or Carruthers. She killed him because he wanted out. Because he was going to kill* her *so he could* get *out.*

She wouldn't have done that, if she'd known the job Kate offered him was a setup. He wouldn't have started that argument to begin with, if he'd *known.*

So... there are parts she doesn't know, about what's been going on. Parts Kat hasn't told her.

Which means Kat hasn't told her everything.

"We don't want no trouble," Ruby repeated, raising her arms in surrender - her vest, El noticed, now half-unzipped. "We haven't talked to no-one about you, and we ain't going to. This don't have to be a fight."

"You started this," Madera said. "Not me. You remember that."

"I didn't start nothing. And I swear to you, swear to you on Mum and Dad's grave - I ain't been talking to the Bill. None of us have."

If Ruby had been betting that the invocation of their long-dead parents would do something to soften Madera's edges, then - from what El could see - she was in for a disappointment. Madera was unmoved; her blue eyes and the tanned, artificially smooth expanse of her face showing no expression at all.

"I know it's been a long time," Ruby went on - still trying, or so El thought, to make a connection, to find some common ground between them. "But we don't have to be at each other's throats like this. You're my sister. You're *family*. That don't just go away, no matter how many years might've gone by. No matter what either of us might've done, in all them years. Christ knows, I done a few things myself I ain't proud 'tween then and now."

The look Madera gave her was something close to pity.

"Fifty-seven years," she said levelly. "That's how long it's been. Too long, Ruby. *Too damn long.*" She turned her attention left, away from Ruby. "Shoot her," she told Kat.

Kat looked genuinely shocked at the instruction; horrified, even.

She wasn't expecting that, El thought. *She must've known it was a possibility, one of us - all of us - getting shot down here. More than a possibility - a likelihood.*

But it never occurred to her she'd have to do the shooting.

"Shoot her?" Kat said, as if she'd misheard. As if she *must have* misheard.

Karen moved closer to Ruby - preparing, El thought, to bridge the gap between Kat and Ruby with her body. To *shield* Ruby, if need be.

"Back," barked Madera, cocking her gun at Karen.

Karen hesitated, seeming to weigh up the likely consequences of obeying versus defying Madera's command - then acquiesced, shuffling back to her original position at Ruby's side.

I could get between them, El thought - calculating the angles, the likely speed and trajectory of any bullet fired. *If I moved fast enough, I could do it.*

If.

"You didn't say I'd have to *shoot* her," Kat said, shaking her head at Madera. "That wasn't the deal."

"That a problem, is it?" Madera asked.

"Well, yeah - it *is* a bit of a problem, actually. It might be *your* cup of tea, but I don't just go around shooting people whenever the urge takes me. I didn't think I'd actually have to *use* this, you know what I mean?" She gestured down at the gun, shaking it very slightly for emphasis.

"And there I was, thinking you wanted to leave them behind. Want back in with them, do you?"

"Look, I told you - I don't give a shit what *you* do, just so long as you leave me out of it. But asking *me* to do it... that's a bit much, isn't it?"

"Let me put it another way." Madera raised her left arm, aiming her second gun - the gun she'd taken from Carruthers - at Kat, but keeping her original weapon on Karen and Ruby. Both hands held steady; Madera's reflexes, El was absolutely certain, as deft at almost seventy as El's had been at twenty. "Shoot her, or I'll shoot *you*."

"Don't do this, Doll." Ruby was pleading now; begging. El didn't think she'd ever seen her beg before; ever seen her *have* to. "Please. You can come back with us, back into town. We can thrash it out there, whatever it is you reckon we need to. There's other ways this can go, you know there is."

"Five seconds, Miss Morgan," Madera told Kat, counting down. "Four."

"Please, Doll," Ruby begged again. El thought she might have been crying; thought she could hear it in the old woman's voice. "Don't."

"Three."

Kat didn't move.

"Two."

Madera's finger pressed down on the trigger of Carruthers' gun, in what seemed to El like slow motion.

"One."

"I'm sorry, Ruby," Kat said, her thumb on the hammer of her cowboy's pistol. "I really am."

She fired, not once but three times in succession. The bullets struck Ruby in the shoulder, chest, head; the first one entering the centre of her forehead neatly, as Carruthers' had Hannah's, but exiting the back of her skull in a mess of blood and gore.

She toppled backwards, landing on her side by Hannah's stiffening body - more blood leaving from her mouth, her nose, her ears.

Someone screamed: a low-pitched, guttural howl of pain that El identified as her own only when her vocal cords began to burn from the strain of it. Her vision blurred, her eyes clouding with tears or blood or both; nearby and on the peripheries of her seeing, more bodies stirred and darted. But they were shadows, vapour. They could have been anyone.

And another shot rang out, somewhere close to her, so loud it stole a portion of her hearing, leaving her almost-deaf as well as almost-blind. Another something hit the ground with a deadened thud.

Time passed, though she had no sense of how much. Then there were hands on her, at her waist; not shaking but gripping, digging urgently into what flesh they could find between the layers of vest and shirt.

"El!" Rose was saying, her face an inch from El's, her breath warm and familiar on El's skin. "El, for Christ's sake, snap *out* of it! We need to *go*, now!"

El blinked; held down her eyelids until there was nothing but darkness there.

Opened them.

Saw.

There were four bodies now, not three: Hannah, and Carruthers, and Ruby - Ruby, not moving but bleeding, still - and Kat a foot from *her*, a spreading patch of red radiating from the place in her chest where her heart must have been, before the bullet that struck her obliterated it.

"Sita," Rose said, seeing El see Kat on the floor. "She…"

She shot her, El thought - not needing Rose to finish the sentence. *Kat shot Ruby, and Sita shot* her.

She would've taken a bullet for Ruby, Sita - El had known that almost as long as she'd known them both. Would've died for her, if she'd had to.

Funny that it had never once occurred to El, in all that time, that she might *kill* for her, too.

"Where?" she asked Rose. Then, following Rose's gaze across the room, saw Sita on the carpet: eyes blank, back slumped against the staircase and legs stretched out in front of her, yet another handgun in her lap and Karen's arms around her, holding her like a child.

And no-one else left in the room.

"Madera. Where's Madera?"

"Gone," Rose told her. She pointed up, to the stairs, the ceiling above their heads; to the path Madera must have taken out of the basement, while El was in her daze.

Rose looked pretty dazed herself, El could see now: shell-shocked, a soldier emerging unscathed from a battlefield strewn with the corpses of her friends. She was holding it together, just about - better than El was, anyway - but it was only a matter of time before whatever adrenaline was powering her depleted completely, and she crumbled.

"We've gotta get out of here," Karen said, meeting Rose's eye. "If that mad bitch is on the move, I wouldn't put it past her to do something to the house on her way out. Torch it, or... I don't even know."

Sita's lowered head whipped up and around.

"No," she said - hollowed-out but absolutely vehement. "We are *not* leaving her. Not like this."

She didn't look to Ruby's body as she spoke; she didn't have to. They all knew who she'd meant; which *she* it was couldn't bring herself to abandon.

"Sita, babe," Karen whispered, gently, as if the old woman really *were* a frightened child, "we can't stay here. You know we can't. Even if that bitch decides *not* to do something to the house, she could come back down here any second armed to the tits with God knows what. And we'd have no way of getting out, if she found a way to block the stairs. We'd be sitting ducks."

"We are *not* leaving her," Sita repeated. "*I'm* not..."

"It won't be for long. I don't want to leave her any more than you do. And we'll need to do something about... all the rest, too. Kat and Hannah and... *him.*"

Karen swept a hand towards what remained of Carruthers.

"Do you have someone in mind?" Rose asked her. "Someone who can... take care of it?"

It had been Dexter and Michael, the last time, El remembered: Dexter and Michael they'd called to help get rid of Marchant's body, Dexter whose connections had made sure that body stayed gone afterwards.

Dexter and Michael, who'd do anything for their mum, if she asked.

The thought of calling the boys now, though, was unconscionable. Bad enough the four of *them* had seen Ruby like that; that they could see her now, the life drained out of her. Dexter and Michael didn't need to see it too. Didn't need the afterimage of it on the back of their eyelids every night before they lost themselves to sleep, the way El had a feeling *she* would.

"Perce," Karen said. "He won't be able to sort it himself, but he'll know someone who can."

El saw why she'd think so. Karen's Uncle Perce, her late father's brother, had spent a solid portion of his life in prisons, and the remainder of it in the company of men more intimidating and more criminally inclined even than Perce himself. The odds were good he *would* know someone equipped to deal with the removal of a quartet of bodies from a given location, before the police turned up and began to ask inconvenient questions; that he *could* help them.

"I said *no!*"

Sita all but roared the final syllable - the sheer raw, commingled power of her grief and rage propelling her to her feet, animating her into lucidity.

"I'm sorry," Karen told her calmly. "It's gotta be done."

"You'd have a *stranger* here, touching her? A *cleaner, handling* her like a slab of meat?"

She won't leave, El thought, with terrible certainty. *She won't leave, not willingly, and we'll have to* make *her, have to* drag *her out and tell ourselves it's for her own good...*

Rose dropped her fingers from El's waist; walked across the floor to Sita and laid a hand on the old woman's forearm.

"Is there someone else?" she asked, voice so soft El could barely hear the words. "Someone you'd rather have... come and take care of her?"

Sita was silent for a very long time.

"Gerry," she answered, finally. "Gerry Adler. He won't like it, but he'll do it. He'll help us. He knows her, you understand? He *knows* her. And he'll... be kind."

Rose nodded.

"We'll call him," she said, not letting go of Sita's arm. "We'll get out of here, and then we'll call him."

They took the staircase slowly, cautiously: Karen leading and El at the rear, with Sita between them, her body collapsed so completely against Rose's that Rose might as well have been carrying her up the stairs.

El tried very hard not to look down, to look *back* at the other bodies they were leaving behind.

If she hadn't been so numb, she reflected - if her capacity for emotional response hadn't been so utterly deadened by what she'd seen, heard, *smelled* in the basement - then she'd be terrified; panicked at the possibility of Madera watching them unseen from some dark corner of the hallway or the kitchen as they climbed, gun in hand, waiting for the perfect opportunity to pick them off, one-by-one.

Maybe she'd done the sensible thing and made herself scarce; maybe she was long gone already. Maybe going up against four armed, unforgiving women in the furnace-heat of loss had seemed too big of a risk even for *her*, without a crew to back her up.

But maybe not.

She was old, yes. But she was clever. She couldn't have survived as long as she had in the circles she moved in without knowing how to beat the odds.

Clever, and fast. What she'd done to Carruthers was proof enough of that.

At the top of the stairs, they paused, then crept forward, their backs half-turned to the wall to their right defensively, as if the plasterboard itself might offer them protection from attack - then sped up their pace at Karen's unspoken instruction, almost but not quite running along the hallway, past the living room and study and on to the kitchen where Stuart Ma had first let them inside.

The back door was open: that was the first thing El saw, as she ground to a standing halt behind Karen and Rose and Sita in the doorway separating the kitchen from the hall. Someone had left it ajar - on their way out, or on their way *in*.

It took her a moment or two to understand the second thing she was seeing, because it seemed - after everything she'd learned about Madera - so very, very unlikely.

But nevertheless, there it was - or rather, there *Madera* was.

Flat on her back on the kitchen floor, as dead as the sister and the protege she'd left in her wake: a bullet wound in her head, another in the palm of her hand, and a pool of blood spreading out around her on the tiles like an aureole.

HAMPSTEAD HEATH, LONDON

June 1998

Without a body, there could be no funeral. And there hadn't *been* a body to find, after Gerry Adler had done whatever he'd done to clean up the carnage at the farmhouse. Not one.

But they held a service anyway: a small remembrance gathering on the Heath, in a wooded section of Golders Hill Park that Ruby and Winston, the husband she'd loved so much, had liked to walk along on Sundays, once upon a time.

There were less than twenty of them, altogether: El and Rose and Sophie and Harriet, who'd known just how much Ruby had meant to her sister; Fergus and Karen, and her brother Theo and their mother, who'd known Ruby since before any one of her children was born; Kate Zhou, her flight home to California postponed; Barbara Potter, the retired Ward Sister who'd patched up more than a few of their work-related injuries over the years, and who'd come along with Ruby's friend Arlena, who still worked as a Staff Nurse at St. Luke's in Islington; Gerry Adler himself, hovering silently and forlornly on the edges of the group.

Dexter and Michael, Ruby's boys, in identical black suits - standing shoulder-to-shoulder beside El, the both of them crying.

And Sita in the centre, in a plain white salwar kameez and dupatta, giving her eulogy from memory.

"She'd have *loathed* all of this," she concluded, smiling dimly through her own tears. "*All this bleedin' sentimentality*, as I daresay she'd have called it. So I shan't belabour things further, except to say that I loved her, as we all did, and that life as I've come to know it will be immeasurably poorer for her passing."

"She never cared much for poetry either, of course. But I believe she'd understand our need to mark her passing, in our own way, and so, if you'll allow me..."

She craned her neck towards the clear sky overhead, pulled back her shoulders and began to sing: a soft, low mantra in a language El thought might have been Hindi or Marathi, or even Sanskrit, and that struck her as astonishingly beautiful.

The boys, lifelong atheists, bowed their heads in what might have been prayer. And Rose, who'd had her left arm wrapped around Sophie as they'd cried, slipped her right around El and drew the three of them together.

"Would you mind terribly driving me home, darling?" Sita asked El afterwards, when the group had begun to disperse. "I don't know that I entirely trust myself behind the wheel today."

She'd rented a car, El remembered - another Rolls, this one minus a chauffeur - and had been using it to transport herself from A to B while she worked out where she'd go next, and how she'd get there.

Her money, like El's and Karen's and Rose's, had been restored to her: Stuart Ma, so frightened that Karen might elect to delete him for good that he'd have done more or less anything she instructed, proving every bit as efficient in returning their assets as he'd been in misappropriating them to begin with.

But her Kensington apartment was still gone, Rohan's hospitality would eventually wear thin - and without Ruby there seemed, she'd told El earlier, less and less reason to build a new, permanent home in the city.

Bereft as she'd be without her, El had understood.

The Ludgate Hill flat was emptier than it had been, she saw when they got there; the lion's share of Sita's furniture and artwork now transplanted, or so El assumed, to a storage facility sufficiently white glove to meet Sita's myriad and extremely detailed demands.

"Tea, darling?" Sita asked, settling El into one of the two red leather Chesterfields that remained in the lounge, then disappearing into the kitchen without giving El a chance to answer.

She's lonely, El told herself. *Her and Ruby: they were together so long - a unit for long, even when they were working different jobs in different countries - that she probably doesn't know what to do with herself without her.*

It's like being widowed. It must be.

A sound came from the kitchen: something fragile breaking, the crack of china or ceramics on hardwood.

She's dropped the cup, El thought - imagining Sita suddenly overcome by a fresh wave of grief by the kettle, her hands shaking so badly she couldn't stop the tea-set from falling from her hands. She stood up, then - after a brief internal struggle - sat back down again, resolving not to intervene, after all, but stay right where she was on the sofa, and let Sita preserve her dignity, for however long it took her to compose herself.

But then, another sound: this time a clatter, the dull thud of a harder and heavier object falling to earth. An ornament, maybe. Something wooden.

I'll just check, she thought, standing up again. *I'll quickly go and check on her, then I'll come back in as if nothing ever happened and we'll never mention it again.*

She crept out of the lounge as discreetly as she could, not wanting to alert Sita to her presence.

And came to a dead stop in the hallway.

She *couldn't* be seeing what she was seeing there, she knew. *Couldn't* be.

Madera on the floor of the farmhouse kitchen with a bullet in her head: that had been unlikely. Improbable.

But Kat Morgan, alive and well and standing stock-still in Sita's borrowed apartment, the walking stick she'd apparently dropped resting by her feet next to a broken teacup... that was impossible. Actually impossible.

She was dead. The bitch, the bitch she'd trusted, the bitch who'd murdered Ruby in cold fucking blood to buy herself a get out of jail free card... she was dead.

El had *seen her die*.

Hadn't she?

Except... *no*, she remembered: she *hadn't*. She'd seen *Ruby* die, and Hannah, and Lucian Carruthers... but she'd been out of it when Kat was shot, in such a fugue state she'd barely registered the gunshot, let alone seen the bullet land.

She'd seen Kat's *body*, yes - seen it splayed and bleeding out on the basement carpet. But she hadn't seen how it'd gotten there; hadn't seen the shot that she and Rose and Karen had been so sure had *caused* that bleeding.

Was it possible that she'd...?

"El," Kat said, breaking into the thought before it could reach any conclusion - looking, it seemed to El, *apologetic* somehow, as if she was gearing up to say sorry for breaking the crockery. "Listen..."

It had been a fog that had descended on her in the basement: a thick mist deadening her perceptions, cutting her off from the sensory data she'd normally rely on to bring her to understanding.

What El felt now, though, was closer to an inferno: a sudden, searing fury, burning away all calm and cognition and flooding her nerves with something dark and molten and incontrovertibly dangerous.

Kat began to speak again, her lips moving but the words lost below the pounding of blood in El's ears.

She sprang: her shoulder tackling Kat in the stomach and forcing her to the ground and her arms grabbing at the dead woman's ankles, snatching them from under her as Kat's lower back hit the floor.

"Fucking *stop*!" Kat shouted, already breathless, but it was too late by far: El's hands were already around her throat, squeezing and choking and...

"For Christ's sake, girl, let *go* of her!" another voice roared, somewhere to El's left. "She can't bleedin' *breathe* with you on her like that!"

El froze, her fingers falling away from Kat's throat almost of their own volition.

She turned her head, her legs still straddling Kat's body.

And there, just behind her, equally impossible, was Ruby.

BLACKHEATH, LONDON

April 1998

She'd expected the postman, or a delivery driver with a parcel; perhaps even, after everything she'd been hearing about the last few days, some sort of Charles Bronson hitman with a sawn-off shotgun.

Who she *hadn't* been expecting on her doorstep, bright-eyed and bushy-tailed at seven o'clock in the morning, was Ruby bloody Redfearn.

"Can I have a word?" Ruby asked, though it wasn't really a question, and what could Kat do except roll out the welcome mat and invite her in?

"I need your help," she carried on, once she was sat down in the conservatory, cross-legged and barefooted on Kat's brand-new, three grand hammock-chair.

"Yeah?"

"Yeah. With our Dolly."

Kat pulled her dressing gown tighter and shivered, wishing she'd put the heating on.

"Not being funny," she said, "but could you not have waited 'til a bit later on in the day to come asking for a favour? I don't know what time *you* get up, but this is still the middle of the night for me."

"Early, as it happens. You don't sleep much, when you get to my age. That ain't the point, though. The *point* is, I didn't want no-one seeing me come down here. What we're talking about - I need it to stay between you and me. I can't have none of the rest of 'em knowing."

"Knowing *what*? What *are* we supposed to be talking about?"

"Don't you bleedin' *listen*? Our Dolly, that's what."

"What about her? What is it you want me to help with that's so fucking *secret*, all of a sudden?"

Ruby winced at the words, and Kat wondered, just for a second, whether the old bag was about to tell her to go and wash her mouth out.

"I been thinking about what to do," Ruby said instead. "Going over and over it in my head, every bleedin' minute since that Hannah come back and opened her gob. And whichever way I look at it, however I turn it 'round, I keep coming back to the same damn thing."

"Which is what?"

"Our Dolly - she ain't gonna stop. She won't hurt *me* - that's what I been tellin' myself, at least, though maybe *that's* only so's I can get to sleep at all. But the rest of you, you and Sita and Rose and Karen and our El, my boys even... she ain't got no reason to hold back with *you*, has she? No reason at all. And if she really is what that Hannah *says* she is..."

She faltered; took a breath.

"If she *is*," she continued, "then we're gonna have to deal with her. *I'm* gonna have to deal with her. 'Cause I can't let her do that, do you see? I can't have her coming after you, any of you. Rose and El... they're like my own bleedin' kids. You and Karen an' all, much as you might hate me sometimes. And as for Sita..."

"Deal with her how?" Kat said, beginning to catch on.

"There's something I been thinking about. Sort of... mullin' over. But it'd only work with you on board - and I mean *proper* on board. You go in half-hearted or half-cocked, and the whole thing's dead in the water."

"When have I *ever* gone in half-cocked? I lost a chunk of my skull on one of your jobs, if you remember. *That's* how bloody all-in I am, when I'm working."

"I know. I ain't forgotten. But this... it's a lot to ask. A *lot*."

Kat looked at the old woman in front of her; really *looked*. Saw the worry-lines on her forehead; the swollen bags under her eyes, from night after night up agonising over what to do and how to do it.

"Ask, then," Kat told her, already knowing what her answer would be. "Ask and get it over with. We haven't got all day."

"Are you *mad*?" Sita asked later, when Ruby had explained what she had in mind, and how she was planning to pull it off. "A *makeup artist*?"

"She ain't a *makeup artist*," Ruby replied. "She's a *special effects technician*. Different kettle of fish altogether."

"The woman turns actors into werewolves and aliens and revenants. Does it *matter* what she calls herself?"

"It does here. I'm talking about a girl who can make it seem like someone's head exploded just from pushing a button, not some bird you'd wheel in to get your face done for a wedding."

"Oh, well, in *that* case..."

"She's bloody good at it, an' all. Won every award going. Can see her picking up one of them Oscars, if she keeps at it."

"And you'd really trust her to keep her mouth shut, would you? She's Len Wolf's daughter, for heaven's sake. I can't imagine the apple fell too far from *that* tree."

Len Wolf, a semi-reformed bank robber who'd since adjourned to the countryside to spend more time with his classic car collection, was an old acquaintance of them both - albeit one for whom Sita, whose preference had long been for the non-violent confidence trick when it came to separating others from their cash above what she continued to refer to as *stick-up artistry*, had little affection.

His daughter Kathleen, both Sita and Ruby had been dimly aware, had worked in the film industry since leaving college: first on the sort of shoestring-budget productions that necessitated she spent more time than anyone could want in abandoned tunnels and repurposed shipping containers, and then, as her portfolio and reputation had grown, on larger-scale features that routinely took her to more exotic locations across the US, South America and Canada. She specialised in horror effects, creating an extraordinary range of demonic and extra-terrestrial visages from scratch, using only her box of tricks and the generically attractive facial canvases of those performers dispatched to her trailer.

She also - very usefully, as Ruby saw it - did blood, and gore, and some very convincing wound-work: replicating every cut and scratch, gouge and soft-tissue injury, disembowelling and decapitation that the studios who hired her demanded.

And bullet-holes. Always, bullet-holes.

"Don't matter whose daughter she is, does it?" Ruby said. "I ain't about to tell her what it's *for*. We could be makin' a bleedin' film ourselves, for all she knows. I just need her to show me how she does it, maybe borrow a bit of equipment for the duration. And it ain't as if she has much to do with her old man, anyway. Way I heard it, she feels the same way about him *you* do. Not so keen on how Len made his money, Kathleen."

"I don't like it. I want to make that very, very clear."

"Didn't think you would. But you'll do it, if we have to?"

Sita sighed.

"When are we meeting her?"

"I don't know if I can do this," Kat told Ruby, the morning before setting out to meet Madera on The Strand. "She sees through me, and I'm done. Game over."

"Then don't let her. You're an actress, ain't you? *Act*."

"Was an actress. *Was*. I don't know *what* the hell I'm supposed to be anymore."

"Just... what do they call it? Channel your emotions. Make it real."

"And what does *that* mean, then?"

'It means... you hate that Hannah, right?"

"D'you even have to ask?"

"And it pisses you off, don't it, us bringing her in on this job? Don't bother answering - it's written all over you, has been for weeks. And me... you ain't *my* biggest fan right now either, are you? You think I've done you over, not kicking her out on her ear the second she showed her face."

Kat didn't reply.

"Listen, girl," Ruby said, conciliatory, "I ain't trying to get at you, alright? I'm just sayin': you're already mad as hell. And *that's* what you gotta show our Dolly, if you want to sell this. All that anger, that bitterness... every bit of hate you've had buildin' up inside you since Marchant - you gotta let it spill out. Let her *see* it."

"And then what? D'you even *know* what you'll be doing, once I'm in with her?"

Ruby scratched her chin - seeming, Kat thought, momentarily forlorn.

"More or less," she said, quietly. "There's a few question marks over everything, a few answers we ain't gonna have until the very last. And a few calls we'll have to make, me and Sita. But I got the shape of it, at least. I bleedin' *hope* I do, anyway."

"I'm sorry, Ruby," Kat said, looking at the old woman down the barrel of the pistol Madera had given her, the one she'd stripped of its live rounds and loaded with blanks when Madera and Carruthers had their backs turned. "I really am."

She pulled the trigger: once, twice, three times.

Now, she thought, willing Ruby to do her part, and do it quickly. *For fuck's sake* - now.

She saw Ruby's hand twitch; saw the old woman's thumb press down on the remote control she'd been concealing up her sleeve.

And then, to her relief, saw Ruby's head succumb to a perfect simulacrum of a gunshot: the tiny packet of blood taped to her skin and hidden below six layers of industrial foundation bursting into life, while the larger packet taped to the back of her scalp - and hidden below her thick, grey hair - unleashed its contents onto the carpet and the wall behind her in a spray of artificial blood and brain matter and God knows what else.

The thumb twitched again, and two more of the pseudo-wounds revealed themselves, at her shoulder and chest.

She fell backwards to the ground, breaking her fall with the side of her body - yet more of the blood she'd acquired from Len Wolf's daughter spilling from her ears and nose and the third, tiny packet she'd kept hidden under her tongue.

Absolute silence descended on the basement, the calm before the inevitable storm.

And Sita, in what had to be the finest performance of her career, growled like a wounded animal before releasing a single bullet of her own into the centre of Kat's chest.

The last thing Kat saw, before she depressed the button on her own control and let herself collapse, eyes closed, beside Ruby, was Madera - scanning the room and, apparently not liking what she found, and then sprinting to the stairs and up, out of the basement.

"Your sister," Sita had said, after their initial conversation with Kathleen Wolf. "She won't let it go, if we let her leave that house. You do know that, don't you? She'll keep on coming for the girls. And me. You too, in all likelihood."

"You think I don't know that?" Ruby had told her. "I said as much myself to young Kat the other day. I *know.*"

"And yet you still believe you'll be able to convince her otherwise? To talk her out of whatever she has planned for us?"

Ruby had shaken her head; looked mournfully down into her cup of coffee.

"Truthfully, Sita? No, I don't, alright? I *don't.* But what am I supposed to do? I've got to try to make her listen, haven't I? She's my *sister*, for crying out loud. I owe her that."

Sita had lit a cigarette; waited several long minutes before she'd spoken again.

"You have a contingency measure in mind, I take it?" she'd asked.

Ruby had looked up from her coffee, her eyes red-rimmed.

"Yeah," she'd said. "Gonna need your help with it, though."

"Of course. But how so?"

"Matteo Randazzo - you still talk to him?"

"Every now and then. He spends most of his time on that ranch of his these days, up in Nye County. But we occasionally have dinner, when I'm in New York."

"You reckon he'd do you a favour, if you asked him?"

Sita had pondered this as she'd smoked.

"I believe so, yes," she'd answered. "We had some rather lovely moments together. I like to think he remembers me fondly."

Ruby had grimaced but nodded, as if she'd expected nothing less.

"Let's give him a bell, then," she'd said. "Me and you, this afternoon. 'Cause if you're right, and our Dolly *don't* want to let it go... we're gonna need all the help he can give us."

OSTERLEY PARK, LONDON

May 1998

The kitchen, Dolly thought. The kitchen was the most sensible place for her to wait for them.

Pasadena kept the front door sealed; God knows, he'd shown her enough times *how*. Kept it locked and bolted with that biometric fingerprint recognition system of his, the one he'd said no-one but him could get through without chopping his hand right off his wrist.

A poor choice of phrase, given her line of work, she'd considered at the time. Very poor.

There was no chance of them getting out of the front of the house, then; no chance at all. They'd have to use the back door - the door they must have come through in the first place.

And to get *there*, they'd have to go through the kitchen.

All *she'd* have to do was stand quietly in the corner, somewhere that gave her a view to the hallway, and she'd have a clear line of sight to all four of them as soon as they made it up the stairs. Four clean shots, one after the other, and they'd go down like dominoes.

She took the stairs at a gallop; as quick as she could, before the smoke cleared and the younger ones decided it was time to start shooting. They didn't know what they were doing with the guns they'd brought, she'd seen that from the first: in normal circumstances, she might've taken her chances. But there were three of them, not including the old girl, and only one of her, and all it took was one bullet to go astray or ricochet off a bit of furniture, and suddenly you were down on your knees with your guts spilling out in your hands.

It wasn't worth the risk.

The ground floor was bright: every lamp and spotlight in the place lit up like a Christmas tree, the way Pasadena seemed to need it. He'd always been afraid of the dark, that boy; she should've known he'd run away at the first sign of danger. He'd even left the lights on over the cooker, she saw as she entered the kitchen.

Spineless little shit.

"Ms. Madera," said a voice from the other side of the room: male, deep, American.

She spun a quarter foot towards him, or where she thought he must have been: not enough to expose any vital organs, but enough that she could see him, get some sense of who he was and what the hell he was doing there.

"Who's asking?" she said.

The owner of the voice stepped forward, showing himself. He was tall, dark, well-dressed; physically fit, from the way he carried himself. And a professional: she could see as much from his stance, the way he was sizing her up. From his easy, familiar handling of the Smith & Wesson in his hand, the one he had pointed straight at her.

He wasn't alone.

The man behind him was shorter, stockier but equally athletic. He was armed, like his friend - but *his* hands, Dolly noted with some concern, held not a pistol but a shotgun. An automatic.

"Mr. Randazzo, Ms. Madera," the taller man said. And fired.

LUDGATE HILL, LONDON

June 1998

You let us think you were dead," El said, holding the bag of ice Sita had given her to her shoulder.

"I know, love," Ruby told her. "And I'm sorry. We weren't sure it was gonna be safe, at first. For me to, you know... come out of the closet, so to speak. She had friends, our Dolly. We didn't know who she'd been talkin' to. Whether there was anyone else we needed to worry about."

"But it's safe now?"

"We reckon so, yeah. Randazzo seems to think so, an' all. And that bloke's got eyes bleedin' *everywhere*."

Kat and Sita had cleared out of the flat, decamping to a coffee shop across the road while Ruby told her story - Kat griping all the way about the stabbing pains in her back and the thumbprint bruises El had left around her neck.

It was just the two of them now, her and Ruby. And try as she might to tamp it down, to tell herself it was nothing personal and that it had to be done... El was furious.

"Dexter and Michael," she said. "Do they know?"

"About me being...?"

"Not dead. Yeah."

Ruby looked away, apparently not able to meet El's eyes.

"No. No, I ain't told 'em, not yet."

"To keep them safe," El said flatly.

"Yeah. Them and Rose and Karen, an' all. I'm *gonna* tell 'em, I am. Only…" She paused. "Truth is, girl: it weren't just about making sure you lot were alright, me going to ground. *I* needed a bit of time away myself. Time to think, know what I mean?" She rubbed at the back of her neck - a self-soothing gesture El had very rarely known her to deploy. "It's been a rough month or two, this has. A rough couple of *years*, what with Marchant and Soames and now our Dolly. I've had… how do them Americans say it? *A lot to process*. A lot of thoughts goin' round in my head."

Even through the haze of her anger, El got it – understood what Ruby was trying to tell her. It had been difficult for all of them, she knew. But somehow, she hadn't stopped to really consider it - the idea of Ruby being affected by it all. Ruby, who always had a trick or two up her sleeve; Ruby, who always found a way to pull off the job, even if was at the eleventh hour.

Ruby, who'd been there for El since El was a kid: solid and dependable - and occasionally as immovable - as a rock.

You forgot she was a person, El told herself. *That she had feelings; stuff of her own going on. An interior life that wasn't just about you and Rose and the boys and the job.*

"I get it," she said, guilt dissolving what was left of her indignation.

Ruby smiled at her; put a hand to El's face and ran a thumb across her cheek.

"Thought you might, darlin'. Thought you might. Been a funny one for all of us, ain't it?"

"Guess so," El agreed - thinking of Madera and Carruthers, lying dead on the floor; of Charlie Soames, and the horrors he'd rained down on his wife and kid; of Ricky Lomax, and Hannah, and Marchant. Of her cottage on fire, and everything she owned burned to a cinder inside it.

Of her Mum - the ghost of her quietened, if not ever really put to rest.

And of Sophie and Rose, finally. Of what the three of them together might mean.

"There's something else, an' all," Ruby said, in a voice that El might have read as nervous, had it come from someone else. "I ain't quite worked out how to tell the rest of 'em *this* yet, neither... but I reckon I might be done."

"Done? Done with what?"

"All of it. The job, the runnin' round... the worry. I'm old, girl. Old and tired. Me and Sita both. We always said we'd stop, one of these days - when it was getting to be more of a headache than it was fun. And... I don't know. I'm starting to get the feeling it might be getting on for that time."

She's leaving, too, El thought. *Her and Sita - they're leaving together.*

"Where will you go?" she asked, the reality of it still a way away from sinking in. "What will you do?"

"*Do*? Christ knows. Ain't sure there's much either of us needs to be *doing*, at our age. Bit of travelling, maybe. Hit a few museums. Actually stop and have a look at some of the stuff we've spent so bleedin' long trying to steal."

"And you'll... stay in touch?" Her own voice sounded desperate, she knew; small, and frightened and sad.

Ruby moved closer to her on the ancient sofa and pulled her into a hug.

"'Course we bleedin' will," she whispered, pushing El's hair out of her face and pressing a kiss to her crown. "We ain't plannin' on dying just yet."

"I'll miss you," El whispered back, embarrassingly aware that she'd begun to cry.

"Yeah? Glad to hear it. 'Cause I'll miss you, an' all. You and that family of yours." She pulled her in tighter, until El's head was resting on her shoulder. "Gonna let you in on a secret though, just between you and me. You'll be alright, girl. Whatever you do - you'll be alright, whether I'm around or not."

El buried her face in the crook of the old woman's neck, her face a mess of tears.

"You sure about that, are you?" she said, snuffling.

"Never been surer, sweetheart. Learned from the best, didn't you? The very bleedin' best."

PALERMO SOHO, BUENOS AIRES

March 1999

t was barely 10am, but Carmen Navarro was exhilarated - the rush of a prospective sale flooding her veins with chemical euphoria.

"It's beautiful," said the Canadian, gazing up at the Castillo with something like wonder. "Just exquisite."

"We're very lucky to have it," Carmen told her. "Castillo's son… you could say he bequeathed it to us, when his father passed on."

"Pretty generous donation."

"He's a very generous man. It helped, of course, that he was married to our owner at the time."

Carmen let out an awkward laugh, hoping that the Canadian would follow suit. But she demurred.

"What do you think?" the woman asked her assistant in English. "You can be honest."

"It's pretty," the girl replied, in a British accent. "Sort of weird, but pretty. For a painting, I mean. You sure it's worth the money, though?"

The fixed, saleswoman smile stayed firmly on Carmen's face, but inside she scowled - cursing the girl's brashness, her lack of taste and, worst still, the bite that lack of taste might take out of what Carmen hoped would be a sizeable commission.

The girl was young: you could say that, at least, in her defence. Probably no more than eighteen, Carmen thought, and obviously new to South America. Her pale, freckled skin had burned to a boiled-lobster vermillion in the early Autumn sun; a situation not helped in the slightest by her bright red hair and long brown dress, which together conspired to give her the look of a children's lollipop on a wooden stick.

"Thiago, Castillo's son," Carmen said, addressing the Canadian in Spanish. "He was offered a quarter of a million dollars for it by a gallery in New York. *American* dollars, that is."

"And he still just... gave it away?"

"His ex-wife... she could be very persuasive, when she tried."

"But a hundred thousand dollars... that's what you're asking for it now? And *in* dollars, not pesos?"

"Just so. We're in a recession," Carmen added, in case the Canadian had neglected to pick up a newspaper, turn on the television or look out of her hotel window since she'd been in the country. "The dollar feels a little more... stable, just at the moment. Or so our owner tells me."

And if I can get this sale done and those dollars stashed away before that wizened old witch comes back from vacation, she thought, *then so much the better. She never so much as* looks *at that fucking painting anyway; she won't even notice it's gone.*

Besides – what does she expect, on what she pays me?

The Canadian leaned in towards Carmen, as if she were about to share a secret.

"It's for my partner," she said. "For her birthday. Pop Art... it's kind of her thing, you know?"

"Ah," said Carmen smoothly - thinking of her cousin in Miami, and the timid young woman she'd brought home with her last Christmas. "Of course.

Well... if she knows anything at all about Castillo, then there's no doubt at all she'll understand the value of this particular piece. Not to say the lengths you went to, to get it for her."

The Canadian took another step back, the better to scrutinise the painting before her.

"Mind if I go away and think about it?" she asked.

"Not at all," Carmen told her. "How long are you here, in Buenos Aires?"

The Canadian, to Carmen's surprise, turned to her assistant for confirmation. The girl looked back at the painting, screwed up her reddened face and shrugged - a gesture the Canadian seemed, against all reason, to accept as an answer.

"Not long," she said. "Couple of days, maybe, before we move on."

"Wonderful. And are you staying nearby?"

"We're at the Palacio Rojo over in Recoleta - you know it?"

"Very well," Carmen said. She resolved to find herself in the vicinity of the hotel that evening - and if she should happen, while she was there, to bump into the Canadian, perhaps strike up a conversation and, who knows, even flirt with her a little over a bottle of Rioja until the deal was done and the Castillo sold... well, who'd be there to call it anything but coincidence? "Very well indeed."

She needed a coffee and a cigarette, after the Canadian and her assistant left: something strong and hot and soothing to wash down the rough caress of the smoke in her lungs.

There was a cafe-bar across the street from the gallery; a pretty little place with outdoor seating and a barista who knew her by name. She left her own assistant in charge - hoping the girl would have the sense to stall if any serious buyers walked in, rather than try to sell them on anything herself - and sped over there, unlit cigarette dangling from her mouth before her feet had even hit the pavement.

A queue had formed at the counter when she got there, which frustrated her; the place wasn't usually so busy so early in the morning. But, thirsty and jittery as her encounter with the Canadian had left her, she stood in line and waited, smoking and taking in - against her will - the fizz and crackle of other people's conversations as they ebbed and flowed around her.

"I thought she did quite well there, our El," the woman at the table next to her was saying - an old woman, white and grey-haired and wrinkled, her harsh English vowels falling discordantly on Carmen's already-strained ears.

"Sophie too, I thought," her companion added. She was brown-skinned, Indian or Pakistani or Bengali, as old as the other woman but more sophisticated; *her* English and her bearing more refined than her friend's, her plain khakis and faded grey tunic fashionably minimalist rather than institutional, as it might have looked on a woman with less obvious style.

"She's comin' along, ain't she? Picks things up quick, that one."

The two old women paused to sip at their coffee, the white one nibbling at the edges of a thick, oozing slice of chocotorta.

"They brought Rose with 'em this time, I noticed," the white one said, several swallows later.

"Yes. Although I suspect she doesn't know *exactly* what they're up to. And she's been off sightseeing with Harriet most days, from what I've seen. They're at the Bosques de Palermo this afternoon, I gather."

"Nice, that, ain't it? All of them and that Harriet getting along."

"Nice for El, certainly."

The Indian one finished her coffee and leaned back in her chair contentedly. Her eyes caught Carmen's, and she smiled broadly.

Tourists, Carmen thought, taking in the woman's camera, the binoculars she wore around her neck like jewellery. *God save us from tourists and their endless rubbernecking.*

"Good morning," the beaming woman said, in perfect Spanish. "Wonderful day, isn't it?"

"Lovely," Carmen replied, smiling insincerely back at her.

The queue began to inch forward and Carmen, relieved to be free of the woman's stare, moved with it towards the counter.

"Come on, then," she heard the white woman say, before the sound of her was swallowed by the grind and gurgle of the coffee machine. "Move your arse. We can't sit here all day, unless you *want* young El to see us and work out we've been keeping an eye on things."

"Very well, then," said her friend, with a world-weary sigh. "Lead on, if you must."

"*Con leche*?" the barista asked Carmen, as if he didn't know already.

She nodded her assent, then turned her own neck to watch the women leave - curious, despite herself, about where they might be heading, and who this El might be that they were so keen to avoid.

But they were gone.

Ah, well, she told herself, mind already turning back to the Canadian and the accidental meeting she'd be engineering later. *How interesting could it really have* been, *anyway?*

ABOUT THE AUTHOR

TC PARKER is a writer and researcher based in the fox-ravaged wilds of Leicestershire, where she lives with her partner and family.

The author of the El Gardener feminist heist trilogy and the horror novels *Saltblood* and *A Press of Feathers,* she's been a copywriter, a lecturer and, very briefly, an academic. Now she runs a semiotics and cultural insight agency by day and dreams up horror and crime fiction at night, when the kids are asleep.

Visit her online at www.tcparkerwrites.com and follow her on Twitter @tcparkerlives